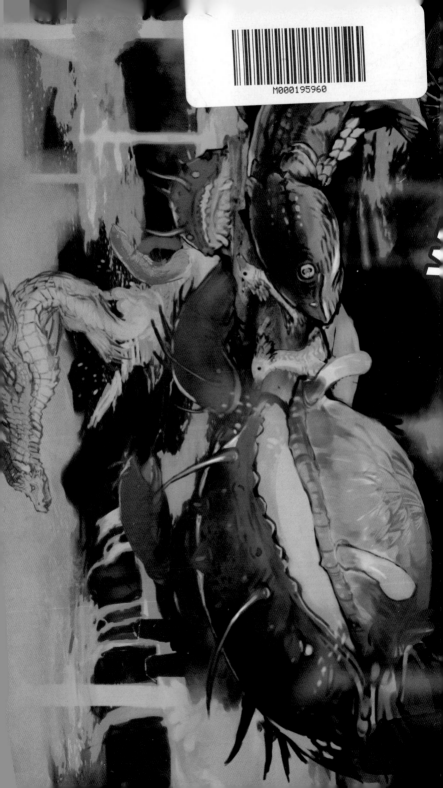

Shun

Katia

Filimøs

WHAAAAA AAAAAAT?!

I don't know if God exists or not, but if so, I'd like to lodge one complaint:

Isn't this a bit much?

A sea of red-hot magma is bubbling in front of me.

So I'm a Spider, So What?

OKINA BABA

Illustration by
TSUKASA KIRYU

2

New York

So I'm a Spider, So What?, Vol. 2

Okina Baba

Translation by Jenny McKeon
Cover art by Tsukasa Kiryu

KUMO DESUGA, NANIKA? Vol. 2
©Okina Baba, Tsukasa Kiryu 2016
First published in Japan in 2016 by KADOKAWA CORPORATION, Tokyo.
English translation rights arranged with KADOKAWA CORPORATION, Tokyo through
TUTTLE-MORI AGENCY, INC., Tokyo.

Yen On
1290 Avenue of the Americas
New York, NY 10104

Visit us at yenpress.com
facebook.com/yenpress
twitter.com/yenpress
yenpress.tumblr.com
instagram.com/yenpress

First Yen On Edition: March 2018

Yen On is an imprint of Yen Press, LLC.
The Yen On name and logo are trademarks of Yen Press, LLC.

The publisher is not responsible for websites (or their content) that are not owned
by the publisher.

Library of Congress Cataloging-in-Publication Data
Names: Baba, Okina, author. | Kiryu, Tsukasa, illustrator. | McKeon, Jenny, translator.
Title: So I'm a spider, so what? / Okina Baba ; illustration by Tsukasa Kiryu ;
    translation by Jenny McKeon.
Other titles: Kumo desuga nanika. English | So I am a spider, so what?
Description: First Yen On edition. | New York, NY : Yen On, 2017–
Identifiers: LCCN 2017034911 | ISBN 9780316412896 (v. 1 : pbk.) | ISBN 9780316442886 (v. 2 : pbk.)
Subjects: | CYAC: Magic—Fiction. | Spiders—Fiction. | Monsters—Fiction. |
    Prisons—Fiction. | Escapes—Fiction. | Fantasy.
Classification: LCC PZ7.1.O44 So 2017 | DDC [Fic]—dc23
LC record available at https://lccn.loc.gov/2017034911

ISBNs: 978-0-316-44288-6 (paperback)
        978-0-316-44293-0 (ebook)

10 9 8 7 6 5

LSC-C

Printed in the United States of America

contents

Class Register

Homeroom Teacher: Kanami Okazaki

Boys

Ken Aikawa
Kanata Doshima
Katia
Kunihiko Ogiwara
Naofumi Kogure
Issei Sakurazaki
Kyouya Sasajima
Kunihiko Tagawa
Douglas Hanfname
Kengo Hayashi
Shinobu Yamada

Aiko Iijima
Mirei Shinohara
Fei
Asaka Kushitani
Sachi Kaido
Shuuko Sera
Saki Temarikawa
Himiko Tonooka
Chie Nanase
Akiko Negishi
Yuika Hasebe
Mio Furuta
Hiro Wakaba

1   Clearly, God Hates Spiders

You know, I just realized I'm pretty unlucky.

In fact, it probably goes beyond just "unlucky." My life as a spider has been such a crazy ride that I have to assume that God must hate me.

I mean, wouldn't most normal people go crazy if they were suddenly reborn as an eight-legged monster for no apparent reason?

Not to mention that my second place of birth is this place, the "Great Elroe Labyrinth"—the largest dungeon in this other world.

All the monsters here are crazy strong, too.

It's definitely an awful eat-or-be-eaten world.

I was doing all right for a while, since I'd managed to use my new spider skills to make a little home for myself, but then a bunch of humans suddenly burned it down.

After that, I wandered around the labyrinth before accidentally falling into the Lower Stratum, which has a much higher difficulty level than my original haunt in the Upper Stratum.

Down there, this ridiculous monster called an earth dragon assaulted me, and I barely managed to escape in one piece.

Then I had to somehow make my way through an area packed with monsters that could kill me without breaking a sweat if I even thought about fighting them.

And then...that monkey army.

A mob of monkeys attacked me like I was their worst enemy, for whatever strange reason.

They're relatively weak compared with the other monsters in the Lower Stratum, but even individually, they're still way stronger than me.

And a whole horde charged me all at once!

I was like, *Is this some kind of joke?*

I was literally fighting for my life.

If my counterattack failed, I seriously would have died.

Really, I think I deserve some praise for surviving that crisis, if I do say so myself.

Good job, me. Yeah. I worked really hard.

So how could I possibly deserve this kind of treatment?!

I don't know if God exists or not, but if so, I'd like to lodge one complaint: *Isn't this a bit much?*

A sea of red-hot magma is bubbling in front of me.

But let's turn back the clock a little. I had just finished wiping out all those monkeys when I noticed something.

It was a little hot.

At first, I wondered if my body temperature had risen following my battle, but that didn't seem to be the case.

Is that a thing that happens to spiders, even?

Okay, not important. The real problem was the sudden change in temperature, which I'd never experienced before.

It didn't seem particularly dangerous.

The only monsters in sight were the corpses of all those monkeys.

It didn't seem like a fire dragon had appeared as a sequel to the earth dragon or anything.

So why was it blazing hot?

Then, as I looked around, I spotted something.

An area sloping upward.

Yes, upward. I'll say it again: *Upward!*

After that long fall from the Upper Stratum, I had spent a while in the Lower Stratum.

And now there was a path leading straight back up.

That could only mean this was the path out of the Lower Stratum and into the Middle Stratum!

Yahoo! It was my chance to escape the extreme danger zone!

With that thought in mind, I excitedly scaled the incline. At the top, I encountered a vast red vista.

And that brings us back to the present.

Whaaaaaaaat?!

What's going on here?

I don't get it.

No, no, no. It can't be!

Why is there magma here?

How can there be magma underground like this?

Well, I guess this is a dungeon beneath the surface, so maybe it makes sense, but…

Unreeeeal.

Wait, it's so hot my HP is actually dropping.

The temperature isn't just a little warm. It's scorching!

Hmm? Something feels hot near my rear.

Gah?! The thread coming out of my butt is on fire?!

Put it out! Put it out! Or at least cut it off!

Whew, that was close. My behind came this close to combusting.

I guess that's on me for not realizing I had silk trailing from my butt again, but still, I can't believe it ignited!

It's not like the whole place is covered in magma, either—there seems to be patches of solid ground I can walk on—but how am I supposed to navigate a place like this when it's already boiling at the entrance?

Someone bring me a cold drink, please!

Huh? There's a monster in the magma.

It looks like a sea horse with arms and legs, just swimming in the stuff. Uhhh, okay.

I'm a bit scared to look, but I'd better Appraise it.

<Elroe gunerush   LV 7
Status: HP: 167/167 (green)   MP: 145/158 (blue)
             SP: 155/155 (yellow)   : 156/165 (red)
             Status Appraisal Failed

>

Oh, I got to see its status on the first try. Lucky me.

Hmm. Going by these numbers, it isn't really all that strong. Still, it's stronger than me!

Guess I might as well investigate further with a double Appraisal.

<Elroe gunerush: A lesser wyrm-type monster that lives in the Great Elroe Labyrinth, Middle Stratum. It manipulates flames and is protected by them.>

There it is! Great Elroe Labyrinth, Middle Stratum! So this really is the Middle Stratum!

<Great Elroe Labyrinth, Middle Stratum: An area located between the Upper Stratum and the Lower Stratum. The terrain of the entire area is scorching hot with flowing magma. Many monsters with resistance to fire inhabit it.>

...For real?

Wow, there's noooo way.

The whole Middle Stratum is like this?

And I have to go through this to get to the Upper Stratum?

How the hell am I supposed to do that?

Terrain that hurts me just by stepping on it. Rivers and ponds of magma that would incinerate me if I fell in.

And if the monsters that live here are resistant to fire, doesn't that mean they might very well be able to make fire, too?

Do you know my spider silk's primary weakness? You do, since it just burned up a little while ago, right?

It's FIRE!!

Seriously, what am I gonna do?

Me without my thread is like *natto* without the *Bacillus subtilis natto* bacterium!

That wouldn't even be fermented beans anymore, just rotten trash!

That's how useless I am if I can't use my silk.

It's not much of an exaggeration to say my spider thread is the only reason I've survived this long.

Without it, I can't make webs, can't trap enemies—I can't do aaanything!

Ah, the sea horse noticed me while I was lost in thought. Our eyes totally met just now.

Well, I'm still pretty far away, so it's no big deal... Wait, what?!

It just took a deep breath and spit something at me?!

Ah, a fireball.

Yaaaaghhhh!!!

I have to dodge. If that hits my body, cinders and ash will be all that's left.

Arrrgh, you gotta be kidding me! How does a fireball even fly through the air like that, huh? What are the physics behind it?

It's the most stereotypical fantasy move I've seen since the earth dragon's breath attack.

Though this doesn't seem as insanely powerful in comparison.

Anyway, how unfair is it that this sea horse guy can use long-distance attacks from the middle of all the magma?

A second fireball shot rockets toward me, but I avoid that, too.

It's not like I can't dodge them. But still, this is not good.

I mean, my only long-distance attack is throwing my spider silk.

Just for kicks, I make some thread and give it a try.

Unfortunately, it catches fire in midair as soon as I throw it.

Ugh, this isn't going to work. I hurry and separate the thread.

While I'm busy with that, the sea horse fires a third shot at me.

I dodge it. Even without taking a direct hit, though, my HP's still going down from all this heat.

Ugh, I hate to admit it, but running away is my only option.

I turn my back on the sea horse, hurrying back down the slope I climbed earlier.

Pulling way back, I don't stop until I'm once more surrounded by monkey corpses.

Phew, now my HP won't keep dropping due to heat.

I have HP Auto-Recovery, so a little break should replenish me.

But man, this is garbage!

Based on numbers alone, I probably could've taken that guy.

The sea horse's stats were technically higher, sure, but that's nothing new.

But this time, I couldn't lay a finger—or a leg, or a thread—on it.

I gotta say, this is pretty serious.

I've fought stronger enemies by making webs before, but never when they had a territorial AND a healthy stat advantage.

This enemy could render everything I've accomplished so far moot.

On top of that, my thread—my strongest weapon—won't work here.

Is it just me, or am I totally screwed?

To get to the Upper Stratum, I have to conquer the Middle Stratum.

But I don't think that's going to be possible.

Should I look for another way, then?

The only other route I know is through that bee-infested pit.

Plus, wouldn't that mean going back to where that earth dragon hangs out?

Nope. No thank you. Not gonna happen.

So should I find another opening? Are there any other convenient shafts like that?

It's not out of the question.

I caught bees in my web when I was still in the Upper Stratum and saw a similar hole somewhere else, so maybe the bees have a nest there, too.

But there's no way of knowing for sure.

So should I try to push through the Middle Stratum?

Or should I explore the Lower Stratum some more, searching for another tunnel that may or may not exist?

What should I do...?

Well, I guess I'll put that aside for now and focus on evolving first.

Thanks to the huge amount of EXP I gained from defeating the monkey swarm, my level instantaneously went waaay up.

It's not like it completely slipped my mind when I found that uphill slope and got ridiculously excited, okay?

I definitely did not forget.

Evolving entails an involuntarily loss of consciousness, so attempting it in the Lower Stratum, where so many dangerous monsters lurk, requires some bravery. But it's not like I won't even try.

For one thing, I'm concerned my ability to level up may be capped.

Despite killing all those monkeys, my level didn't go higher than 10.

It'd be one thing if I simply hadn't gained enough EXP to boost it, but what if my species has level restrictions that won't let me advance further unless I evolve?

If this were just a game, I could test it by trying to level up once before evolving, but my life is on the line here.

I don't really wanna risk dying for the sake of an experiment.

Anyway, I have two options for evolution: taratect and small poison taratect.

Hmm, which should I choose?

Since the "small" part of my current name is missing from the "taratect" evolution, I'm guessing that choice will make me bigger.

The first time I evolved, I had the option of going from "small lesser taratect" to "lesser taratect," so it's probably safe to assume that I'd just grow if I picked this one.

The real problem is the "small poison taratect" option.

Since it adds the word "poison," it must strengthen my poison specialty, right?

Man, it's times like this I really wish I could Appraise my species options...

Wait... Appraisal?

Glancing at my status, I noticed something strange.

At the bottom of the stat list, the words "Evolution Available" were displayed in blinking letters.

What's this?

I'll try double-Appraising it.

<Available Evolutions: Taratect OR small poison taratect>

Whoa! Appraisal, are you for real?!

Holy crap! Since it's being displayed in letter format, that means I can double-Appraise it!

Now I can Appraise the species I can evolve into!

Appraisal is getting so useful that it's starting to scare me.

Anyway, I'll investigate my choices right now.

<Taratect: A standard adult of the spider-type monster species taratect. A carnivore with poisonous fangs.>

<Small poison taratect: A rare young species of the spider-type monster species taratect. Has extremely powerful poison.>

Yep. I've made up my mind. It's gotta be the Poison one.

I mean, it's a rare species! Rare!

Who would choose a "standard" species over a "rare" one, am I right?

And with that, I hurriedly construct a simple little home on the wall.

Time to evolve! Good night.

And good morning.

Hmm. Looks like I woke up all right.

I survey the area from my humble home.

All I can see are the corpses of the monkeys, no other monsters. Nice, nice. Since I seem to be safe, let's have a look at my postevolution status, shall we?

<Small poison taratect   LV 1   Nameless

Status:

HP: 56/56 (green) 2UP   MP: 1/56 (blue) 2UP

SP: 56/56 (yellow) 2UP   : 1/56 (red) 2UP

Average Offensive Ability: 38 2UP   Average Defensive Ability: 38 2UP

Average Magical Ability: 27 1UP   Average Resistance Ability: 27 1UP

Average Speed Ability: 537 21UP

Skills:

[HP Auto-Recovery LV 3]	[Poison Attack LV 9 NEW]	[Poison Synthesis LV 3]	[Spider Thread LV 9 1UP]
[Cutting Thread LV 4]	[Thread Control LV 8 1UP]	[Throw LV 3]	[Concentration LV 5 1UP]
[Hit LV 4]	[Evasion LV 2]	[Appraisal LV 8 1UP]	[Detection LV 4]
[Stealth LV 6]	[Heretic Magic LV 3 1UP]	[Shadow Magic LV 2]	[Poison Magic LV 2 1UP]
[Overeating LV 4]	[Night Vision LV 10]	[Vision Expansion LV 2]	[Poison Resistance LV 8 1UP]
[Paralysis Resistance LV 3]	[Petrification Resistance LV 3 1UP]	[Acid Resistance LV 4]	[Rot Resistance LV 3]
[Faint Resistance LV 2 1UP]	[Fear Resistance LV 6]	[Heresy Resistance LV 2 1UP]	[Pain Nullification]
[Pain Mitigation LV 6]	[Life LV 2]	[Magic Mass LV 2]	[Instantaneous LV 2]
[Persistent LV 2]	[Herculean Strength LV 1]	[Sturdy LV 1]	[Skanda LV 2]
[Taboo LV 2]	[n% I = W]		

Skill Points: 200

>

Ooh. There's some kind of new "UP" display.

This must be because my Appraisal level went up, right?

There's a skill point display now, too, and Appraisal seems to be working happily.

Does the UP thing compare it with before evolution, maybe?

Awesome! My stats got better! Just a little bit...

I thought they might rise a bit more dramatically, since I evolved into a rare species, but I guess not.

Although my speed is stupidly high as usual.

Well, that's fine. My status hasn't changed that much in all this time.

My skills certainly have, though.

Those improved while I was fighting the monkeys, too, so I got a bunch of new ones.

Poison Fang turned into Poison Attack somehow?

Thanks to Appraisal, I know what changed at a glance, but it's still pretty inconvenient.

Whoops, my SP went down from evolving and all, so I better eat some of my monkey stash and refuel.

I'll keep checking my status while I eat.

I knew my SP would go down, but it looks like my MP did, too.

That didn't happen last time I evolved, so I almost didn't notice.

Since I need it for Poison Synthesis and Thread Control and stuff now, I'll have to start paying more attention to my MP now.

Man, Poison Synthesis really saved my hide in the monkey battle before.

When I first picked it up, I thought it was kind of strange, but it's surprisingly useful. I'll probably rely on it more from now on.

Speaking of Poison Synthesis, since it leveled up, the fields Amount of Damage and Duration have been added.

Apparently, I can now control how strong my poison is and how long it lasts.

So if I want the enemy to suffer for a long time, I can extend the duration, and if I want to do a lot of damage all at once, I can add to the power.

Basically, I can customize my poison as much as I like.

However, the degree to which it can be customized is apparently dependent on the skill level.

When I tried customizing my spider venom, the power and duration wouldn't go past 9.

Boy, that spider venom is strong.

Speaking of poison, let's Appraise that Poison Attack thing now.

Since Poison Fang is gone and now I have this, it must be a variation of Poison Fang, right?

<Poison Attack: Adds the poison attribute to attacks>

Huh? That's the whole explanation?

Hmm? Wait, isn't that kind of a crazy effect?

Does that mean I can add poison to all my attacks now?

In that case, can I also poison my threads?

What a scary skill. I'll have to try it as soon as my SP recovers.

Aah! But my silk burns in the Middle Stratum, so I can't use it!

Noooo! I got such a wonderful skill, but it's useless!

Ugh, all right, let's put that aside for the moment.

The last poison-related skill is Poison Magic, right?

I'm sure I can't use it anyway, but its skill level went up, too.

Now I have the Poison Shot spell. It's a magic spell that lets you fire a ball of poison.

This is a long-range attack, isn't it?

I think back to the sea horse in the Middle Stratum.

To defeat it, I'd have to either drag it out of the magma or shoot it with a long-range attack.

Dragging it from the magma would be pretty much impossible with the means currently at my disposal.

As for long-range attacks, since I can't use my thread there, all I'd be able to do is throw whatever rocks I could find.

Even with the Throw skill, tossing a rock with my low stats definitely wouldn't be enough to put a dent in a monster.

Given that, coming up with a new long-range attack is my only option.

All things being equal, this new long-range ability seems very attractive indeed.

Yep. I don't really want to go roaming around the Lower Stratum rubbing elbows with monsters like that earth dragon, looking for an exit that might not even exist.

That settles it, then. I'll push on through the Middle Stratum.

Besides, having proven so ineffective against that magma sea horse still irks me.

My pride won't allow me to just ignore the Middle Stratum and search for another route now.

I'm totally getting my revenge.

But first, I'll spend some time here strategizing countermeasures.

I have to find some way to avoid taking damage from the heat of the Middle Stratum.

Then I'll acquire a long-range attack.

Once I clear those hurdles, my conquest of the Middle Stratum will commence!

file.06

ELROE GUNERUSH

LV.01

status

HP
132 / 132

MP
106 / 106

SP
128 / 128

128 / 128

Average Offensive Ability : 70
Average Defensive Ability : 70
Average Magic Ability : 68
Average Resistance Ability : 67
Average Speed Ability : 73

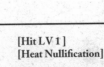

skill

[Fire Wyrm LV 1] [Hit LV 1]
[Swim LV 1] [Heat Nullification]

Also known as a sea horse. It looks like a sea horse with limbs. A low-ranking wyrm species. It generally swims through magma, looking for food. It physically attacks other monsters from the Middle Stratum but will confront intruders from other stratums mainly by launching fiery projectiles. Because of its low intelligence, though, it will resort to physically attacking any opponent once it runs out of MP. Its behavior is often reckless, but it has also been known to retreat when the enemy it faces is too strong. Danger level D.

J1 HERO PARTY

Led by our guide, Mr. Goyef, we press on through the Great Elroe Labyrinth.

The reason for our excursion this time is a report of an unusual taratect, a spider-shaped monster species.

Our job is to hunt it down. However...

"Yaana, would you let go of me, please?"

"N-no, thank you! You know how much I hate bugs, don't you, Julius?!"

Yaana, a saint, clings tightly to my clothes. She is literally dragging me down.

She's always hated bugs, so this is her usual reaction whenever we face off against insect-type monsters.

The Great Elroe Labyrinth is home to many such foes.

And to top it all off, Yaana's afraid of the dark.

Clearly, this is the last place she wants to be.

Yaana has an unparalleled gift for Light Magic and Recovery Magic, but she isn't in any state to use them at the moment.

"See? This is why I said you should stay behind. You're just gonna hold us back."

"Hyrince. I told you I can't do that, yes? A saint must be by the hero's side at all times. How could I disobey the Word of God?"

Hyrince stares at Yaana in disbelief.

Then he grudgingly shrugs and hefts the large shield in his hands.

Hyrince is a childhood friend of mine.

He's also the second son of Duke Quarto, from my birthplace, the Analeit Kingdom.

So Hyrince is nobility, but only as a duke's second son. I am also royalty, but the son of a concubine and second in line for the throne.

Since we are similar in both age and unusual social standing, it's only natural that we became close.

Beyond those ties, Hyrince is second to none in putting up an iron defense with a shield in his hands, so even after I became a hero, he's stayed by my side as a powerful warrior.

He's very reliable, and my best friend—even if he does have a bit of a sarcastic streak.

"Well, I suppose it's not just you, little Miss Yaana. Just about the only members of this group who can tolerate dismal surroundings like these are Hawkin and myself, no doubt."

"Y'know, boss, I can't say I blame ya for assumin' that, but I ain't actually all that fond of places like this, either."

Jeskan and Hawkin share a quick exchange.

"Wait, really?"

"Yep. I always did my best thievin' from other people, y'see. I can sniff out a fishy business deal with no trouble at all, but I ain't so good with dark caverns and the like."

Hawkin is a former thief who had apparently been caught and made a slave before being picked up by Jeskan.

Though a former thief, Hawkin had lived with a code, stealing only from corrupt aristocrats and sharing the wealth with the needy.

Hawkin may have been weaker than the others in terms of combat, but as an ex-thief, his skills and detailed knowledge of the underbelly of society make a great addition to our party.

Hawkin's employer, Jeskan, is a resourceful former adventurer.

As the eldest in the group, his abundant experience makes him a big brother figure to our young entourage.

Me, the hero; Yaana, the saint; Hyrince, the shield knight; Jeskan, the former adventurer; and Hawkin, the former thief.

With the addition of a sixth person, the labyrinth guide Goyef, our group sets out to bring down the monster.

The Great Elroe Labyrinth is home to all kinds of troublesome creatures, but the greatest challenge is its sheer size.

It's said that without a proper guide, people become permanently lost, even with a map.

"Everyone, please be careful. There's a monster ahead."

Our labyrinth guide issues a warning.

Dropping the idle chatter, we prepare for battle.

A deerlike creature appears, with a horn that looks like a sharp blade.

"An Elroe mowajitz. Danger level C. Be careful of their horns and flames!"

Mr. Goyef shouts a brief assessment.

The horns certainly look sharp. And it can use fire, too?

There are eight of these deer monsters in total.

A flame lights the end of each of their horns.

With their burning prongs thrust forward, the eight deer line up side by side and charge!

Yaana and I use Light Magic to intercept them before they reach us.

Yaana's spell pierces two, perforating their bodies and killing them instantly.

I hit the four that had pulled in front, bringing them down.

Jeskan stops another by swinging a sickle and chain, and Hawkin finishes off the beast with a throwing knife to its head.

Hyrince meets the final deer's charge head-on with his shield, using the creature's own momentum to ram it against the wall.

Then he lops off its head with a sword swipe while it's still dazed.

"Splendidly done. So even a group of C-ranked monsters are no trouble for the hero and his party."

Goyef sounded genuinely impressed.

"I knew you were quite gifted with a sword, Sir Hero, but your magic skills are excellent as well."

"Sir Goyef, Julius may be known throughout the world as a sword-wielding prodigy, but he doesn't actually know his way around a blade all that well."

"It's true. In terms of pure technique, I'm probably stronger, really. Though I would still lose because of the difference in our stats if we were ever to fight in earnest."

Hyrince and Jeskan aren't pulling any punches.

They're right, but I wish they wouldn't spread that information around so freely.

I have a reputation to protect, after all.

"He's beside himself just trying to make sure his brother and sister don't overtake him."

Hyrince grins, as if having heard my thoughts.

At times like these, having a childhood friend can be awfully annoying.

"If anything, he's better at magic. Right, Julius?"

"I suppose. The master who taught me was a mage, so that could be why. Master really was amazing."

In more ways than one.

Still, I didn't actually get to learn all that much from my master.

Since Master was from another country, we weren't able to study together as teacher and student for very long, for political reasons.

But my master's teachings are still firmly imprinted on my mind.

"Ahh, so that's why the structure of your magic was so perfect."

"That's right. Even though he's a hero and I'm a saint, Julius is somehow even better at magic than I am. Since the whole point of my existence will be rendered meaningless if he uses too much magic, I've asked him to refrain from using it outside as much as possible."

"Julius, you know you don't have to listen to this foolish woman, right?"

"Who are you calling a fool?!"

Watching Yaana and Hyrince go at it like a comedy duo, I can't help but smile.

Meanwhile, Jeskan and Hawkin have finished breaking down the monster corpses.

"Mr. Goyef, can we get anything else off these besides meat and the horn?"

"It'd be ideal to take the whole body, since the hide and such are usable, too... But that's not very practical, so yes, that should be enough. The horn can be used to make an excellent knife."

"It's much lighter and stronger than it looks, huh? Betcha I could use it for a throwin' knife."

The pair's knowledge as a former adventurer and thief, respectively, never ceases to amaze me. They are always on the lookout for a chance to turn a profit from monster corpses.

Beastly remains often turn out to be a treasure trove of materials.

They can produce weapons, armor, daily necessities, and even food.

"Sorry, Mr. Goyef. 'Fraid our lot is always like this when left to ourselves."

Hawkin's whispered apology reaches my ears thanks to the Auditory Enhancement skill.

"Not at all. Everyone is quite friendly, perhaps more so than I expected. It only makes my job all the easier."

"I'm glad to hear ya say that. People're always watchin' us just 'cause we're the hero's party. Times like these are our only chance to just be ourselves, y'know? Aside from me an' the boss, this is a pretty young crew, too. Havin' this kinda childish conversation really suits 'em."

"I see. Having heard so many legends about him and all, perhaps I'm guilty of viewing Sir Hero through rose-colored glasses myself."

"Most people do. And it don't help that Julius is pretty good at livin' up to expectations. 'Parently his little bro's started lookin' up to him, too, so he can't even be at ease with his own family."

There's a strange tone to Hawkin's words.

All of us have Auditory Enhancement.

Naturally, we all hear what is being said.

Hawkin must know this, too.

So we were meant to overhear it.

Is this Hawkin's way of showing concern for me, telling me I should try to relax a bit more?

I don't know whether to feel grateful or offended.

"Well, shall we move on?"

Mr. Goyef stows the materials gathered from the deer and starts walking.

The rest of us follow.

"Mr. Goyef, how many days will it take to reach our destination from here?"

The Great Elroe Labyrinth is enormous, so it takes days to get anywhere, even without taking monster battles into consideration.

I was told how far our destination was beforehand, but underground, where day and night blend together, it's all too easy to lose any sense of the passage of time.

"Let me see… About three more days, perhaps?"

"Three days, huh…?"

Another three days to achieve our goal.

However, there's no telling whether our target will stay put for that long.

If it moves on, it will take much longer than planned to complete this assignment.

"I hope it doesn't go anywhere."

"Indeed. Especially since the area where the creature was sighted is so close to the Middle Stratum. If it flees there, we won't be able to follow, of course. It's no place for human beings to enter. But since taratects are vulnerable to fire anyway, it's preposterous to think one would enter the Middle Stratum."

I nod in agreement with Goyef, and we keep walking toward our destination.

I wanna use magiiiic!

If a little white demon came up to me right now and said, "Make a contract with me and become a magical girl," I'd totally say yes at this point.

But then I'd have to get rid of him afterward, of course.

Actually, if something like that really did rear its head, I'd kill it first and ask questions never!

All right, enough messing around. I have to seriously think about what to do for a long-range attack.

Being able to use magic would of course be ideal, but there are several problems with that.

First of all, there's the reason I can't use magic in the first place—which is I don't know how.

It's like I have a game but don't know how to turn on the power. This is a pretty fundamental problem.

Aside from that, I'm also starting to suspect that there are skill requirements to enable magic usage.

Why? Because I just found one that seems to indicate precisely that.

It's called Magic Power Perception.

I mean, magic exists, and so does MP, so I guess it makes sense that "magic power" would exist, too. Actually, that might be what "MP" stands for.

But does that mean that without this skill, you can't properly sense magic power or something?

That could very well be the case. In fact, I can't think of any other explanation.

So is this "magic power" required to use magic?

Inquiring with the Divine Voice (temp.), I discovered a skill that seems to fit the bill.

It's called Magic Power Operation.

So I need to perceive magical power and manipulate it. Then I can invoke magic.

That's what it looks like to me, anyway.

In other words, without these skills, maybe it's not possible to use any spells?

I'm guessing that's the case.

Then basically, I've been trying to play a game without a power source or a controller.

Luckily, as it happens, I have 200 skill points.

I need two skills, and 200 is the exact number I'd need to acquire them both.

This is basically like God telling me to get those skills, right?

Hold your horses for a second, though.

Remember all the hardships I've endured so far.

Has God ever been that kind to me? No. Absolutely not!

I can't underestimate just how bad my luck is. There's definitely a catch.

And this time, I know exactly what that is.

It's called Detection.

I got the Detection skill at the same time as Thread Control.

After defeating that snake and evolving for the first time.

Since I always relied on surprise attacks, I couldn't afford to fall prey to one myself.

Hoping for a skill that would alert me to enemy presences right away, I opted for Detection.

As it turns out, that was a big mistake.

Basically, Detection is too powerful.

<A skill that combines all perception systems. Summary: Magic Power Perception, Physical Perception, Material Perception, Presence Perception, Danger Perception, Motion Perception, Heat Perception, Reaction Perception, Space Perception.>

Isn't that wild?

All the perception-based skills in one go.

And it only cost me 100 points. Unfortunately.

The problem with this skill is it invokes all those sensory skills at once.

You can't pick and choose or employ them individually.

So what happens when they all kick in at once? Well, I get a really horrible headache.

It doesn't feel like my head's going to crack open so much as just violently explode.

My guess is that Detection is simply too high in regard to performance, and my brain's processing speed can't keep up.

And unlike other skills, there isn't much improvement after leveling up.

I mean, since it's already too damn overwhelming to begin with, making the skill stronger only worsens my headaches. That makes it even more useless than before.

Though as a bonus, since it perceives so many things simultaneously, Detection advances really easily.

The only times I've ever used it are when I first got it and once more after that, when I got a headache and went "What the hell was that?!" before cautiously testing it again.

Then there was the time when Appraisal gained the ability to display skills, so I decided to try it again after checking its description.

With just three uses, it leveled up three times.

Seriously, I wish I could apply that growth rate to some of my other skills instead.

And of course, each time Detection levels up, it gets even harder for me to use.

There's no saving it at this point.

Which is why I decided to semipermanently seal off the skill.

But here's the big problem.

To use magic, I probably need to use Magic Power Perception.

And Magic Power Perception is tied to Detection.

Strength and Herculean Strength, Solidity and Sturdy: They're both pairs of upwardly compatible skills.

I got Strength and Solidity when I gained the Monster Slayer title, while Herculean Strength and Sturdy appeared when I got the Monster Slaughterer title.

Strength and Solidity raise my attack and defense power, respectively, by their number of skill levels, while the improved counterparts raise the skills by ten times the number of skill levels. On top of that, they also increase my level-up stat increases.

They basically seem to be lesser versions of the Skanda skill, which I seem to have had since I was first reincarnated here.

Anyway, when I acquired these skills, Strength merged into Herculean Strength and Solidity into Sturdy.

It seems to me that once I acquire a superior skill, the lesser versions get incorporated into it.

In which case, I get the feeling that if I acquire Magic Power Perception, it'll wind up merged into Detection, since the latter is clearly higher ranked.

Meaning it's impossible for me to use any parts of Detection individually.

Aggghhh, does this mean that if I don't do something about Detection, I'll never be able to use magic for the rest of my life?

Noooooo!

After coming this far, a skill I semipermanently sealed off is going to stand in my way?!

Hmm. Isn't there anything I can do here?

Since my brain's processing power can't keep up, I guess it'd be good if I had some kind of skill to compensate for that.

That doesn't mean I'm stupid, though. It doesn't, okay?

Detection simply goes overboard.

But it seems like I just discovered a new feature of Appraisal.

I already knew that skill points are displayed when I level up now, but it turns out that if I double-Appraise that, I can see a catalog of all the skills I can acquire with my current skill points.

Man, Appraisal is no joke.

Now I don't need to check in with the Divine Voice (temp.) every time I want to know if a specific skill exists or not.

And since the list is displayed in Appraisal, that means I can double-Appraise the skills, too.

So I can investigate the effects of a skill before I acquire it.

Now I'll never take a useless skill by accident…I hope.

So I immediately look over the skill list, hoping to find one that will let me do something about Detection.

But along the way, I am distracted by the discovery of a truly insane skill.

I'm so shocked that I do a double take, close the Appraisal, then Appraise it again for good measure.

That's how massive the difference is.

In more ways than one.

‹Pride [Skill Points Required: 100]: n% of the power to reach godhood. Upon acquiring, experience points and proficiency will greatly increase, along with improved growth capacity for every ability. In addition, the user will gain the ability to surpass the W system and interfere with the MA field.›

I don't really get it.

Neither the meaning of the summary nor the reason a skill like this can be acquired for a mere 100 points.

I try Appraising all the vocabulary I don't recognize, like "n%," "W," and "MA field," but the result for all of them is just ‹cannot be Appraised›.

All I can really glean from the description is that this skill will grant me more experience points and proficiency, and that it will have some kind of effect on growth.

That alone sounds pretty extraordinary.

"Pride" is a word you hear often as one of the seven deadly sins.

It's said to be the gravest sin of all—even the root of all other sins.

When it shows up in a game, it's usually the name of a last boss-level enemy or a strong but cursed weapon. You know, that sort of thing.

Judging by the name, this skill can't be a good thing.

The fact that I can't find anything else that increases experience or proficiency only heightens my skepticism.

If this were a game, it wouldn't be too unusual for there to be a few skills like that, but no. Pride is the only one.

So instead of a bunch of minor skills like that, there's nothing but a single super-advanced skill with a sketchy-sounding name.

If I learned anything from Detection, it's that being technically superior doesn't necessarily mean it's good.

Aside from the fact that it's basically preventing me from using magic, Detection can't hurt me again unless I activate it.

But something that increases EXP and proficiency is probably the kind of skill that's constantly in effect, right?

What if it's another trap like Detection, but this time I can't switch it on and off?

I can't shake the feeling that that's exactly what'll happen.

However, its known effects are certainly attractive.

Even knowing that it's probably a trap, there's still this temptation to jump right in. Legit, it's like a deal with the devil.

The description of the Pride skill reminds me a bit of my "n% I = W."

They're similar enough that it's probably no coincidence.

I still don't know what the mystery skill does.

At least it doesn't seem to have any negative or positive effects.

So it's possible that this one has no downsides, too, yeah?

…It'd be better if I don't jump to conclusions like that.

But in my heart, I've already decided. Honestly, I probably decided as soon as I first saw it.

I have a funny feeling about this.

Like, I almost have to take it.

For better or worse, I think I've gotta have this skill.

There's this sense like it's not really up to me.

I don't know why I'm so drawn to Pride.

Sometimes fate works in mysterious ways, though, so I want to trust my intuition here.

Anyway, I really don't have a choice.

The instant I laid eyes on it, my intuition told me, "Grab!"

<Number of skill points currently in possession: 200. Number of skill points required to acquire skill [Pride]: 100. Acquire skill?>

Yes.

<[Pride] acquired. Remaining skill points: 100.>

All right.
I did it!

<Proficiency has reached the required level.

Skill [Taboo LV 2] has become [Taboo LV 4].>

Uh-oh!

<Condition satisfied. Acquired title [Ruler of Pride].>
<Acquired skills [Abyss Magic LV 10] [Hades] as a result of title [Ruler of Pride].>

Now I've done it!

Hoooo, boy.

How did it come to this?

I mean, come on. Is this really happening?!

What the hell? What the hell? I'm gonna say it one last time, okay? What the hell?

My Taboo skill level rose. By two levels, no less. What'd I do?

And some crazy title popped up. Yay?

And I mean, Abyss Magic definitely sounds like a superior kind of magic to me. And it's level 10!

This is weird, right?

Anyway, I guess I'll start by Appraising the effects of Abyss Magic and Hades.

Wait. Something weird is going on in my status.

My MP, average magical ability, and average resistance ability.

Wait a sec, aren't these way higher than they were a minute ago?

Why? Is this another effect of Pride?

I mean, well, it's not like getting better stats is a bad thing...

Yeah. Better not overthink it.

Okay, Appraisal time.

<Abyss Magic: The highest form of Dark Magic. Manipulates the darkness of the abyss. The kinds of magic that can be used depend on the skill level. LV 1: Hell Gate, LV 2: Hell of Unbelievers, LV 3: Hell of Lust, LV 4: Hell of Gluttony, LV 5: Hell of Greed, LV 6: Hell of Wrath, LV 7: Hell of Heresy, LV 8: Hell of Violence, LV 9: Hell of Fraud, LV 10: Hell of Treachery.>

<Hades: Manifests Hades>

Uh...yikes. What should I even say?

Unreal. This sounds all kinds of dangerous.

What's the deal with this "hell" series? I mean, clearly "manifesting Hades" sounds pretty dicey, but what about the rest of it?

<Hell Gate: The beginning gate>

<Hell of Unbelievers: Hell for the ignorant and unbelievers>

<Hell of Lust: Hell for those stained with lust>

<Hell of Gluttony: Hell for those who glorify gluttony>

<Hell of Greed: Hell for those who devote themselves to greed>

<Hell of Wrath: Hell for those who are ruled by wrath>

<Hell of Heresy: Hell for those who idolize heresy>

<Hell of Violence: Hell for those who exert violence>

<Hell of Fraud: Hell for those who whisper fraud>

<Hell of Treachery: Hell for those who stir up treachery>

What kind of Appraisal results are these?

I mean, it's got nothing to do with the effects of the spells. Who wrote these results? That's what I'd like to know.

Just out of curiosity, I try to see if I can use Hades, but not a single thing happens.

I'm not sure whether I feel disappointed or relieved.

Man... I seriously feel like I did something messed up.

What kind of terrible, hidden side effects is this freaky skill hiding?

Just as I feared, it doesn't seem like I can switch it on and off.

And it's pretty weird that I got a title just for acquiring it, right?

It doesn't exactly sound like a good one, either.

And leveling up the Taboo skill is supposed to be bad, too...

The Appraisal description even talked about not raising it.

I've definitely seen numerical values that you're not supposed to raise in games before.

Like karma meters and that sort of thing.

The kind of stuff where, as it rises, the story heads toward a bad ending or villagers start acting afraid of you and the like.

I mean, not that there's any story, in this case, or people for me to meet, but still...

Thinking about it, the only two skills I've seen with Appraisals that don't clearly explain their effects are Taboo and n% I = W.

And Taboo is something I'm not supposed to raise.

There's definitely something going on here.

If I keep pushing it, I just know something horrible will happen.

Maybe if I max out Taboo, the wrath of God will kill me on the spot or something.

Ahhhhh! That's too scary!

A-all right, there's no need to panic just yet.

It's still only level 4. And it's not as though I know for sure that'll happen.

Hmm. The fact that this new skill has no immediately obvious downside is scary in itself.

Taboo doesn't seem to have any effect right now, and it looks like Pride isn't doing anything bad, either, but...

...the last thing I need is suddenly realizing I'm being strangled little by little with silk floss or something.

On the other hand, that most likely means nothing's gonna happen anytime soon.

Well, there's no helping it now, so I may as well save my panic for when the time comes.

Though, hopefully, I won't panic too much then, either...

Anyway, I should probably save the rest of my skill points for now.

Since I just learned this crazy magic and all, I definitely want to try it, but I don't think I'm going to get anywhere until I figure out what to do with Detection.

The Magic Power Operation skill is probably necessary, too, in which case I need two skills: Magic Power Operation and something to deal with Detection.

Since I only have 100 points left at the moment, I'd have to choose between one or the other.

So for the time being, I may as well wait until I have 200 points to spend again.

Boy, it sure is quiet.

Usually, I can hear all kinds of sounds in the distance, but right now, I don't hear much of anything.

I don't see any monsters around, either, which is peculiar in itself.

Maybe it's because of the monkeys?

I'm sure a huge mob on the move would chase away other monsters.

So that's probably why it's so quiet.

<Proficiency has reached the required level. Acquired skill [Prediction LV 1].>

Hmm? I got a skill?

Let's see.

<Prediction: When making predictions, adds a bonus to thinking ability>

Huh. Well, I certainly don't mind having it, but it doesn't seem super-useful, either.

I mean, it's not like it lets me automatically know the answer to things or anything.

It just means the gears in my head turn a little faster—and only in specific circumstances.

Wait, I think this was on the list of skills I can get with 100 points, too.

So this is worth the same number of points as Pride...?

Doesn't that seem strange?

Anyway, there really isn't a single monster around here, huh?

I'm not sensing any danger, so I don't think it's because there's a really strong monster scaring the others off or anything.

Even squinting, I don't see a thing.

<Proficiency has reached the required level. Acquired skill [Vision Enhancement LV 1].>

Oh? Another skill?

Let's see.

<Vision Enhancement: Enhances vision>

Thanks a lot!

I mean, I guess that's fair.

But I don't think I really need this, either. Spiders' eyes are already pretty good, y'know?

And this was on the 100-point skill list, too...

Come to think of it, there were some for enhancing the other senses, too.

If squinting really hard was the only condition for acquiring Vision Enhancement, maybe I could increase the proficiency of the other ones by focusing on them one at a time, too?

Well, let's give it a try.

First, ears.

What sort of ears do spiders have anyway? I should probably know this, but I have no idea.

<Proficiency has reached the required level. Acquired skill [Auditory Enhancement LV 1].>

Oh, hey, it totally worked.

All right, let's try the rest of them, too.

<Proficiency has reached the required level. Acquired skill [Olfactory Enhancement LV 1].>
<Proficiency has reached the required level. Acquired skill [Tactile Enhancement LV 1].>

I'll do the taste one next time I eat something, I guess.

Man, though, I can't believe skills come this easily.

I guess I hadn't really thought about it, since a spider's five senses seem solid to begin with.

The key to gaining proficiency is consciously focusing on the action, I guess.

Otherwise, I probably would've gotten these skills a long time ago.

<Proficiency has reached the required level.
Skill [Prediction LV 1] has become [Prediction LV 2].>

That was fast! Didn't I just get this skill a minute or two ago?!

How did it go up already?

I mean, I guess that's fine. I totally knew that would happen anyway.

<Proficiency has reached the required level. Acquired skill [Parallel Thinking LV 1].>

Wait, again?!

This is one of the skills I thought might be able to help with Detection, too!

<Parallel Thinking: Grants the ability to think about multiple things at the same time>

Awesome! Doesn't that mean my brain's processing power's improved?

How exactly did I get this, though?

I don't think I was really thinking about multiple things at once...

Ah, it must've been my old friend Appraisal.

I always have Appraisal on.

The Appraisal results of whatever's around me are constantly flowing into my head.

I usually just ignore it, so I barely even notice anymore, but I guess you could call that thinking about multiple things.

And I can't think of any other explanation, so that's gotta be it.

Still, kinda weird, right?

I'm getting an awful lot of skills at once.

You have to admit, it's pretty unusual to suddenly start getting skills one after another, yeah?

I mean, not that I don't know why.

Pride.

A skill that greatly increases the amount of proficiency you gain.

Yep. Gotta be it.

Still, though, it's gone up by a pretty crazy amount...

I don't know the specific numbers, so I can't say for sure, but this definitely seems like a lot.

<Proficiency has reached the required level.

Skill [Prediction LV 2] has become [Prediction LV 3].>

See what I mean?

Well, since I got this new skill that might help with Detection and all, I may as well give it a shot right away.

Huff... Whew. Okay.

Detection on.

GAHHH! It's too much! Off, offffff!

<Proficiency has reached the required level.

Skill [Parallel Thinking LV 1] has become [Parallel Thinking LV 2].>

<Proficiency has reached the required level.

Skill [Detection LV 4] has become [Detection LV 5].>

Wheeze... Owww. My head hurts.

Right, right. My Parallel Thinking skill was only level 1.

Based on my experiences so far, I shouldn't have expected much from a level-1 skill.

Nothing really feels any different this go-around.

That raised Parallel Thinking, but it raised Detection, too.

Detection leveling up doesn't help me at all!

All that'll do is add to the amount of information and make things even worse!

If both of them level up at the same time, it's like taking one step forward and two steps back.

And my stupid Detection seems to have an insane growth rate that raises its level every single time I activate it, so really, it's more like three steps back.

Plus, it'll grow even faster now because of Pride.

Seriously, what's up with this damn Detection skill?

What a monstrous foe. I can't believe it's outsmarted even me!

Who knew there was an enemy as strong as that earth dragon lurking so close by?

I don't think I'm gonna win this one.

Anyway, maybe I should just wait for my Parallel Thinking skill to level up for now.

It certainly doesn't seem like I can use it to partition my thoughts or anything at the moment, so the only way I can think of to earn more proficiency is by thinking about something else while looking at Appraisal results.

Apparently, activating Detection raises it, too, but I really don't want to mess with that anymore.

Hmph. Still, I don't think the idea itself was a bad one...

If my thinking ability improves, then I should be able to use Detection eventually...probably.

Man, when I looked at the skill list before, I thought the Parallel Thinking skill was my best bet, though...

Hmm. Let me look at the list again.

Since I have fewer points now, there aren't as many on it as before.

But there are still quite a few.

It seems like most skills can be acquired with 100 points.

Aside from certain high-performance and totally broken skills.

Although I was able to get one broken skill, Pride, for 100 points.

Anyway, the only skills that seem like they might help with Detection are:

<Arithmetic Processing: Enhances mental processing ability>

<Memory: Enhances memory ability>

I think that's about it.

Not a lot of options. And I don't think the Memory one is quite right, either.

In which case, Arithmetic Processing is the most likely candidate, but would taking that really be enough to let me use Detection?

Hmm, hmm, hmm. I mean, I thought Parallel Thinking was the best option, and that hasn't helped much so far...

Arithmetic Processing would probably be pretty useless at a low level, too.

Oh, wait a sec.

"Arithmetic" is basically math, right?

If I do some mental math, maybe I'll get the skill for free?

Yeah. That's probably worth a try.

Okay, maybe I'll think about powers of 2 for a while...

2, 4, 8, 16, 32, 64......

......8,192; 16,384; um...32,768 maybe?

This is getting pretty tough.

What's next? Hmm...

<Proficiency has reached the required level. Acquired skill [Arithmetic Processing LV 1].>

Oh! Nice, nice. My plan worked perfectly.

Hmm. Should I give it a shot?

It's probably not gonna work, but nothing ventured, nothing gained, right?

Huff... Whew. Okay.

Detection on.

GYAAAH! Still too much! Off, off!

<Proficiency has reached the required level.
   Skill [Arithmetic Processing LV 1] has become [Arithmetic Processing LV 2].>
<Proficiency has reached the required level.
   Skill [Parallel Thinking LV 2] has become [Parallel Thinking LV 3].>
<Proficiency has reached the required level.
   Skill [Detection LV 4] has become [Detection LV 5].>
<Proficiency has reached the required level.
   Skill [Heresy Resistance LV 2] has become [Heresy Resistance LV 3].>

Wheeze... Owww. My head hurts. Again.

This isn't gonna work, huh? It's just too much. My head feels like it's gonna burst. I don't like pain.

Ugh... Unreal.

Wait, what happened to my Pain Mitigation?

I've gone through a bunch of near-death experiences, so why is this pain too much for me to handle?

And hey, why did my Heresy Resistance skill level up anyway?

What does that mean? Is it because Mr. Detection's assault on my head is so demonic?

There's nothing weird about calling it an "attack," right?

I mean, my resistance even became better.

Let me think about this.

The heresy attribute is something about attacking the soul directly, right?

So if my Heresy Resistance improved, that means the results of Detection aren't affecting just my brain, but my soul itself.

Does that mean that half of this headache is actually my soul aching?

That's scary!

My soul's not gonna wear out if I keep doing this, right? I don't wanna suddenly go brain-dead, okay?

<Proficiency has reached the required level.
   Skill [Prediction LV 3] has become [Prediction LV 4].>

Oh, okay. Good thing the effect of Prediction isn't based on correct answers!

It's fine. That was just a prediction, nothing to worry about. Let's go with that.

Hmm. But in that case, doesn't that mean a soul-related skill would help me withstand Detection?

I don't see anything like that on the list, though.

All there is, is Heresy Resistance.

So I'll just have to keep leveling up Heresy Resistance, then?

…How do I do that?

Ahh… It's no use.

I should just stick to the original plan: Keep raising Parallel Thought and Arithmetic Processing.

After all, they both advanced when I activated Detection, which means they must be involved in the process somehow. Until then, I'm putting Detection back off-limits. I'm a little scared of using it.

Okay, so now that I sort of have a plan for Detection, what am I going to do about the heat in the Middle Stratum?

Maybe it'd help a little if I had Fire Resistance or something?

But I think my whole body might be weak to fire, not just my thread…

I didn't see Fire Resistance when I looked at the list before.

Does that mean it's not something I can obtain with 200 skill points?

There were other resistances on the list, but no fire.

This is just a guess, but I think maybe since I'm weak to fire, it's harder for me to obtain Fire Resistance.

<Proficiency has reached the required level.
Skill [Prediction LV 4] has become [Prediction LV 5].>

Oh, hello there again. You sure level up fast, huh? It's probably the effect of Pride in action again.

Well anyway, since I know it won't be easy, let's aim to acquire Fire Resistance while training my HP Auto-Recovery skill.

To that end, I'll go to the Middle Stratum a couple times a day, then come back when my HP goes down.

Taking damage probably means I'm gaining proficiency for Fire Resistance, or maybe Heat Resistance, if that's a thing.

I don't know how long it'll take, but sooner or later, I think I'll probably get a Fire or Heat Resistance skill.

And when my HP goes down, HP Auto-Recovery will kick in, so that's two birds with one stone.

If my defense and recovery exceed the passive damage I take, I should be able to walk around, at least.

In the meantime, I'll work on my other skills.

Parallel Thinking and Arithmetic Processing for the Detection plan, for starters.

I may try to improve my stat-increasing skills while I'm at it, too.

In particular, Skanda, Herculean Strength, and Sturdy all improve the growth rate of my stats, so I should give them top priority.

But... I know running around should increase my Skanda skill, and doing push-ups or leg-ups or whatever should increase Herculean Strength, but what about Sturdy?

Since it's for defense, does that mean I have to get hit with attacks?

Hmm. Maybe if I do some Thread Control practice and use it to whip my own body or something?

I hate pain, but I guess it might be worth a try...

Also, if I'm going to be staying here for a while, I should probably secure some food.

My stamina isn't decreasing right now thanks to Overeating, but sooner or later, I'll have to eat.

Probably a good idea to look around a little and make some preparations for hunting.

It may even be worth setting up a few webs for capturing prey.

I can lay some traps with thread that's as close to invisible as I can manage.

Yeah, there's an idea. Let's go with that.

Even if a strong monster capable of breaking through my thread gets caught by mistake, I won't be there, so no harm done.

All right, then, let's put this plan in action.

My HP's recovered, so I guess I'll go back to the Middle Stratum and work on reducing my HP again.

...Man, when I put it that way, it sure doesn't sound fun.

So... Hello from the Middle Stratum!

It's hot, folks! I'd tell you how hot, but it's impossible to measure! Mostly because I don't have a thermometer!

Today's forecast predicts magma spewing around all day!

It'll be much too hot for even this intrepid weather reporter to venture outside!

This has been a live on-site report from the Middle Stratum! Back to you in the studio!

Whew. It's reeeally hot.

Neither of my skills has gone up yet, either. Guess I might as well take my time.

I mean, it's not like I'm being chased or anything.

S1 ACADEMY

There's something called an academy in this country.

In our old world, the expectation is that everyone goes to school, but in this world, getting a formal education is fairly unusual. The only people able to afford it are aristocrats and other members of the privileged class, particularly wealthy commoners or people otherwise blessed with a great deal of natural talent.

Because I'm a member of the royal family, I can attend school without a problem.

Sue is in the same boat, of course, as well as Katia, who clears the conditions by being the daughter of a duke.

And so the three of us were sent off to academy together.

Just like school in our old world, there are general studies taught here.

At the same time, though, there are classes that teach us how to fight.

If anything, the latter is the main focus.

This continent, Daztrudia, is human territory, but the other continents are still embroiled in violent battles against demons and monsters.

There are monsters here on Daztrudia, as well—to the point where there's always a need for more capable fighters.

So we spend a lot of our time at school learning about combat.

Sue, Katia, and I are at the academy entrance ceremony.

Fei is considered my pet (or rather my familiar), so I can't bring her along.

Apparently, I can bring her to class, but she isn't allowed to participate in events like these.

Looking around, I see other incoming students my age, sitting in chairs and waiting for the ceremony to begin.

This is the largest academy in the region, so a lot of kids come here from other countries, too.

As I size up the other students, most of them either hurriedly look away or stare directly at me.

I can feel eyes on me, too, and hear the whispered rumors.

"That's the prince of this country sitting over there."

"I heard he's some kind of genius, but he doesn't look that strong to me..."

"I wonder if we can get close to him somehow?"

Because of my Auditory Enhancement skill, I can hear every word they're saying.

Now I'm feeling really uncomfortable.

"Gooood morning!"

A nonchalant voice breaks through the strained atmosphere.

Turning to look, I saw the elf Filimøs, formerly known as Ms. Oka.

"Good morning. It's strange to see you as a student now."

"I'm very excited to experience youth all over again, you knooow!"

With that, she sits down beside me.

Sue, who is seated on my other side, regards Ms. Oka with an expression that borders on a scowl.

In fact, she's definitely scowling at Ms. Oka.

Oh, right. This is Sue's first time meeting my former teacher.

"Come on, Sue, don't glare at people. Sorry, ma'am. This is my sister, Sue."

"Oh-ho! I see, I seeee. Verrry cute."

Ms. Oka scrutinizes Sue with a smile that elicits a bad feeling in my gut.

She's definitely not thinking anything decent.

"Brother, who is this suspicious-looking person?"

Understandably, Sue is trying to shield herself behind me a little.

"Shun, dear, you haven't done anything strange to your poor sister, have you?"

Teacher, please don't ask me that with such a serious expression.

Of course I haven't done anything.

"Sue, this is Filimøs, an elf who'll be joining us at school. Shun and I have met her before, you see. Though she looks like a child, it's only because elves age quite slowly—she's actually the same age we are. She's also worked in many different places, so if anything, she knows more of the world than any of us."

Katia steps in to explain things to Sue for me.

I'm not good at laying things out so clearly, so Katia's support is a big help.

"Nice to meet youuu!"

"…You too."

Sue still looks rather guarded, but she reluctantly exchanges greetings with Ms. Oka.

"Katia, does my brother prefer childish women like this?"

"Oh, it's not like that at all, don't worry. Despite her looks, Ms. Filimøs is quite dependable, so Shun simply views her with respect."

You know I can hear you whispering, right?

I'm absolutely not a lolicon, thank you very much.

I'll have to thank Katia for backing me up later—and have a few words with Sue.

Apparently, Ms. Oka overheard this conversation, as well. I muster a wry smile despite my sulky mood, and she returns it in kind.

The entrance ceremony ends without any issues.

Afterward, most of the students return to the dormitories or set out to explore the campus.

The academy is a boarding school.

I'm no exception to this rule, so I'll be living in a dorm while I'm attending.

Unless there are special circumstances, students can't leave school grounds except during long holidays.

"What shall we do next?" Katia poses the question in socialite mode.

We've already gotten our dorm rooms set up.

I'd like to see the academy grounds if possible, but I have a feeling Fei would scold me later if I left her alone for that long, so I should go back to the dormitory first.

"There're a few people I'd like to meeeet. Would you all come with meee?"

Just as I'm about to head back to my dorm, my former teacher calls out to us.

"Someone you'd like to meet?"

"Oh, yesss. The future saint and the future sword-king. It wouldn't hurt for you to get to know them as well, you knooow!"

The saint and the sword-king.

The saint is a symbolic figure from our neighboring kingdom, the Holy Kingdom of Alleius.

Often called the hero's counterpart, the woman designated as the saint in each generation is obliged to work alongside the hero.

The saint is selected based purely on ability, not pedigree.

And since the Holy Kingdom of Alleius is the main seat of the religion called the Word of God, all the followers of that religion gather there.

In other words, the saint is chosen from an elite group of female followers of the Word of God.

The current saint, of course, accompanies my older brother Julius.

Her name is Yaana, I believe. A master of Light and Recovery Magic, she's the only woman in my brother's party.

I've only met her a handful of times, but I remember thinking she was pretty tomboyish for a saint.

So this person at the academy would be Yaana's successor, then.

The sword-king is the title of the ruler of the Renxandt Empire, the country with the highest human population on the continent of Kasanagara.

The Renxandt Empire is adjacent to demon territory, so it's endlessly under siege.

To lead that country, the most important requirement is strength.

As a result, it's said that subsequent generations of rulers have taken the alias of the first king, the "sword-king," as their title.

While the saint is chosen from a pool of talented candidates regardless of their lineage, the sword-king is based purely on bloodline.

Which means the current sword-king's son is enrolled at this academy.

"Ah yes, the crown price of the Renxandt Empire. I've certainly heard the rumors. I believe he's a first-year at the academy this year, just like us. He's said to be a sword master to rival the memory of the original sword-king, or such is the claim."

Katia, how do you know about this?

This is the first I'm hearing about it.

"Shun, you should try paying attention to the world around you a little more, too."

Katia raises her eyebrows at me. My expression must've betrayed my thoughts.

Damn. She's got me there, I guess.

"But... If you're going out of your way to meet them, ma'am, does that mean...?"

"It sure doooes."

"Well then, I suppose we simply must meet them."

Katia and Filimøs continue the conversation on their own.

Sue and I don't follow their meaning, so we simply look on in silence.

"Come along, then, Shun... Wait. Why the long face?"

"Oh, I just wasn't sure what you were talking about..."

"Really? Sue I can understand, but you..."

Katia and our teacher both look at me pityingly.

C-come on, do you really have to make that face at me?

"I mean, I know she said it'd be good to meet them sooner rather than later, so I figured I'd go, but..."

"Shun, you're something else."

Katia presses a hand to her forehead as if fending off a headache.

"Do you really trust Ms. Oka that much?"

"Huh?"

I stare at Katia blankly, not understanding her pointed whisper.

Seeing this, Katia heaves a deep sigh.

"Ah, looks like we don't have to go and find them after aaaall!"

I look up and follow the teacher's gaze to see a boy and a girl approaching us.

The boy has dark brown hair that's nearly black and eyes of the same color, with tough, masculine features.

The girl has wavy blonde hair and blue eyes with an air of mysterious beauty.

"Yo. So that puny elf is Ms. Oka?"

"Don't be rude, Natsume. That's no way to talk to a teacher! It's good to see you, ma'am."

Both of them are speaking Japanese.

With that, I finally realize what Katia and our teacher were getting at.

These two are reincarnations, like us.

"Good to see you, toooo! Natsume, Hasebe, I'm so very glad you're wellll."

Our teacher's words reveal the pair's original identities.

The boy's name used to be Kengo Natsume, the de facto leader of the boys in our class.

Honestly, though, I never really liked Natsume much.

He was really athletic, with good reflexes, and while he never actually did anything violent, he had a tendency to show off his strength and use it to get people to do what he wanted. On top of being pushy, he came off sounding like he looked down on others.

Most kids in our class either followed his lead or did their best to avoid him.

I was always the latter.

"Ha-ha! Ms. Oka was always tiny, but now she shrank even more! That's hilarious!"

"Natsume!"

The girl scolding Natsume was formerly Yuika Hasebe, who used to sit next to me.

Unlike Natsume, Hasebe never made much of an impression as being particularly good or bad.

Among the girls, the clique that stood out most was the one that included Fei, aka Mirei Shinohara. But Hasebe was closer with the relatively quiet girls, like Temarikawa and Furuta.

Of course, that's just compared with Fei—she was still a pretty bright and active person herself—but Hasebe certainly never struck me as the type who secretly held the potential to be a saint or anything like that.

"I'm an elf, so I can't help being small, you knooow. Besides, you're not so much taller than me yourself now, Natsumeee."

"I'm gonna have a huge growth spurt soon, just you wait. Anyway, this guy's the prince of this country, right? Who's in there?"

Natsume looks my way like a predator sizing up its prey.

His eyes glitter as if he might attack me at any moment.

I do remember this guy being pretty nasty in our former life, but did his eyes always seem this dangerous?

"Shunsuke Yamada."

"And I'm Kanata Ooshima. Long time no see."

After I answer, Katia steps forward deliberately to introduce herself.

"Huh? Ooshima?"

"Yes, that's right. I'm Ooshima. Big surprise, right? Guess I got reborn as a woman."

Hasabe stares at Katia in shock.

From there, the conversation picks up, and Natsume looks away from me.

Thanks, Katia.

Natsume's name may be Hugo Baint Renxandt now, but just like in our previous lives, I want as little to do with him as possible.

Interlude

THE DUKE'S DAUGHTER AND HER TEACHER

"Ma'am, why exactly are you going to school in the first place?"

"Why, to enjoy my youth all over again, of course!"

"I'm serious, you know."

"I'm joooking. I suppose you could say I'm trying to watch over those of you reincarnations whose social status is too high for me to take you into my care, you knooow."

"I knew it."

"Ooooh? You'd alllready guessed?"

"To an extent anyway, since so many of us reincarnations are in one place. I don't know how you managed it, but I'm guessing you elves must've done some negotiating to gather all the reincarnations at this academy."

"That's true as far as Natsume goes, but Hasebe being here is sheer coincidence, honessst."

"So you don't entirely deny it."

"That's because I know I can't fool you, clever Miss Katiaaa."

"Well then, since I'm so clever, maybe you'll let me ask you a question. Are the last six of us still alive?"

"...We know for certain that four have died. I've located the other two, but I have no way of going to them directly at the moment."

"I see. I had a feeling..."

"I'm sorry."

"There's no reason for you to apologize, ma'am. Do you mind if I ask...the names of the ones who died?"

"Of course… Kouta Hayashi, Hiiro Wakaba, Naofumi Kogure, and Issei Sakurazaki."

"…I see. Well, that does explain why you have the time to attend school like this. You don't need to search for the others anymore."

"That's right, although I am still taking action to protect the other two, you knooow."

"So who have they become that's created a situation where you can't get to them?"

"That's a seeecret."

"Ma'am, I'm being serious here."

"I am, too. It seriously has to be a seeecret."

"Does it have anything to do with why we can't meet the others that you have been able to look after?"

"Hmm. That's a different matter, sooo it's not really related, nooo."

"I see. Are they doing well, at least?"

"They're fiiine."

"And what are their names?"

"I caaan't tell you."

"Why not?"

"Well, you might find out eventually, but I don't think now is the right time."

"That doesn't make any sense."

"I'm sorry. But it's how it has to be. And on that note, I have a warning for you."

"What is it?"

"Please don't train your skills too much."

"Why not?"

"I can't say."

"Ma'am, I can only imagine what you've seen in the outside world, but you know Shun's older brother is a hero, right? I've heard all about his work as a hero from Shun. How he protected a village from a horde of monsters all by himself and fended off a demon even after it made him drink poison. That sort of thing."

"Whaaat about it?"

"This world is extremely dangerous. We may not be heroes, but Shun and

I still have roles to play. It's very possible we may have to stand on the battlefield ourselves someday. Since I'm a woman, those odds are still relatively low… But even if Shun's royalty, he's not the heir to the throne. It's more than likely. So by telling us not to train our skills, aren't you basically asking us to be killed in the future?"

"Of course not!"

"Right. And I know you wouldn't say a thing like that, ma'am. But without any reason or explanation, I can't just agree, either."

"I…suppose not."

"I'm sorry. I shouldn't have been so harsh."

"No, it's all right. I'm the one who's keeping so many secrets."

"And I'm guessing you can't tell me why you have all these secrets, either?"

"I'm sorry."

"Does it have something to do with the elves?"

"Hmm?"

"It's pretty strange. Why would elves help protect us reincarnations? It seems like you've explained the situation to them, but can they really be trusted? They're not forcing you to comply with some weird conditions or anything, are they?"

"Not at aaaall. You'll just have to trust me on that, okaaay?"

"Even with all the secrets you're keeping?"

"I'm afraid sooo."

"I can't just trust people based on gut instinct like Shun can. I want to trust you, of course, but as long as you're keeping all these secrets, I can't quite manage it."

"I don't think you're wrong about thaaat. If anything, Shun is too trusting, you knooow?"

"Yeah, I agree. Sometimes I think he'd be lost without me, honestly."

"Oh-ho-hooo? Perhaps not a bud yet, but is that a seed I smellll? What an interesting development that would beee."

"Huh? What're you talking about? Ma'am, please don't smile so creepily. Since you look like a little girl now, it's really disturbing."

"Divine punishment tiiime!"

"Huh? Ow!"

3 MIDDLE STRATUM PLAY-THROUGH, START!

I'm here in the Middle Stratum! Yay!

Today I'm gonna start exploring it! Yay!

I haven't perfected my long-range attack or my anti-heat measures yet, but here I go anyway! Yay!

Ugh… No way can I do this unless I hype myself up about it somehow.

It's been several days since I first discovered the Middle Stratum.

In the meantime, I've been training my skills, and I've gotten pretty strong. This is what my status looks like now.

<Small poison taratect   LV 5   Nameless

Status: HP: 57/83 (green)   MP: 181/181 (blue)

SP: 51/82 (yellow) `2UP`   : 82/82 (red) `2UP`

Average Offensive Ability: 92   Average Defensive Ability: 92

Average Magical Ability: 135   Average Resistance Ability: 168

Average Speed Ability: 830 `1UP`

Skills:

[HP Auto-Recovery LV 5]   [MP Recovery Speed LV 3]   [MP Lessened Consumption LV 2]   [SP Recovery Speed LV 2]

[SP Lessened Consumption LV 3 `1UP`]   [Destruction Enhancement LV 1]   [Cutting Enhancement LV 1]   [Poison Enhancement LV 1]

[Mental Warfare
LV 1]

[Energy Conferment
LV 2]

[Deadly Poison
Attack LV 3]

[Poison Synthesis
LV 7]

[Threadsmanship
LV 3]

[Spider Thread
LV 9]

[Cutting Thread
LV 6]

[Thread Control
LV 8]

[Throw
LV 6]

[Hit
LV 7]

[Evasion
LV 3]

[Spatial Maneuvering
LV 3]

[Stealth
LV 7]

[Concentration
LV 9]

[Prediction
LV 8]

[Parallel Thinking
LV 4]

[Arithmetic Processing
LV 6]

[Appraisal
LV 8]

[Detection
LV 6]

[Heretic Magic
LV 3]

[Shadow Magic
LV 2]

[Poison Magic
LV 2]

[Abyss Magic
LV 10]

[Destruction
Resistance LV 1]

[Impact Resistance
LV 2]

[Cutting Resistance
LV 3]

[Fire Resistance
LV 1]

[Dark Resistance
LV 1]

[Deadly Poison
Resistance LV 2]

[Paralysis Resistance
LV 3]

[Petrification
Resistance LV 3]

[Acid Resistance
LV 4]

[Rot Resistance
LV 3]

[Faint Resistance
LV 2]

[Fear Resistance
LV 7 1UP]

[Heresy Resistance
LV 3]

[Pain Nullification]

[Pain Mitigation
LV 7]

[Vision
Enhancement LV 8]

[Night Vision
LV 10]

[Vision Expansion
LV 2]

[Auditory
Enhancement LV 8]

[Olfactory
Enhancement LV 7]

[Taste Enhancement
LV 4]

[Tactile Enhancement
LV 6]

[Life
LV 7]

[Magic Mass
LV 8]

[Instantaneous
LV 8 1UP]

[Persistent
LV 8 1UP]

[Herculean Strength
LV 3]

[Sturdy
LV 3]

[Protection
LV 3]

[Skanda
LV 3]

[Pride]

[Overeating
LV 7]

[Hades]

[Taboo
LV 4]

[n% I = W]

Skill Points: 180

>

Man, I really have gotten pretty strong.

I've got quite a few new skills, too.

Since my beloved Appraisal has started displaying a list of skills I haven't acquired yet, I've been setting my sights on anything that seems decent, then doing things related to that skill to earn proficiency and acquire it naturally.

So now my repertoire has increased considerably, including some additions I've had my eye on for a long time.

Though this is all probably thanks to the huge effect of Pride.

I collected all the MP- and SP-related skills.

Namely, Recovery Speed and Lessened Consumption.

Recovery Speed, of course, quickens natural recovery, and Lessened Consumption reduces the amount used.

SP Lessened Consumption seems to work on both red and yellow stamina, too.

Specifically, my red total stamina has gotten harder to reduce, and my yellow stamina decreases less when I'm running.

I also randomly got a new skill called Spatial Maneuvering.

I think because I built a home near the ceiling, I got the skill climbing up and down the wall.

As a result, I can jump around and stuff now.

I don't need that, though. I was already able to do those things…

I guess I'll explain the rest of the skills as they come.

Anyway, the little UP markers seem to indicate skills that have changed since the last time I looked at my Appraisal results.

This time, SP Lessened Consumption, Fear Resistance, Instantaneous, and Persistent all improved.

Instantaneous and Persistent are the SP version of Strength and that type of skill, with the former working on yellow SP and the latter on red SP.

Looks like my speed and SP stats rose, too.

In the past few days, I've figured out that, like skills, stats can actually increase outside of leveling up if I focus on training them.

This discovery came to me when I was running around to increase my Skanda skill and saw that my speed stat had also gotten better.

Why didn't my stats make any progress before when I was being chased around by monsters and stuff? I probably didn't run enough, or my growth rate has increased because of Pride.

It's too hard to tell which is responsible, but one thing I can say for sure is that Pride is definitely working.

Since I constantly have Appraisal active, the display of an UP symbol must mean that the skill or stat in question increased very recently.

The UP display automatically disappears a little while after I've seen it, which means the skills and stats that rose this time must be due to whatever decisive action I just took.

Heh-heh-heh. It's pretty amazing how much my skills and stats grew in one go, right?

Well, yeah.

That's 'cause I was running at top speed. For my life.

<**Earth dragon Kagna   LV 26**
Status: HP: 4,198/4,198 (green)   MP: 3,339/3,654 (blue)
              SP: 2,798/2,798 (yellow)   : 2,995/3,112 (red)
       Status Appraisal Failed   >

It's a dragon.

Compared with the one I saw before, earth dragon Araba, this one comes off as a bit short and stout. And apparently, it's more powerful to match.

Its wings are different from Araba's.

The guy totally appeared out of nowhere.

Just as I was getting ready to go hunting like usual, my home was suddenly blown away behind me.

The aftershock alone was enough to send me tumbling, and then I caught sight of the earth dragon on the edge of my vision.

After that, I ran away at top speed, fleeing into the Middle Stratum, which is the real reason I'm here now.

Ha-ha-ha. Yeah, I desperately ran for my life, all right.

But at least that desperation was enough to raise my skills and stats!

Anyway, damn, what is it with dragons and destroying my spiderwebs on sight?

That's so scary.

Was the Lower Stratum actually an earth dragon den all along and I just never noticed?

That's even scarier.

No, no, no. There's no way there can be that many of those awful things just hanging around.

Now I'm remembering the glimpse I got of the beast's status Appraisal.

It was all four-digit numbers. That's just ridiculous. There's no way I can beat that.

On top of that, even after it used a powerful attack that destroyed my entire home, its MP and SP were barely even diminished.

In other words, it could attack like that endlessly if it wanted to.

I can't deal with that. What a horrifying monster. Earth dragons are scary.

Still, though, that one was different from the earth dragon Araba that I saw before.

While this one's level was lower, I wasn't able to Appraise Araba, so I don't know which is stronger.

But regardless, it's not like I'd stand a chance against either of them, so I guess it doesn't matter.

I wonder if there's some kind of connection between them, since they're both called earth dragons?

Maybe they started out as the same species and evolved apart or something?

Ooh, that could be it.

Dragons are like the definition of a superior race, so it wouldn't be surprising if they had a wide variety of evolutionary options.

Otherwise, maybe each earth dragon is its own unique species? That could be it, too.

Like, there are only a few because of how elite they are, but each individual is hyper-strong? That kind of thing.

I mean, "hyper-strong" doesn't even begin to cover it.

If that's the case, then it's likely my odds of running into more are pretty low, at least…

No, wait a second.

That would mean that I've now been attacked twice by creatures I should have an extremely low chance of ever meeting.

Does that mean I just have ridiculously bad luck?

Th...th-th-th-that can't be it, r-r-r-right...?

I've had plenty of near-death encounters before, but I always survive in the end, so that means I'm lucky, probably.

Hold on a second. Wouldn't someone lucky avoid flirting with death so many times in the first place?

Hmm?

...Forget it. I shouldn't think about this anymore.

Really, I escaped by the skin of my fangs that time. It's a good thing I'd already been about to leave.

I haven't quite shaken this streak of bad luck yet.

Yeah, let's go with that.

Please, someone tell me I'm right.

<Proficiency has reached the required level.
    Skill [Prediction LV 8] has become [Prediction LV 9].>

Hey, nobody asked you!!

What's with the too-perfect timing?!

Were you waiting for your chance to jump on me like that?!

You think you're some kind of comedian, do you, Divine Voice (temp.)?!

Whew. Okay, I got a little worked up over nothing there.

Yeah. I'm just gonna ignore the absurdly ominous beginning and start slowly working my way through the Middle Stratum.

I definitely want to put as much distance between me and that earth dragon as possible.

Anyway, let's check in on the current situation.

I'm surrounded on either side by boiling hot magma. The ratio of land to magma is more or less the same.

Still, I kinda just charged ahead in a panic. I wonder if I'm going the right way?

Well, I have no way of knowing, so I may as well just carry on like this.

So thanks to the aftershock from the earth dragon's attack and the fact that I kept running far past my limits, my HP's been reduced a bit.

Not by very much, but because the heat around here's constantly causing enough damage to cancel out my HP recovery, I don't think I can expect to rebound anytime soon.

I was able to acquire Fire Resistance by traveling back and forth between the Middle and Lower Stratum, at least, but it's still only level 1.

As of now, with Fire Resistance at level 1 and HP Auto-Recovery at level 5, I can break even with the heat's drain on my HP.

Which is great, but it also means that if I incur any additional injuries, it'll be hard to patch myself up.

My only options are either making a full recovery by leveling up or raising one of these skill levels so my healing outpaces the rate of damage I receive from environmental hazards.

But since the magma is so close by now, there's also the dreaded possibility that the heat damage may get a leg up, instead.

I'd like to avoid such hot places if possible, but what can I do?

Judging by the stratums I've visited so far, it's probably best to assume the Middle Stratum is also pretty massive.

This is the biggest labyrinth in the world, after all.

It connects two continents and everything, so it could easily take days to traverse the Middle Stratum.

I've got a long ways ahead of me, but I was forced to start this journey in quite a rush. Not a good sign.

Oh well, guess I better keep going.

Whew. Sure is hot, though.

Ever since I was reborn as a spider, I've lived in a pretty comfortable temperature. It was never too hot or too cold, y'know?

Having the environment suddenly change on me like this is a huge downer.

It's not so bad that I can't bear it, since I practiced coming here to get the Fire Resistance skill and all, but still…

I can barely even stand the thought that the entire Middle Stratum is probably gonna be like this. Ugh.

Especially for my poor feet.

I mean, magma's flowing right there!

Of course the ground's blazing hot.

Asphalt heated by the summer sun doesn't even compare.

Forget frying an egg on the ground. In this place, it'd burn right up.

And I'm walking barefoot out here!

It's so hot, it's actually quite painful.

I wouldn't be able to do this without Pain Mitigation and HP Auto-Recovery.

Oh, hey, a monster.

<**Elroe gunerush**   LV 5

Status: HP: 159/159 (green)   MP: 145/148 (blue)

SP: 145/145 (yellow)   : 116/145 (red)

Average Offensive Ability: 83   Average Defensive Ability: 81

Average Magical Ability: 79   Average Resistance Ability: 77

Average Speed Ability: 88

Status Appraisal Failed   >

Heh-heh-heh. Now that Appraisal's leveled up more, I can even see the enemy's attack power and stuff!

Ahhh, this rules!

Although, the success rate still isn't very high...

That's the same kind of monster I saw when I first arrived in the Middle Stratum.

The sea-horse-looking thing.

Just like the one I spotted on the first day, my quarry is swimming in magma. Unreal.

It doesn't seem to have noticed me yet, so I'm kinda tempted to just ignore it, but I have to pass right by it.

What should I do? Hmm...

Oh. While I was busy worrying about it, I guess it noticed me.

Like last time, a fireball launches from the magma.

Yaaah! I dodged it.

Hmph. That isn't fast enough to hit me.

There was a time when I couldn't even dodge those frogs' spit attacks, but I'm way stronger now—my speed's gotten much higher, and I have the Evasion skill and everything.

Now I have godlike agility that would be the envy of any game character!

Even if a single hit would reduce me to cinders with my paper-thin defense, that doesn't matter if I never get hit!

Still, though...

Neither of us has the upper hand at this rate.

I mean, those fireballs aren't gonna hit me.

But since I can't use my threads here, I have no way of attacking him.

It's a stalemate.

Oh, wait. The other guy's about to run out of MP. Those fireballs apparently use a lot of it.

So once its MP is exhausted, it won't be able to shoot any more fireballs.

Appraisal really is like cheating. I mean, I know all my opponent's info while we're fighting.

All right, avoided the last fireball. With that, he's out of MP.

The sea horse's next move will change the course of this battle, but how?

Oh, it crawled out of the magma.

And it's charging me.

What an idiot. If I ran out of MP, I'd be making a strategic retreat right away.

From my point of view, the rush is suuuper slow, so I slip by it easily.

Then I attach myself to the sea horse's back, piercing it with a poisoned claw.

Now that I mention it, this thing's body is crazy hot! My HP's even gone down a little! My precious HP!

Well at any rate, the deadly poison killed the sea horse in no time flat.

Phew. I managed to win my first match.

Fireballs streak past me, tracing arcs through the air.

Two at once. But even then, dodging them is simple.

Glancing ahead, I see two sea horses.

Apparently, this place is just crawling with them.

They don't flock together—they just wander around individually doing as they please. Still, once in a while, they happen to end up close to one another and attack me simultaneously.

Well, as long as they're not gonna swarm me like those monkeys, it's no problem.

I evade another pair of flying fireballs.

They don't cooperate very well, probably because they're normally pretty solitary. It's like they're launching fireballs at random.

If they weren't, this might actually be a hard fight.

All I have to do is avoid getting hit, but on the flipside, if I do get tagged…

I'm vulnerable to fire, so if one of those attacks lands, I doubt I'll get off with minor scrapes and bruises.

On top of that, shuffling around the missiles is simple on its own, but I'm doing it in the middle of a magma field.

If I accidentally fall in, I'm sure my body wouldn't even catch fire. It'd just melt.

So even as I avoid the fireballs, I have to keep a close eye on the ground beneath my feet.

It feels like I'm down to my last heart in a bullet hell game.

Except this is my real life on the line.

It really sucks that I don't have a way to fight back right now.

As soon as I produce thread, it just burns up and disappears, especially now that I'm so close to the magma.

So while they can attack me as much as they like, all I can do is dodge. Like a fish in a barrel.

But that's just until they run out of MP.

Once that happens, the sea horses climb ashore.

That's right. They opt to abandon their advantageous position and put themselves on my level voluntarily.

What gentlemen. What idiots. What meatheads.

Even now, the first sea horse has run out of MP and is ambling toward me.

I quickly pack a claw with poison and finish it off.

It helps that I gained the new skills Destruction Enhancement and Cutting Enhancement in my earlier quest for knowledge.

Destruction Enhancement, as the name implies, increases my destructive power. The meaning is a bit vague, but I'm assuming it's a skill that generally increases my attack power.

Cutting Enhancement is the same sort of thing, just limited to slashing attacks.

The second sea horse crawls out of the magma with perfect timing, so I finish it off the same way.

<Experience has reached the required level. Individual small poison taratect has increased from LV 5 to LV 6.>
<All basic attributes have increased.>
<Skill proficiency level-up bonus acquired.>

<Proficiency has reached the required level.
  Skill [Poison Enhancement LV 2] has become [Poison Enhancement LV 3].>
<Proficiency has reached the required level.
  Skill [Evasion LV 3] has become [Evasion LV 4].>
<Skill points acquired.>

Ooh! I leveled up!

I'm extra-grateful for this, since my HP has gotten a bit low. After I finish molting, my HP is fully recovered.

I can beat those sea horses pretty easily, but if I make contact with their bodies, I take damage.

It's not a big deal with one or two, but after I fight a bunch of them, it starts adding up dangerously.

Since leveling up is my only way of healing right now, I'd rather not incur any other injuries, no matter how small.

By the way, they cool down after a little while, so I wait for that to happen before eating them.

It'd be great if my Fire Resistance or HP Auto-Recovery advanced with that last level-up, but of course, the world's not so kind.

Fire Resistance is still level 1, and HP Auto-Recovery hasn't improved, either.

Well, it's no surprise that Fire Resistance isn't making any progress. It seems like my species is naturally vulnerable to fire, so there's no chance I overcome that in a single day.

And HP Auto-Recovery is such a handy skill, it naturally takes a long time to grow.

I mean, automatic recovery is an ability you wouldn't normally have until near the end of a game anyway.

I'm lucky I was able to get it without spending any skill points. It's probably too much to ask for it to level up quickly, too.

I have to remember that just having it at all is a godsend.

In fact, without HP Auto-Recovery, I couldn't have even considered a trip through the Middle Stratum.

I mean, how could I?

Entering an area where you constantly take damage without an auto-recovery skill would be a suicide mission.

I'm not interested in committing suicide, so without HP Auto-Recovery, I'd probably still be puttering around in the Lower Stratum looking for another shaft to climb up.

In the Lower Stratum with those dragons? No waaay. I'd be dead in no time.

I'm actually making fairly smooth progress in clearing the Middle Stratum.

I've run into a few other kinds of monsters besides those sea horses, but none of them were a big deal.

If I wasn't at a disadvantage in this terrain, I could beat all of them easily.

However, the handicap I have here is pretty inconvenient.

First of all, the magma. What a pain.

If I'm facing a monster that's immersed in the magma, all I can do is throw rocks.

Since I have the Throw skill and all, I thought I'd try imitating those monkeys, but it doesn't do much damage at all.

Ultimately, unless the enemy comes ashore, I basically can't do a thing.

It'd be fine if every monster acted like the sea horses and made landfall as soon as they ran out of MP, but some simply stay in the magma or run away.

The worst are the ones that start out on land but duck into the magma when I have them where I want them.

And not being able to use my silk is rather stressful.

This is right after I got the Threadsmanship skill, too, which increases the power of any thread-related moves...

I can at least pick up rocks and toss them with my silk, but if it's out for too long, it catches fire even on relatively safe ground.

The real problem's the thread that I often produce unconsciously.

Whenever I move, I automatically spin silk, but in the Middle Stratum, it ignites.

The lit thread acts like a fuse, until even my backside starts getting hot.

It definitely freaked me out the first time. There was literally a fire lit under my butt.

My HP went down quite a few points from that, and using Poison Synthesis to put it out lowered my HP even more.

I mean, that was the only thing I could think of to put out a fire.

In the end, my only choice is to keep severing the thread as I produce it.

I have to do something, or it'll turn into a real pain in the ass. Literally.

Bedding is a problem, too.

If I try to build a web here, it'll undoubtedly go up in flames and take me with it.

So I decide to make do and sleep in the shadows of some rocks.

Not that I can really sleep anyway.

Not in this hellscape, where I'm always passively taking damage and have to stay on the alert for monsters.

I may be bold, but even I have my limits.

Even so, I still have to sleep.

I'm not sleeping very often, as you might imagine, but I've been trying to rest whenever I find an appropriate hiding place.

But even though this area is worse than the Lower Stratum in a lot of ways, the one silver lining is that the monsters are much weaker.

In terms of threat, they're not far removed from those found in the Upper Stratum.

There are probably some relatively strong monsters here, like the snakes that live in the regions above, but so far, all the creatures I've encountered have been no big deal.

The largest difference between the threats here and in the Upper Stratum is the way they use their environment.

That's what makes these normally weak monsters dangerous.

Since I don't have much in the way of recovery options, just getting grazed by an attack could put me in serious trouble.

Besides, they've all been rather manageable so far because they're so puny, but it's still possible that there could be some Lower Stratum–class big game here, too.

The terrain alone is a challenge for me, so if that sort of opponent appears...

Well, I just have to hope there aren't any.

Man, if only I could use magic, it'd turn this whole thing around.

But to use magic, I have to quell Detection, which might be an even more formidable enemy than this god-awful terrain.

In any event, I'm not likely to solve either problem anytime soon.

Aaargh, I really wanna use magic!

J2 THE NIGHTMARE'S VESTIGE

A few days after entering the Great Elroe Labyrinth, we finally arrive at the spot where an adventurer reported seeing an anomalous taratect.

From here, we enlist Goyef's help searching the surrounding area to find and destroy our target.

"Please be careful. Because the passages in this area are so wide, large monsters like earth dragons sometimes turn up."

Earth dragons, is it? Dragons are generally strong.

Low-ranking wyrm species usually aren't much more dangerous than other monsters of the same level, but the higher-ranking the species, the greater the danger becomes.

They may even be a match for my stats, despite my hero status—or even outrank me.

"It's too quiet around here."

I nod in response to Jeskan's remark.

It's good that we're starting our hunt, but we haven't encountered a single monster since we got here.

And this is the Great Elroe Labyrinth, renowned for being teeming with them.

Something strange is definitely going on.

Suddenly, I feel a sharp prickling sensation on my skin.

I draw my sword immediately.

Hyrince raises his shield, and Yaana concentrates so she can use her magic at a moment's notice.

Jeskan and Hawkin look around warily.

I can see cold sweat streaming down Goyef's face.

"The hero's here."

Then a voice echoes in my mind.

It doesn't make a sound, reaching me like a thought.

I whirl around.

There, I find myself face-to-face with a giant spider monster.

"G-greater taratect…"

Goyef speaks in almost a whimper.

A greater taratect can be just as strong as an upper-class wyrm.

And there are three.

But my gaze goes right past the three giant monsters, captivated by the sight of a small form.

A little white creature, lurking behind the greater taratects, as if in hiding.

"Th-there it is! That's our target! The Nightmare's Vestige! This is the monster said to have been left behind by the Nightmare of the Labyrinth!"

The Nightmare of the Labyrinth. A monster that appeared some ten-odd years ago.

It had been indescribably strong, hence its title.

A spider that crushed humans like insects.

And the first monster that taught me the pain of defeat.

Our target this time is the Nightmare's Vestige, a mutant taratect—stronger than an upper-class wyrm or even a dragon—said to have been left behind by the Nightmare.

Apparently, it attacked a group of adventurers and partially wiped them out, which is why we were sent in to destroy it.

"Die, hero."

The Nightmare's Vestige disappears from sight.

Or, at least, it moves with such ferocious speed that it seems to have disappeared.

Instantly, I grab Yaana beside me and jump to one side.

Then something cuts through the air where we were standing just seconds ago.

The two front legs of the creature's eight morph into a pair of scythes.

I tumble to the ground, towing Yaana along.

Then I use the momentum from my roll to stand again, pulling Yaana back up with me.

"Yaana, support us with your magic, please. It's best to assume that attacks won't hit this thing."

"Understood!"

Such speed. Without powerful accuracy-boosting magic, I doubt any strikes would land.

My master probably could have done it, but I can't expect the same results from Yaana.

Master was outside the norm in many ways, after all.

My comrades move according to my instructions, and the three greater taratects set out at the same time.

Greater taratects have average stats somewhere around 2,000.

But the most dangerous monster here is undoubtedly the Nightmare's Vestige accompanying them.

"I'll take care of the greater taratects! The rest of you, focus on taking down the Nightmare's Vestige!"

I shout orders as I charge the approaching greater taratects.

Jeskan aims his sickle and chain toward the Nightmare's Vestige.

The creature dodges it by leaping upward.

Reaching the ceiling, it clings upside down.

Hawkin immediately throws a knife, but the Nightmare's Vestige runs along the ceiling with terrifying speed, an impossible target.

The throwing knife simply bounces off the rock surface of the cavern with a dull thud.

"How the hell is it movin' that fast on the ceiling?"

Hawkin's voice cracks a little, but I can't blame him.

It seems best if I finish off the greater taratects quickly and rejoin the rest of the group.

My sword fills with a holy light.

The greater taratects spray webbing at my feet, trying to slow my approach.

My shining blade severs it with ease.

Spider monsters' silk may be dangerous, but it's no match for my holy light.

I press my advantage to gain ground on the closest greater taratect.

The beast tries to guard itself with its front legs, but my sword slices its limbs neatly in half, along with its head.

Fluid gushes from the body of the first spider as it falls.

The second greater taratect counters immediately, leaping over the giant corpse.

But I have magic at the ready to take it out.

Holy Light Sphere. The small, floating ball of light blows the second enemy away.

The attack tears the greater taratect to shreds before it hits the ground.

One left!

As the battle continues, the effects of Yaana's magic begin taking hold.

Magic increases all our stats while also boosting our resistance to poison.

When fighting spider monsters, the most important things to be wary of are poison…and thread!

Glancing behind me, I see a rain of silk showering down from the ceiling at my comrades.

Jeskan swings his now-flaming sickle and chain.

Spider thread is vulnerable to fire. An experienced adventurer like Jeskan isn't likely to get caught like that.

The sickle and chain arcs toward the Nightmare's Vestige.

But by the time the weapon reaches the ceiling, the monster is no longer there.

The Nightmare's Vestige launches itself directly at Jeskan.

Hyrince jumps between them, stopping the attack from the Nightmare's Vestige with his shield.

The heavy sound of the creature's scythes clashing with Hyrince's shield hurts my ears.

Hyrince falls back a step from the sheer weight of the assault, and the Nightmare's Vestige leaps backward in turn, putting some distance between them.

At that moment, Hawkin slashes at the monster with a short sword.

The Nightmare's Vestige dodges Hawkin's blade by a hairbreadth, trying to get a bit more distance.

In these short moments, the battle unfolds like a tug-of-war.

I only spare a second to assess their struggle.

The greater taratect sees this as an opening and charges.

Its giant, poisonous fangs bear down on me.

How foolish.

The spider's fangs crash against a wall of light right before my eyes.

It's a Light Magic spell called Light Barrier.

Normally, it's a thin shield only effective against low-powered attacks like arrows.

But with my stats behind it, that defense becomes much stronger.

A Holy Light Sphere bursts over the thwarted greater taratect.

I quickly turn on my heel.

The Nightmare's Vestige isn't looking in my direction.

Thinking it's my chance, I strike at it from behind.

The Nightmare's Vestige reacts to my attack so quickly, dodging my sword with ease, that it's as if it has eyes on its back.

However, I'm prepared for this possibility.

Aiming at the Nightmare's Vestige as it leaps back, I let loose with some Light Magic.

This—along with Lightning Magic—is among the fastest magical attacks.

No matter how quick the Nightmare's Vestige might be, there's no way it can dodge this.

I'm confident I'll land a direct hit, but something blocks my strike.

It's been canceled out by a Dark Magic spell cast by the Nightmare's Vestige.

"What?!"

I can't contain my shock.

The fact that the creature uses magic isn't surprising in itself.

As soon as I realized it understands human speech, I could tell it's very intelligent.

That being the case, it's no wonder it can use spells.

But how can it dispel a hero's magic? Against a technique that activates in an instant, no less?

It must have stats that rival a high-class wyrm—or maybe even a dragon.

Sweat drips unpleasantly down my forehead.

The Nightmare's Vestige dodges Hawkin's throwing knife only to be met with Jeskan, who swings a flaming sword at it.

Jeskan can employ all kinds of different weaponry, depending on the situation.

Usually, he favors a giant ax, but he appears to have opted for a sword in this instance to match his opponent's speed.

However, the Nightmare's Vestige avoids even Jeskan's blade, proceeding to slice at my comrade's body with its scythe-like front legs.

"Ngh!"

Jeskan drops to one knee with a short grunt.

The Nightmare's Vestige turns to attack him again, but Hyrince stands in its way.

"Yaana!"

"Right!"

Yaana responds to Hyrince's cry.

She hurries toward Jeskan to heal him.

Aiming for the moment when Hyrince stops the attack from the Nightmare's Vestige with his shield, I cast another spell.

This time, the monster doesn't bother dispelling it, simply reading my movements and ducking the attack instead.

But I'm prepared for that as well.

I cast again, aiming in the direction the Nightmare's Vestige is leaping and tapping into magic that I'd prepared simultaneously.

Light Magic level 10—Light Field.

Against an enemy this fast, the best approach is an attack with a wide effective range that gives the target nowhere to run.

Light Field is exactly that kind of spell. It bathes a broad area with light and causes damage.

Even the Nightmare's Vestige couldn't avoid it if there was no chance to escape.

Still, at top speed, that thing might manage.

Which is why I forced my prey to dodge my initial attack—to throw the beast off-balance when I cast this one.

The light envelops the Nightmare's Vestige, just as I planned.

It was a perfect strategy.

And yet a poisonous fog spreads out, eclipsing the light. Poison Magic.

The Nightmare's Vestige launched a counterattack, even as the light seared it.

"Ugh!"

Pain assaults my whole body.

I can feel my HP rapidly decreasing.

Such a powerful poison. My resistance should be heightened thanks to Yaana's magic, and yet...

"Julius!"

All at once, the pain eases. It isn't Yaana. Goyef?

"This is the best I can do, but poison is my strong suit. Leave it to me!"

Apparently, Goyef saved me with some kind of detoxification magic. Thank goodness.

I look back. The Nightmare's Vestige is crawling out of the light.

It's definitely wounded, but its injuries are far from fatal.

Not only that, but the monster seems to be gradually healing. Maybe it has HP Auto-Recovery or some kind of recovery magic?

Either way, it seems like ordinary methods won't be enough to bring down Nightmare's Vestige.

"Good grief. Our attacks rarely connect, and when they do, they barely make a dent. Really brings you down, doesn't it?"

Hyrince's casual observation makes me smile.

In reality, the situation is far too grim for such light commentary. Hyrince must know this, so he plays it off as an attempt to keep the party's mood from becoming despairing.

If the Light Magic attack with the broadest effective area won't slay it, then my only option is to use even more powerful spells.

I do have something stronger than Light Field.

The strongest spell in my arsenal: Holy Light Magic level 7—Holy Light Beam.

However, while this magic is powerful, it only deploys in a straight line.

How can I land a hit...?

But I'm not fighting alone.

My friends will create an opening for me.

Trusting in my companions, I begin preparing the spell, when I notice something strange.

The Nightmare's Vestige is behaving oddly.

Is it afraid of something?

Whatever the cause, it's the perfect opening.

Jeskan restrains the immobilized Nightmare's Vestige with his sickle and chain.

As if coming back to itself, the beast starts moving again, struggling to escape.

Then it's pierced by one of Hawkin's throwing knives.

Hawkin's weapon carries an attribute that inflicts paralysis on its victims.

The Nightmare's Vestige spasms and stops flailing.

That's when I cast the spell I've prepared—Holy Light Beam.

"Excellent work."

Goyef's praise seems to be coming from far away.

Looking around, I only see the members of our party.

What in the world made the Nightmare's Vestige seize up like that?

If that hadn't happened, we might have lost this battle.

"Julius, I know you might be concerned, but we won. Let's just focus on that for now."

I nod slowly at Hyrince's words.

He's right. There's no use getting hung up on things I don't understand.

Why did the Nightmare's Vestige target me, the hero?

Why did it suddenly stop?

Why did I feel so uneasy, despite the fact that we won?

I have no way of unraveling any of this, so there's no use worrying about it.

After all, no matter what happens next, I'll have to keep fighting as the hero.

"Well, looks like our job here is done."

"Indeed. Let us leave this place as quickly as we can."

"Ah, there's a spider behind you!"

"What?! Where? Where is it?!"

"Sorry, my bad. I was just seeing things."

Yaana puffs up her cheeks in rage at Hyrince's teasing.

Jeskan looks on blandly, and Hawkin gives a dry smile.

They're all their usual selves.

Right. I might not feel 100 percent reassured, but everything is fine.

Now the Nightmare's Vestige can't cause any more harm.

Protecting the people's safety is the hero's duty.

So our accomplishment should be cause for celebration.

In the wake of the battle, we're able to leave the Great Elroe Labyrinth without further incident.

☆

"Was it quite to your liking?"

"Hmm? Well, it seems like one of them got a false start, so I'll have to deal with that…"

"Pardon?"

"Ah, it's all right. Nothing to do with you, so don't even worry about it."

"Very well, then…"

"More important, what would really please me is if you'd make some headway on your own work, y'know?"

"As you wish, O Demon Lord."

4 WYRM? NOT FISH?

Man, I knew I had a bad feeling about this.

Because apparently, sea horses are wyrms.

<Wyrm: A variety of monster said to be a lesser species of dragon. Despite this qualifier, some wyrms are comparable to dragons in strength.>

Yep. It's a lesser version of that earth dragon's species.

Guess that would make it a kind of fire dragon?

I mean, if earth dragons exist, fire dragons must, too...

There aren't any in the Middle Stratum, are there?

Let's hope not.

Okay, I'm getting a little off track here. Time to seriously focus on dealing with the immediate issue at hand.

<Elroe guneseven   LV 7

Status: HP: 461/461 (green)   MP: 223/223 (blue)

SP: 218/218 (yellow)   : 451/466 (red)

Average Offensive Ability: 368   Average Defensive Ability: 311

Average Magical Ability: 161   Average Resistance Ability: 158

Average Speed Ability: 155

Status Appraisal Failed

>

<Elroe guneseven: A lesser wyrm-type monster that lives in the Great Elroe Labyrinth, Middle Stratum. An omnivorous creature, its large mouth swallows anything and everything.>

That's the monster swimming slowly through the magma right now.

For a low-ranking wyrm, its shape resembles a catfish more than anything else.

The name "seven" doesn't really suit it, either.

Not that griping about the naming system in this world will do me any good.

That huge, catfish-like mouth is definitely its most notable feature.

If it catches me with that...yikes. At my size, it'd definitely swallow me whole.

It's great that status Appraisal worked, though.

The probability is usually about one in three.

So I'm lucky it came through this time.

It'd be way too dangerous trying to get past this thing without knowing its exact stats.

All the Middle Stratum monsters I've run into have been weak, but this is definitely the strongest so far.

If possible, I'd like to just ignore it.

But it's swimming around right next to my path.

Going by experience, chances are high that it'll attack me.

Hmm. What should I do...?

I mean, if I try to run away, I'm pretty sure I could outpace it given my speed, but it'd be a pain having that thing chasing me for ages with its crazy-high red stamina gauge.

And even if its yellow gauge is smaller, it's still several times the size of mine.

Most importantly, I can't see its skills.

If the catfish has a high-level SP Reduced Consumption skill or something, I may not be able to outrun it, after all.

I doubt that's the case, but still....

It's a bit strong to consider a straight fight.

Should I run away after all, then?

Yeah. I don't wanna push it.

Things have been going pretty well lately, but every time I get overconfident, it always ends poorly for me.

See, I've learned a thing or two by now. I know better than to get carried away.

I have to proceed with the utmost caution!

And so, I'll start moving slo-o-o-wly.

If it sees me, I'll just take off at top speed.

Now…wait. Another catfish just emerged from the magma nearby.

Eh?

What?! This wasn't part of the deal!

I didn't get carried away this time, but I still wound up in trouble?!

The catfish locks eyes with me. After staring blankly for a moment, it opens its huge mouth.

Backstep!

The catfish's huge mouth clamps shut on the spot where I was just standing.

It keeps advancing, sliding up on land.

The damn thing has limbs. I didn't notice in the magma.

Not only that, but its whole body is covered in dragon-like scales.

By all appearances, it's extremely well protected.

Yep. I'm gonna run for it.

Geh?!

When I turn in the direction of the escape route I'd mapped out, I see the other catfish crawling onto land.

Wait, now I'm flanked on either side! How am I supposed to run away?!

What do I do now?!

Oh geez, my only choice is to beat the one in front of me to the punch!

I wrap poison thread around the catfish's body.

I already confirmed while I was training that Poison Attack enables me to add poison to my threads.

Not that it's much use here, since they burn up right away!

But even so, hopefully it'll poison this guy some in the process!

Of course, the thread catches fire right away.

I check the catfish's HP to see if the poison is having any effect.

It worked. Its HP has gone down a little.

In which case, I just have to poison it properly.

The catfish opens its mouth wide.

And charges right at me.

Nooo! Scaryyyy!

But I have to hang in there as long as I can!

Just as it's on top of me, I activate Poison Synthesis!

Then bail in the nick of time!

Instead of me, the catfish gets a mouthful of synthesized Spider Poison.

My Poison Attack skill reached level 10 while I was training and turned into the advanced version, Deadly Poison Attack.

So my Spider Poison, which was already powerful enough to bring down a giant monkey, evolved into Deadly Spider Poison.

The moment the catfish swallows the toxic cocktail, its HP starts dropping at an incredible rate.

We're talking the speed of sound here.

As a result, the catfish writhes around in apparent agony.

Wow, I didn't know my poison had gotten this potent...

I knew it'd be strong, but it's actually terrifying, if I do say so myself.

Okay, what about the other one?

Turning to look, I see the other catfish recoiling a bit fearfully at the sight of its comrade's condition.

Wh-whoa. I mean, I guess it makes sense to be scared if you see one of your own kind suffering like that.

I'd assumed that dragons never run away, but maybe that was just the sea horses.

The still-healthy catfish turns around and flees, just like that.

Man, for real? I thought I'd be the one to skitter off first.

Guess I really turned the tables on them.

Maybe it's okay for me to be a little cocky after all?

I'm actually pretty strong, aren't I?

For the time being, I'll put the suffering catfish out of its misery.

I spray more poison in the flapping creature's face.

With one last spasm, the catfish stops moving.

<Experience has reached the required level. Individual small poison taratect has increased from LV 6 to LV 7.>
<All basic attributes have increased.>
<Skill proficiency level-up bonus acquired.>
<Proficiency has reached the required level.
　Skill [Concentration LV 9] has become [Concentration LV 10].>
<Condition satisfied.
　Skill [Thought Acceleration LV 1] has been derived from skill [Concentration].>
<Proficiency has reached the required level.
　Skill [Evasion LV 1] has become [Evasion LV 2].>

\<Proficiency has reached the required level.

Skill [Life LV 1] has become [Life LV 2].>

\<Skill points acquired.>

Hmm? Apparently, I maxed out my Concentration skill with this last level-up.

Concentration. I had rather high hopes for that one.

It's pretty basic, but this skill has been supporting me from behind the scenes all this time.

So I'm expecting great things from its successor.

May as well start out by Appraising this new skill.

‹Thought Acceleration: Accelerates the thinking process, prolonging the user's available perception of time›

…Wow.

Seriously, is that amazing or what?

I mean, is this what I think it is?

Like, I'll basically be able to slow down time for myself?

This is like the thing top athletes sometimes experience where the ball seems to move in slo-mo, right?

So I can use that whenever I want now?

Holy crap.

I'm gonna try it right away.

Hmm. Looks like I was able to activate it without a problem.

So how's this work?

Hmm? Is the magma moving a bit slower?

Also, something feels off.

Like various sensations in my body are moving too quickly and too slowly at the same time. It's hard to describe.

To test it out, I try moving my body.

It feels heavy, like I'm moving through water.

Not being able to control my body the way I want is frustrating.

This is the default for Thought Acceleration?

I've been screwed over by own speed before, so I may want to activate this when I'm sprinting, at least.

Huh? Wait, this isn't consuming anything?

My MP and my SP haven't gone down at all.

So is this a passive skill that can be active all the time?

I do seem to be able to turn it off and on if I want, but there's no disadvantage to having it on all the time, is there?

Wow, is that wicked or what? I totally thought this was gonna eat up MP or something.

Like, you have to spend MP just to activate it for a few seconds at a time, or something.

But I can use it anytime at no expense?

That makes this skill pretty ridiculous, doesn't it?

There isn't really any downside.

Aside from maybe a slight discomfort until I get used to it.

I might've just gotten a crazy cheat skill!

<Proficiency has reached the required level.
　Skill [Prediction LV 9] has become [Prediction LV 10].>
<Condition satisfied.
　Skill [Prediction LV 10] has evolved into skill [Foresight LV 1].>

Oh, hey, Foresight. What's up?

I guess I maxed out Prediction, too.

Well, it was never a particularly necessary skill, but maybe now that it evolved, it'll be a bit more useful?

<Foresight: Increases effectiveness of predictions. In addition, grants the ability to see slight glimpses of possible futures.>

Hmm? Possible futures? What does that mean?

Well, let's try it out.

Okay. Looks like I can activate this one just fine, too.

But it doesn't really seem like anything's changed?

Oh, wait. The magma's moving a bit strangely.

Like it's kind of blurry in places?

No, it's more like my vision is overlapping.

So are these overlapped bits showing me what could potentially happen?

In other words, I can see into the future now?

Well, it's just what's possible, so I have to take it with a grain of salt, but this skill may be really useful if I train it up more.

Though it doesn't seem too helpful at the moment, since all I see is a few patches of overlapping magma.

Huh? Wait a sec. This one's not consuming anything, either?

So, another passive skill?

...That's crazy.

Who knew that a useless, childlike Prediction would produce something so amazing?

I'm sorry, Prediction. I guess even useless kids can learn to be competent if they try hard enough.

<Proficiency has reached the required level.
Skill [Appraisal LV 8] has become [Appraisal LV 9].>

Speaking of formerly useless children!

Appraisal! Did you enjoy this most recent level-up?

Let's see what you've learned to do this time!

<Small poison taratect   LV 7   Nameless

Status:

HP: 88/88 (green)	MP: 185/185 (blue)
SP: 88/88 (yellow)	: 88/88 (red) +612
Average Offensive Ability: 109	Average Defensive Ability: 108
Average Magical Ability: 139	Average Resistance Ability: 173
Average Speed Ability: 956	

Skills:

[HP Auto-Recovery LV 5]	[MP Recovery Speed LV 3]	[MP Lessened Consumption LV 2]	[SP Recovery Speed LV 2]
[SP Lessened Consumption LV 3]	[Destruction Enhancement LV 1]	[Cutting Enhancement LV 1]	[Poison Enhancement LV 3]
[Mental Warfare LV 1]	[Energy Conferment LV 2]	[Deadly Poison Attack LV 3]	[Poison Synthesis LV 7]
[Threadsmanship LV 3]	[Spider Thread LV 9]	[Cutting Thread LV 6]	[Thread Control LV 8]
[Throw LV 7]	[Spatial Maneuvering LV 4]	[Hit LV 8]	[Evasion LV 5]

[Stealth LV 7]	[Concentration LV 10]	[Thought Acceleration LV 1]	[Foresight LV 1]
[Parallel Thinking LV 4]	[Arithmetic Processing LV 6]	[Appraisal LV 9]	[Detection LV 6]
[Heretic Magic LV 3]	[Shadow Magic LV 2]	[Poison Magic LV 2]	[Abyss Magic LV 10]
[Destruction Resistance LV 1]	[Impact Resistance LV 2]	[Cutting Resistance LV 3]	[Fire Resistance LV 1]
[Dark Resistance LV 1]	[Deadly Poison Resistance LV 2]	[Paralysis Resistance LV 3]	[Petrification Resistance LV 3]
[Acid Resistance LV 4]	[Rot Resistance LV 3]	[Faint Resistance LV 2]	[Fear Resistance LV 7]
[Heresy Resistance LV 3]	[Pain Nullification]	[Pain Mitigation LV 7]	[Vision Enhancement LV 8]
[Night Vision LV 10]	[Vision Expansion LV 2]	[Auditory Enhancement LV 8]	[Olfactory Enhancement LV 7]
[Taste Enhancement LV 5]	[Tactile Enhancement LV 6]	[Life LV 8]	[Magic Mass LV 8]
[Instantaneous LV 8]	[Persistent LV 8]	[Herculean Strength LV 3]	[Sturdy LV 3]
[Protection LV 3]	[Skanda LV 3]	[Pride]	[Overeating LV 7]
[Hades]	[Taboo LV 4]	[n% I = W]	

Skill Points: 220

Titles:

[Foul Feeder]	[Kin Eater]	[Assassin]	[Monster Slayer]
[Poison Technique User]	[Thread User]	[Merciless]	[Monster Slaughterer]
[Ruler of Pride]			

>

Oh, whoa! I can see my titles now!

I've been wondering about that for a while.

Also, could it be that this new number next to my red stamina gauge is my stock from overeating?

I didn't realize I'd stocked up so much.

That's not gonna run out for a long time.

All right, may as well Appraise my titles.

Since Appraisal lets me inspect my titles now, I'll take a look at all of them.

‹Title: Enhancement code obtained by satisfying certain conditions. Up to two skills can be acquired at the time of obtaining a new title. Some titles have special effects, increase certain stats, and so on.›

Ooh. So titles do more than just giving out skills.

I'd assumed that was all there was to it.

Which means some of my titles may have special effects that I just never noticed.

Now I'm really excited to Appraise them.

Let's go!

‹Foul Feeder: Acquired skills [Poison Resistance LV 1] [Rot Resistance LV 1]. Acquisition condition: Consume a large amount of poison or similar substances within a certain period of time. Effects: Digestive system becomes stronger. Description: A title awarded to those who will eat even poison.›

Oh, okay. Makes sense, since I've been eating poisonous monsters since I was born.

Guess I can't really complain about it being called "foul."

So it makes my digestive system stronger…

Well, I did eat tons of poison, so maybe it helped without my noticing.

If I hadn't gotten Rot Resistance by acquiring this title, I might've kicked the bucket as soon as I took a bite of that snail-bug, so I guess it might've saved my butt, after all. Although I wish the name were a bit more pleasant.

‹Kin Eater: Acquired skills [Taboo LV 1] [Heretic Magic LV 1]. Acquisition condition: Consume a blood relative. Effects: None. Description: A title awarded to those who eat a relative.›

No effect.

So was there any point in getting this title?

I mean, it gave me the Taboo skill, which clearly has a negative effect, so maybe you're not supposed to get this title?

And since I can't use Heretic Magic, there's no benefit there, either.

Seems like a total negative to me at the moment...

‹Assassin: Acquired skills [Stealth LV 1] [Shadow Magic LV 1]. Acquisition condition: Succeed in a certain amount of assassinations by way of surprise attack. Effect: Damage bonus to surprise strikes. Description: A title awarded to those who accomplish repeated assassinations.›

Ooh. Just like the skills I got from it, this title's effect is totally ninja-like.

This is definitely a ninja skill.

Ninjas also worked as assassins at times, so I'm not wrong.

Does that mean I'll eventually be able to do stuff like break someone's neck with a bare-handed surprise attack?

Ah, I guess I can probably do that already, since I have claws instead of hands.

‹Monster Slayer: Acquired skills [Strength LV 1] [Solidity LV 1]. Acquisition condition: Defeat a certain number of monsters. Effect: Slight increase in damage to monster opponents. Description: A title awarded to those who bring down a large amount of monsters.›

Ahh. So it does have something to do with the number of monsters I killed.

I don't know how many a "certain number" is, exactly, but I did get this title after defeating quite a few of them.

The effect is pretty sweet, too, so I'm glad I got this title.

‹Poison Technique User: Acquired skills [Poison Synthesis LV 1] [Poison Magic LV 1]. Acquisition condition: Use a certain quantity of poison. Effect: Strengthens poison attribute. Description: A title awarded to those who use poison.›

This is probably the most useful one yet.

I'm totally indebted to Poison Synthesis.

Actually, that's a great effect, too. It's like this title was made just for me.

Though, it'd be nice if I could actually use Poison Magic...

Since it just requires a certain quantity, does the strength of the poison have nothing to do with it?

My poison is pretty strong, so I feel like I might've actually not used that much in terms of quantity.

Maybe that's why it took so long for me to get this title, even though I've been using poison since I was born.

<Thread User: Acquired skills [Thread Control LV 1] [Cutting Thread LV 1]. Acquisition condition: Use threads to attack a certain number of times. Effect: Increases power of thread-based attacks. Description: A title granted to those who use thread as a weapon.>

And this one's the second-most useful.

This title strengthened my other weapon of choice—thread.

Not that I get to show it off in this stupid Middle Stratum!

But I didn't realize it was specifically for thread-based attacks until I saw this description.

In my case, sticky thread was a mainstay for a long while.

I think that's more of a support-based use than an attack.

So that's why a lot of time passed before I scored this title.

Sticky thread must not have counted toward the thread attack tally.

Maybe once I started using Morning Spider and the casting net and stuff, those counted?

If I'd known the acquisition conditions sooner, I might've had an easier time getting it.

<Merciless: Acquired skills [Heretic Magic LV 1] [Heresy Resistance LV 1]. Acquisition conditions: Merciless behavior. Effect: Negates any feelings of guilt. Description: A title awarded to merciless individuals.>

Oh, come on. Can't you elaborate on these explanations a little more?

How are these acquisition conditions even remotely informative?

Hmm. The effect is pretty weird, too, so it's just a weird title overall.

<Monster Slaughterer: Acquired skills [Herculean Strength LV 1] [Sturdy LV 1]. Acquisition condition: Defeat a certain number of monsters. Effect: Increase damage dealt to monster opponents. Description: A title awarded to those who bring down an extremely large number of monsters.>

Yeah. This is definitely an advanced version of the Monster Slayer title.

You probably get it for killing more monsters than Monster Slayer.

The effect and explanation and everything fit the bill, too.

<Ruler of Pride: Acquired skills [Abyss Magic LV 10] [Hades]. Acquisition conditions: Obtain [Pride] skill. Effect: Increases MP, Magic, and resistance stats. +Correction to mental skill proficiencies. Grants ruling class privileges. Description: A title granted to one who has conquered Pride.>

Wait. Hold the phone.

What's up with this effect?

So you're the reason my stats skyrocketed all of a sudden?!

And on top of that, it adds a bonus to proficiency levels?!

On top of all the bonuses from Pride?

So that's why Prediction and those other skills improve so fast!

And wait, what are "ruling class privileges"?

<Ruling Class Privileges: Authority given to rulers to control a portion of the world>

Huh? What's that mean? Can I use that, too?

<Ruler of Pride's request to exercise special privileges has been received.
Currently, the Ruler of Pride has no authority available for use.>

Whaddaya mean, I don't?!

Seriously, what is going on here?

The Pride skill is way too mysterious.

Well, I guess I learned a lot about titles, at least.

Appraisal always has my back.

The catfish cooled down while I was Appraising, so I may as well eat it now.

It's a real pain that you can't eat Middle Stratum monsters until you give them time to sit for a while like this...

Not to mention, half the time, it's only the surface that cools down, and the inside still stays hot.

It can even decrease my HP if I'm not careful, and I don't wanna be in pain while I eat.

Oh. The catfish is delicious.

What, seriously?!

This is the first time I've had delicious food in my whole life as a spider!

Oh man. I shouldn't have let that other one escape.

Maybe I can still catch up if I chase it now?

These things are pretty slow, so I might still make it.

Aah, but I guess there's nothing I can do once it slips into the magma.

Damn, that was a mistake.

Oh well. I'll just savor the one I have here.

<Proficiency has reached the required level.

Skill [Taste Enhancement LV 5] has become [Taste Enhancement LV 6].>

It's sooo good! Makes me glad I was born. Seriously, yum.

I mean, it still doesn't compare to what I ate in my previous life, but everything I've had so far in this world has been gross, so...

Finally, finally, I've found something I can honestly call delicious.

Although I wasn't so concerned about food in my old life as a human...

I didn't realize how lucky I was until I came back as a spider.

I'm so tired of eating gross monsters.

I wanna eat tasty food!

All right. I'm gonna hunt catfish.

They're a little strong, but who cares?

I don't mind putting my life on the line to satisfy this desire.

For real, it's worth it.

Just you wait, catfish. I'm gonna eat every last one of you!

Catfiiiish! Catfiiiish! Where aaaare youuu, catfiiiiish?

I wander through the labyrinth, looking for catfish.

There aren't any.

They're all over me when I don't want to see them, but now that I do, they're nowhere to be found?

Hurry up and come out. Come out so I can eat you.

Ugh. Of course something else turns up at a time like this.

<Elroe gunerush   LV 8

Status: HP: 170/170 (green)   MP: 161/161 (blue)

SP: 158/158 (yellow)   : 156/167 (red)

Average Offensive Ability: 87   Average Defensive Ability: 84

Average Magical Ability: 84   Average Resistance Ability: 81

Average Speed Ability: 91

Skills:

[Fire Wyrm   [Hit   [Swim   [Heat Nullification]
LV 1]   LV 4]   LV 4]

>

There are three sea horses in total.

And something new happened when I Appraised one of them.

Ooh, nice!

Since my Appraisal skill went up, now I can see my opponents' skills, too!

Whoa! Finally, it's starting to work like a real cheat skill!

Man, though, sea horse, where are all your skills at? You've only got four?

That's way too few. So that's why you seem weaker than your stats.

Plus, they're all low-level except for Heat Nullification, which is clearly a maxed-out version of Fire Resistance.

I should probably Appraise the skills I haven't seen before.

‹Fire Wyrm: A special skill possessed by fire wyrm species. It grants special effects based on its level. LV 1: Fireball Breath.›

‹Swimming: Positive correction to swimming movements›

Hmm. So Fire Wyrm is a species-specific skill that only fire wyrms have.

Just like my Spider Thread.

I guess all it can do at level 1 is shoot those fireballs, though.

Actually, why is its Fire Wyrm skill at level 1 when the sea horse itself is level 8?

Is it that difficult to raise its skill level, or is this guy just slacking on earning proficiency?

And Swim is just a skill that makes you better at swimming.

Hmph. Now that I've seen this thing's skills, I'm even more confident. There's no way I can lose to this guy.

So let's just finish this off...not very smoothly, I guess.

I mean, these guys are still in the magma.

All I can do is chuck little rocks at them for the moment.

Hmm. Maybe I can try poisoning the stones?

I give it a shot, but it doesn't really do much more damage than before.

My Deadly Spider Poison causes two different kinds of damage: contact damage and ingestion damage.

Contact damage occurs when the poison makes contact with skin and such, while ingestion damage is when the poison penetrates into the opponent's body.

Between the two, ingestion damage is way, way higher.

Contact damage isn't very effective at first, but if the poison stays there long enough, the amount of damage increases explosively.

That's because poison seeps into the body after a while.

In other words, contact damage eventually becomes ingestion damage. Unless it gets rinsed or rubbed off beforehand, of course.

So when I'm fighting a monster that can't wash away the poison, I don't need to bother aiming for the mouth. I just have to smear poison somewhere on its body.

If I want to be quick about it, it's best to aim for the mouth or the eyes, but for safety's sake, it's better to apply it as many places as possible. Everything depends on the situation, of course.

Once the sea horses run out of MP and come ashore, I douse them all with poison. Their mouths are so small, they're hard to target. It's easier just to slosh it all over them.

Catfiiiish! I've been looking for you everywhere, catfiiish! I finally found you, catfiiish!

Now then, gimme that meat of yours! Give it here right now!

I have no choice but to kill you and eat your flesh! Reunited with my beloved catfish at last!

The catfish is blithely swimming through the magma.

First, I have to drag it out.

Incidentally, I was able to Appraise the catfish's skills, too.

Its stats aren't that different from the last one.

This catfish's skills are [Fire Wyrm LV 2], [Dragon Scales LV 1], [Hit LV 7], [Swim LV 6], [Heat Nullification], and [Overeating LV 2].

The ability it can use with Fire Wyrm level 2 is called Heat Wrap. As the name implies, the catfish wraps its body in heat.

I assumed it was a defensive thing, but according to Appraisal's explanation, it mostly serves to increase movement speed when used.

However, since it heats up your body, it'll actually cause damage if the user doesn't have Fire Resistance. Not that it matters in this case, since the catfish has Heat Nullification.

Dragon Scales is a skill that makes special scales grow all over the creature's body.

They're special because, on top of having high defense, they negate magic to a certain degree.

Like, instead of just blocking it, apparently, it interferes with the composition of magic itself and lowers its potency or something.

Well, I can't use magic anyway, so they're just a bunch of hard scales to me. And we all know what the rest of those skills do by now.

Something just occurred to me, though. Is it possible that the catfish is an evolution of the sea horse?

They're both fire wyrms, and the catfish has skills that are advanced versions of the sea horse's.

It just has higher levels—and the additions of Dragon Scales and Overeating.

Between that and their respective species names, it does seem possible.

But if that's true, that means it evolves from that form into this one?

Biologically speaking, isn't a sea horse technically more evolved than a catfish?

I mean, I don't really know enough about the subject to argue either way, but still.

They look pretty different, but I suppose…if you stretched a sea horse's mouth reeeal wide and made its body big and heavy, maybe it'd look like a catfish?

Hmm. I dunno.

Well, that doesn't really matter anyway.

My only concern right now is gnawing on that catfish's flesh.

So let's get things started with a poisonous stone throw!

The rock bounces off the catfish's back.

Yep. It didn't do much damage. No surprises there.

Guess I'll have to stick with the strategy of nailing it with Poison Synthesis when it charges again.

Or so I thought. Now the stupid catfish is launching a fireball at me from the magma.

For real? This is way bigger and faster than the sea horses' fireballs.

It's still not gonna hit me, though. I hop lightly to avoid the shot.

For the most part, Thought Acceleration just stretches out my sense of time by a tiny bit, but it does make everything else seem a bit slower than normal.

Thanks to my insanely high speed stat, I can still move pretty quickly compared with the rest of the world even in this inhibited state.

I assume, though, that when Thought Acceleration levels up, time will get even slower, so I'm not sure what'll happen then.

For now, it seems like 1 second is stretched to 1.1 seconds, maybe?

I don't know the specifics, but that's what it feels like to me.

The catfish fires a second volley.

I can't believe this guy. Same tactics as those sea horses.

I guess maybe the catfish really is the evolved form of the sea horse.

Was the one that decided to jump on land earlier just an outlier? Do they normally use the same strategy as the sea horses?

Ah, but now they have the Heat Wrap ability and stuff, so maybe they change things up depending on the circumstance.

Maybe the one before reacted like, "Oh, I popped my face out, and now there's something right in front of me. Guess I'll attack it," or something.

I dodge the catfish's next fireball.

It should run out of MP soon. What'll it do then?

The sea horses crawl ashore when they run out of MP, but what about catfish?

I really want it to beach itself, but judging by what happened last time, it seems like they run if they sense danger.

I won't allow that, okay? I'll chase you to the ends of the earth, got it?

Oblivious to my concerns, the catfish stops attacking.

Hmm? But it still has a little MP left…

Ah, it went under. Did it use Heat Wrap?

It's pretty cool that I know this stuff about my opponents now. Appraisal really is a wonderful cheat.

Eh? The catfish is opening its mouth?

What's it gonna do?

Once its mouth is completely open, I hear a sound effect from its belly that can only be described as a rumble.

Huh? What's it doing?

I don't remember seeing any skill like this?

As I stand momentarily dumbfounded, I feel something like wind on my body.

Wait, am I getting sucked into the thing's mouth?

What are you, that round pink character from the stars?!

Is this some new use of the Overeating skill or something?!

Crap, I'm gonna get sucked in and dragged away through the magma… or not.

Oh. The sound is really loud, and there's wind and all, but it's not actually strong enough to budge me.

The catfish stops hoovering. Guess it noticed.

Then our eyes meet.

Well, this is awkward...

Maybe it's a little nervous—or it could be the sort of vacant expression catfish always seem to have, but is this guy, like, the friendly mascot character of the Middle Stratum or something?

Next, the catfish comes wriggling out of the magma. It's actually kind of cute, I have to admit.

Then it opens its huge mouth and lunges toward me.

Oh, well, that's not cute at all. But it's exactly what I was waiting for!

Once it gets close enough, I use Poison Synthesis.

At the same time, I quickly jump out of the way.

The catfish swallows the deadly poison as it moves straight ahead.

I stand off to the side and watch. Oh, it fell over.

Now it's flopping around.

Deadly Spider Poison sure is strong.

I don't think any ordinary venom would have this big of an effect. When you combine Poison Synthesis with the spider poison I've had all my life, seems like it makes something way potent.

Really, this skill is just perfect for me.

Anyway, I'll spray more poison on the suffering catfish.

The big lug gives one last shudder and dies.

Now I just have to wait for the effects of the magma, Heat Wrap, and such to wear off so it cools.

Then it's dinnertime!

Up to now, I've been eating monsters strictly for survival, but this time it's different!

I can actually enjoy the delicious taste.

Ah, what a time to be alive!

I hope it cools down soon.

I can't wait to eat it!

file.07

ELROE GUNESEVEN

LV.01

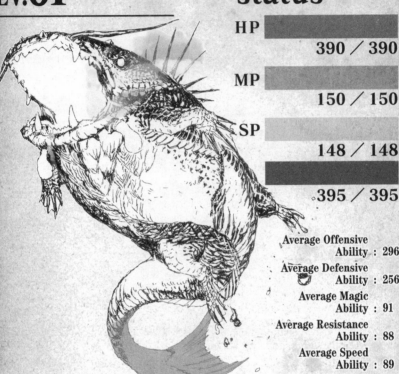

status

HP
390 / 390

MP
150 / 150

SP
148 / 148

395 / 395

Average Offensive
Ability : 296

Average Defensive
Ability : 256

Average Magic
Ability : 91

Average Resistance
Ability : 88

Average Speed
Ability : 89

skill

[Fire Wyrm LV 1]
[Swim LV 5]

[Dragon Scale LV 1]
[Overeating LV 1]

[Hit LV 6]
[Heat Nullification]

Also known as a catfish. This monster looks like a catfish with limbs.
A lower-class wyrm species. Evolved form of the sea horse. It will eat
anything with its enormous mouth. It is generally more cautious than the
sea horse and will flee if it senses its opponent is even a little bit strong.
Danger level C.

S2　Magic Lesson

Today's class is magic practice.

After learning the fundamentals, we were permitted to take practical lessons to actually use magic.

"We will now distribute staffs for magic training. For safety's sake, we've chosen water-magic-imbued staffs for today."

Our instructor, Professor Oriza, speaks in a slightly disinterested voice as he hands out staffs.

The students scramble to be the first to receive them.

"You all have Magic Power Perception and Magic Power Operation, correct? Because students without those skills can't take this lesson. If anyone doesn't have them, please come forward now."

All the students in the class have Magic Power Perception and Magic Power Operation, of course.

In fact, Professor Oriza taught them to us himself last time.

"Now, please concentrate your magic power."

Obeying his instructions, I focus on gathering my magic.

"Once that is done, try to let it flow into your staff. Then the magic in the staff will activate on its own."

Huh? That's it?

"These staffs are enchanted with the level-1 Water Magic spell Water Ball. It is a simple spell that projects spheres of water, but please be sure not to point it at anyone. There are targets for that purpose."

Professor Oriza points at an area where several targets have been set up.

Without further ado, the students begin casting magic.

Most of them don't have enough magic power, or their spells are incompletely formed, or some other issue occurs, and their spells dissipate before reaching the target.

"You can use as much magic as you'd like during this period. If you use it enough, you may even gain the Water Magic skill. However, please do pay attention to the amount of magic power you have remaining and stop as soon as it reaches a dangerous level. Otherwise, don't come crying to me if you overdo it and pass out."

How irresponsible.

But I guess there are probably people who collapse every year.

A lot of the students are using magic for the first time, and some of them are extremely excited about it.

It's no surprise that one or two might get too hyped up and push past their limits.

"Water Magic, huh? I would've preferred Earth Magic, myself."

Fei complains from her position on my shoulder.

Fei is an earth wyrm, so she probably has a higher aptitude for Earth Magic than Water.

I know my own aptitudes, too, having seen them during the Appraisal ceremony.

Light Magic is the highest, followed by Water.

In that respect, you could say this lesson is worthwhile for me.

However, there are only a handful of Appraisal Stones in existence powerful enough to show one's compatibility with different attributes.

Instead, people who don't have access to such high-quality items use enchanted tools to invoke magic and acquire skills that way, like we're doing now.

You can figure out whether you have a knack for that kind of magic based on how quickly you acquire the skills.

However, that isn't an option unless you have access to magic tools with multiple attributes. In many cases, impoverished magic-user families only have one kind of magic tool to their names.

In that situation, you'd have no choice but to use that attribute whether you have an aptitude for it or not.

But at this school, there are magic tools with every kind of attribute, so no such problem exists.

"I simply don't have a knack for Water. On the contrary, I seem to be inclined toward Fire."

"That's funny. I'm bad with Water and good at Fire, too."

I overhear a conversation between Katia and Hugo.

Despite her claims, Katia's conjured balls of water are striking the targets perfectly.

Considering that most of the students haven't even gotten their spells to reach their marks yet, I'd say that solid strikes are pretty good already.

Looking around, the only people I've seen successfully hit are Katia, Hugo, and Yuri, formerly Hasebe.

Yuri is focusing intently on blasting water balls at the targets.

I have to wonder if it's safe to shoot that much, but I suspect that even if I speak to Yuri now, she won't hear me.

She's probably planning to stick with it until she gets the skill, even if her MP runs out.

By the way, Ms. Oka isn't around.

She shows for class or doesn't as she pleases.

And she won't tell us what she's doing when she isn't around.

Anyway, I feel like Sue would be able to do it if she tried, but she's just hanging out behind me, making no attempt to use magic at all.

"Sue, don't you want to practice?"

"Oh, I mustn't go ahead of my older brother. Instead, I shall wait until you demonstrate your incredible magical prowess, then sneak in my own practice while everyone fawns over you admiringly."

Hoo, boy. Way to raise the bar.

I did always want to be an older brother who my sister could be proud of, but lately, that's translated into a crazy amount of pressure.

In the meantime, some of the students have run out of magic power and started taking breaks.

That means that some targets have opened up, so I guess I'll try, too.

Now that I think about it, this will be my first time experimenting with magic.

Until now, Anna always stopped me from practicing anything but controlling magical power, so I've never actually used it.

Now I'm getting a little excited.

Though at the same time, the pressure from my sister makes me a little nervous.

"Hmph, I don't see the point of practicing magic I know I'm gonna suck at." As if to deflate my excitement, Hugo tosses away his staff. "It's way more efficient to improve what you're already good at than practice on your weaknesses."

Hugo gathers his magical power. What's he planning?

The next moment, he casts. Without a staff.

The result is a fire spell. So he already had Fire Magic as a skill?!

The flames engulf the entire row of targets.

What incredible destructive power.

For the students who couldn't even reach the targets, this must be a clear display of how strong he is.

In fact, it was perfect timing for showing off. Hugo must have realized that and pulled his stunt on purpose as a demonstration of his ability.

Still, this is way too much!

Flames swirl around the spot where the targets once stood.

If no one does anything, the fire might spread and engulf the entire class.

I pour all my magical power into the staff in my hand and unleash it toward the flames.

The staff absorbs my magic, activates the Water Magic spell enchanted into it, and launches a water ball.

The projectile lands directly in the flames and bursts open with a huge splash.

…Pretty impressive, if I do say so myself.

The water ball created by my magic power was massive. Enough to make a column of water when it exploded.

The flames are completely swallowed by the resulting deluge and disappear.

<Proficiency has reached the required level. Acquired skill [Water Magic LV 1].>

I just gained the Water Magic skill.

Maybe my extremely high aptitude is why I was able to get it with a single spell.

Or was it because the magnitude of that spell was so large? Or a little bit of both, I suppose.

"That's my elder brother for you! Who else could cancel a level-5 Fire Magic spell with level-1 Water Magic?"

As if to pull me back to reality, Sue praises me in a particularly loud voice. So that was level-5 Fire Magic?

Wait, Sue, you're doing this on purpose, aren't you? You usually don't speak so loudly.

Sure enough, Hugo glares at me for stealing his thunder.

Before he can do anything, however, Professor Oriza suddenly looms up behind him.

"May I have a word, Hugo?"

"What? Why should I have to talk to you?"

"Just come with me for a moment, please."

Professor Oriza more or less drags Hugo away, leaving behind only the charred remains of the targets and the group of very confused students.

"Yikes, Natsume's lame."

Fei's murmur echoes in my ear.

At the edge of my vision, I see Katia reining in the noisy students. *Thanks as usual, Katia!*

This is the day Hugo begins regarding me as his enemy.

Interlude

The Duke's Daughter and the Prince's Sister

"Katia, why did you quell everyone's excitement about my brother's success?"

"Sue, do you really think Shun wants that?"

"Well...no, I suppose not... You're a crafty one, Katia. What is your relationship with my brother, exactly?"

"What do you mean? We're friends, of course. What's wrong with that, I wonder?"

"Liar. You're not just regular friends, are you? It's the same with that elf you all call 'ma'am.' And the future saint and sword-king, too. What's going on with all of you?"

"Should I really be the one to answer that for you, do you think?"

"What's that supposed to mean?"

"Well, do you honestly want to hear it from me, or is there someone else, perhaps?"

"Well, I—"

"You should ask Shun directly about that sort of thing."

"But—"

"I certainly don't mind explaining, if you wish. But would it truly satisfy you, hearing it from me?"

"It would."

"I think not. Or do you really view Shun so lightly that you don't care what his answer is?"

"It's not like that at all!"

"Well then, you ought to ask Shun, not me. It's better that way for the both of you, no?"

"…Maybe so."

"I believe I do understand your feelings right now, if only a little. And that's precisely why I think it's best you confront the source of those feelings."

"…All right. I'm sorry. And…thank you."

"You're quite welcome. Ah, incidentally, we do indeed have a special relationship, but there are no romantic feelings there whatsoever. So please don't concern yourself with that."

"R-riiight…"

"What is it? Why the halfhearted reply?"

"Oh, nothing. You don't seem to realize it yet, so I don't think I'm the one who should say it."

"? What on earth…?"

"After all, why should I encourage someone who might end up being my rival?"

"Huh? What did you just say?"

"Nothing at all."

"I guess all I'm really doing is shoving it off on someone else, but so what? I mean, this is between the two of them as siblings. I don't want to get dragged into something that's got nothing to do with me. Yep, it's not my problem. Not at all… I should probably say something to Shun tomorrow, just in case."

That catfish was delicious. What a feast.

My Taste Enhancement skill even rose to level 7.

I guess I was really focused on eating, huh?

But you can't blame me!

Everything I've eaten until now has been disgusting!

Obviously, I want to savor it when I get to eat something good!

In addition, Overeating rose to level 8.

I still have plenty of stock left, but since it probably increases the amount I can conserve, there's certainly no disadvantage to raising that.

Plus, I'm curious to reach level 10 and find out what the derivative or evolved version of Overeating might be.

It's a very convenient skill as it is, so my hopes are high.

There's something else I'm concerned about, though.

That would be the Pride skill.

Pride is one of the seven deadly sins.

And there's also a deadly sin called Gluttony.

Overeating. Gluttony. They're rather close in meaning.

I can't help but be leery.

What if the evolved form of Overeating is Gluttony?

The effects of Pride are almost disturbingly powerful, and if Overeating evolves into Gluttony, it's possible it would have similar effects as another skill from the "deadly sins" series.

In that case, I'd feel as anxious about it as I do about Pride.

Well, it's still only level 8. No point in worrying about that yet.

Besides, it's gonna level up whether I want it to or not, so it's not like worrying will do me any good anyway.

Well then, guess it's time to keep exploring and search for more catfish.

Catfiiiish!

I wander around the Middle Stratum on the lookout for catfish.

However, I don't see a single one.

Hmm. I guess if they're submerged in the magma, I wouldn't notice them.

The first time I ran into one, it just so happened to be peeking out of the flow, after all.

If they normally run deep, they'll be hard to find.

If you ask me, I should have a useful skill for enemy detection by now.

Thinking back, it does seem like I've been able to pick things up more accurately than you'd expect with mere intuition.

I mean, I've never once been caught off guard by a surprise attack, and whenever I feel like I'm in danger, I'm usually right.

This is just a guess, but I think it's probably just my natural instincts as a spider.

I'm probably detecting stuff like the flow of air without even realizing it.

In that case, it makes sense that I didn't notice there was a catfish so close before.

If my senses rely on the flow of air, then of course I can't detect threats that are underneath magma.

I may not be able to sense surprise attacks coming from underwater or underground, either.

In which case, being near the magma is dangerous.

If something suddenly jumps out and drags me in, that'll be the end of the story right there.

Plus, it's risky being near magma in general anyway, so I've been trying to avoid it.

From now on, I'll have to stand far enough away that I'll be safe even if a monster appears.

You know, like right now.

If I had to sum up the creature that just leaped out of the magma, I'd call it... Hmm, an eel?

Yeah. An eel-like monster with scales and limbs.

<Elroe gunerave   LV 2
Status: HP: 1,001/1,001 (green)   MP: 511/511 (blue)

SP: 899/899 (yellow)   : 971/971 (red) +57

Average Offensive Ability: 893   Average Defensive Ability: 821

Average Magical Ability: 454   Average Resistance Ability: 433

Average Speed Ability: 582

Skills:

[Fire Wyrm LV 4]	[Dragon Scales LV 5]	[Fire Enhancement LV 1]	[Hit LV 10]
[Evasion LV 1]	[Probability Correction LV 1]	[High-Speed Swimming LV 2]	[Heat Nullification]
[Life LV 3]	[Instantaneous LV 1]	[Persistent LV 3]	[Strength LV 1]
[Solidity LV 1]		[Overeating LV 5]	

>

Uh-oh. This eel is really strong.

<Elroe gunerave: An average wyrm monster that lives in the Great Elroe Labyrinth, Middle Stratum. Omnivorous, but has a preference for eating other monsters.>

It's this strong, and it's only "average"?

Actually, judging by its skills, I wonder if this eel is also part of the catfish's evolutionary line?

No, now's not the time to worry about that sort of thing.

The eel is about fifty feet away.

It's already noticed me and has totally locked on.

I have the higher speed stat, but its other stats totally leave mine in the dust.

Worst of all, its red stamina gauge completely outweighs mine, even considering my Overeating stocks.

Even if I can outrun it, there's a good chance it'd catch up to me when my stamina runs out.

Hopefully, it loses interest before that happens, but...

My yellow stamina is low anyway, so I can only maintain my top speed for short bursts.

Once my instantaneous stamina runs out, I'll get short of breath, so I might get caught that way, too.

Can I get away?

Just as the question occurs to me, my vision of the eel splits in two.

Foresight must be activating.

The blurred version of the eel looks like it's about to spit something out.

Moments later, the real thing does the same, expelling a fireball.

So the basic tactics are the same.

But this blast is even faster and larger than the ones the sea horse and catfish made!

I move out of the way in a hurry.

Thought Acceleration is working, but the missile's velocity is so high I can barely tell.

It lands right where I'd been standing a moment before with a *boom*.

Even with the help of Foresight and Thought Acceleration, I was just barely able to avoid it.

What the heck? I thought I'd gotten away more quickly than that.

<Probability Correction: Adds a positive correction to any skills with power related to probability>

So it's this skill's fault. Maybe it increases the eel's accuracy rate.

In which case, it could be hard to keep evading even for me.

I may be in serious trouble here.

I dodge another fireball.

The next one flies at me, though, before I can recover.

At this rate, escaping won't even be an option.

The aftershock of the explosion shaves off a little HP.

If I move at top speed, I can definitely dodge these, but my yellow gauge will drain rapidly.

If I'm constantly sprinting, my yellow stamina bar will deplete before I can blink, leaving me short of breath.

Then I'll be finished.

Foresight and Thought Acceleration help me predict the path of the flaming missiles and avoid them.

But the eel can anticipate my movements, too, and corrects the trajectory of its shots.

Who will outwit who? It's like a high-speed, high-stakes game of chess.

The big difference is that while the eel doesn't lose much if it misses, I'll die if I make a single misstep.

<Proficiency has reached the required level.

Skill [Thought Acceleration LV 1] has become [Thought Acceleration LV 2].>

<Proficiency has reached the required level.

Skill [Foresight LV 1] has become [Foresight LV 2].>

I'm extremely grateful for my skills leveling up at a time like this.

The velocity of the incoming fireballs seems to slow down just a tad.

That said, my perception of my own movement speed slows down, too, so I have to be careful.

I evade more fireballs.

Then, thanks to Foresight, I see the eel try something different.

It still looks like it's going to exhale something, but it's sucking down way more air than before.

Time to let loose that peak speed I've been holding back.

I dash past the monster at a clip that blurs the scenery around me.

Behind me, powerful flames burn everything to a crisp.

<Flame Breath: Spews flames over a wide range>

This is a move that can be used when the Fire Wyrm skill reaches level 4.

I didn't get hit directly, but my back feels scorched by convection alone.

My HP decreases bit by bit.

At this rate, things'll only get worse, and if I take a direct hit even once, I'm done for.

But I can't come up with a single plan.

All I can do right now is keep bobbing and weaving and wait for my chance.

The feeling that my life is being slowly taken from me has me hot under the collar, no pun intended.

Another fireball flies toward me.

Between the eel's level-10 Hit skill and Probability Correction, its aim is incredibly accurate.

If I didn't have Evasion, Thought Acceleration, and Foresight on my side, I doubt I could dodge it.

<Proficiency has reached the required level.
  Skill [Evasion LV 5] has become [Evasion LV 6].>

All right! It's not enough to turn the whole situation around, but I'll take whatever advantage I can get.

I check the eel's remaining MP as I avoid the fireball.

It's definitely gone down, but it still has over half remaining.

Since Flame Breath has such a wide range, it seems to use a lot more MP than Fireball.

That's great and all, since it means it can't shoot that one after the other, but I kinda hope it tries to preserve its MP by not using it at all.

There's no guarantee that Foresight will save me every time, so I'm not sure if I can keep avoiding it.

I'll have to keep as close an eye as possible on the eel.

Before I finish that thought, Foresight shows me the image of the eel charging another Flame Breath.

I dash off at top speed once again.

But this time, instead of firing it straight forward, the eel swings its head sideways and sweeps the ground with fire!

Flame Breath already has a huge attack range, so now it's spreading ridiculously far.

Crap! It grazed me a little.

Even though it barely touched me, my HP goes down by 10.

Part of my back and one of my hind legs got hit.

The leg is in a bit of pain, but I can still move it fine, I think.

Still, this might slow me down a little bit. Shoot.

<Proficiency has reached the required level.
  Skill [Fire Resistance LV 1] has become [Fire Resistance LV 2].>

At this point, my stubborn Fire Resistance skill level finally goes up.

Great timing.

With higher Fire Resistance, my HP Auto-Recovery rate should exceed the rate of heat damage.

The amount of recovery will probably be minuscule, but it's a world of difference from having none at all.

I check the eel's MP.

Good. It's less than half now.

The rate of MP consumption seems to be about 10 for Fireball and 50 for Flame Breath.

But even with half its MP gone, I'd guess the eel could still use Flame Breath about four more times if it wants to.

That's not good.

I move to put some distance between myself and the monster.

Trying to prevent that, the eel launches a fireball as it follows me.

Just as I intended.

I doubt it can charge that Flame Breath while moving.

If I keep juking around and goad it into spitting more fireballs, it'll eventually run out of MP.

If I can hold out until then, I should get a chance to strike back, hopefully.

For now, I keep evading.

I'm constantly doing my best to get as far away as I can, but avoiding getting hit takes top priority.

I carefully choose my escape routes so I won't get cornered by the magma.

One wrong step, and I'm toast.

It's like I'm on a tightrope.

<Proficiency has reached the required level.

Skill [HP Auto-Recovery LV 5] has become [HP Auto-Recovery LV 6].>

YES!

My skills keep leveling up, probably because I'm so concentrated on this battle.

Fire Resistance and HP Auto-Recovery are the two skills I've been hoping to level up, and now it's happening!

I celebrate for only an instant. But that instant is nearly fatal.

The eel initiates Flame Breath.

This is completely unexpected. Foresight didn't even warn me.

There's no way I can dodge this.

The breath erupts from the eel's mouth.

Immediately, I kick off the ground with all my might, jumping into the air.

The stream of fire scorches my legs.

Fighting back the pain, I use Energy Conferment while extending a thread toward the ceiling.

Energy Conferment consumes red SP to strengthen things.

With this skill, I can spin some thread capable of withstanding the heat of the Middle Stratum for a short period.

Still, it'll only last a limited time, so I quickly pull on the thread to raise myself to the ceiling.

Then I cut the silk before it burns.

<Proficiency has reached the required level.

Skill [Spatial Maneuvering LV 4] has become [Spatial Maneuvering LV 5].>

I stare down at the eel from the ceiling.

It glares at me from the magma.

It's great I escaped to the ceiling and all, but overall, this situation is still untenable.

When I'm sticking to the ceiling, I inevitably move more slowly than when I'm on the ground.

I already had my hands full avoiding the eel's attacks on terra firma. There's no way I can keep it up on the ceiling.

I have to get back down ASAP, or I'll get shot down instead.

However, the eel isn't in such great shape, either.

Its MP has gone down considerably.

Looks like it could summon three more Flame Breaths or sixteen more Fireballs.

Compared with when we started, that's pretty low.

But it's still more than enough to knock me off my perch.

Will I make it back down to the floor, or will it nail me first?

This is no time to be stingy with my skills.

Mental Warfare, activate!

Mental Warfare is a skill that consumes red SP to temporarily increase physical stats.

Red stamina is my lifeline, so I've never activated this before. But in this situation, I can't be reluctant about spending SP.

I set off right away, aiming for the nearest wall.

But apparently, the eel anticipated this.

It launches a fireball as if to hedge me in, seemingly knowing exactly where I wanted to go.

This would be tough to dodge while clinging to the ceiling.

I'll have to stop worrying about my red stamina bar for now.

I avoid the approaching fireball with the highest speed I can muster.

My best option is to push through Mental Warfare and hope that SP Reduced Consumption and SP Recovery Speed will offset the loss.

I have to get to the wall before my yellow gauge runs out.

It keeps firing, and I keep dodging.

However, this is making it difficult to get close enough to the wall.

While I'm busy with acrobatics, my yellow stamina bar keeps dwindling.

Crap. If I run out, it'll be even harder to stick to the ceiling.

I have to avoid that outcome at all costs.

But it's no use. The eel's flawless aim prevents me from getting anywhere.

Finally, the yellow gauge runs out.

Fatigue immediately assails my body. Before I can think, another fireball homes in on me relentlessly.

Damn! I can tell that I won't be able to dodge it, so I deliberately release by grip, leaping into empty space.

The fireball explodes in my immediate vicinity, the blast brushing against my body.

I manage to prevent myself from going into a tailspin, drawing on Energy Conferment again.

The reinforced thread shoots out, adhering to the wall, and I instantly scuttle along it.

Another shot passes through the space I'd just evacuated.

Swinging through the air like a pendulum, I narrowly avoid falling in the magma and manage to land on the ground.

Without so much as a beat, another fireball flies at me.

I use the momentum of my landing to roll out of its way.

This is rough. As punishment for continuing to move even after my yellow gauge expired, my breath is ragged and my exhausted body aches.

I force myself to ignore it with the powers of Pain Nullification and Pain Mitigation...

...because I can see the eel is about to unleash another Flame Breath.

Whipping my spent body into action, I take off at maximum velocity.

The edges of my vision fill with red flames. The heat approaching from behind is palpable.

I keep running, trying to shake it off.

Somehow, I've avoided the Flame Breath.

<Proficiency has reached the required level.
  Skill [Evasion LV 6] has become [Evasion LV 7].>

I let out the air I was unconsciously holding in my lungs.

My yellow stamina gauge starts to recover.

There'll be no more fireballs now.

The eel is finally out of MP.

With no more means of attacking from a distance, the eel slithers onto land.

As it turns out, its head is the only eel-like thing about it.

The rest of its body bears an uncanny resemblance to a Chinese dragon.

Even with its MP gone, its eyes are still fixed on me.

This thing has definitely decided I'm its enemy.

At first, it felt like it might've just decided to crush me because I was a bit of an eyesore, but somewhere along the way, its fireballs took on a more serious tone.

By the time it started using Flame Breath, it was definitely coming at me for all it was worth.

Seems it didn't care for having its attacks continuously dodged.

Even if I ran away now, I doubt it'd let me go.

Its MP might be gone, but its SP is still going strong.

My stamina, on the other hand, has been whittled down considerably.

Since I kept moving after my yellow bar ran out, my red stamina bar has gone down too much for comfort, too.

I still have my surplus from Overeating, so it's not like I'm completely immobile or anything, but if it comes down to a battle of stamina between us, the eel will definitely be the winner.

I can't run.

That leaves me with one choice. I have to fight and win.

Based solely on the numerical values of our stats, I don't stand a chance.

But numbers aren't everything.

If there's one thing I've learned in my battles here, it's that skills are the biggest deciding factor, for better or for worse.

I mean, considering the huge difference in our stats, it's a miracle I've survived at all.

And the source of that "miracle" has to be my set of skills.

It's only because I've been exploiting them to their fullest that I've been able to compensate for the inherent difference in our strength and even forced the eel onto land.

The gap in our stats is definitely huge, but it's not enough to decide the battle.

If I play my cards right, I can still traverse the gulf.

Not to mention, I can see all of the eel's skills, too.

Since it's out of MP now, the only ones I have to worry about are the combination of Hit, Evasion, and Probability Correction.

That, and the defensive power granted by Dragon Scales, the last level-3 ability granted by Fire Wyrm.

The final threat is the sheer physical size of the eel's massive body.

That alone is enough to make it a formidable enemy.

But I still have a few tricks up my sleeve. Namely, my strongest means of attack: Deadly Poison.

The target's defense means precious little in the face of my powerful venom.

It can erode even Dragon Scales, eating away at the flesh beneath.

In the end, my skills are all I can rely on.

That's the only area where I outperform the eel.

Although, even that's debatable depending on how well I use them.

Both of us are lacking in the defense department.

This'll be a sudden-death match, where whoever lands an attack first wins.

Which means my winning move would be…

The ground-based second round begins without a bell.

The eel's long body coils back and forth.

After our exchanges thus far, it seems quite wary of me.

This eel is pretty smart compared with most other monsters, though not as smart as those monkeys.

Which only makes my job harder.

<Proficiency has reached the required level.
  Skill [Thought Acceleration LV 2] has become [Thought Acceleration LV 3].>
<Proficiency has reached the required level.
  Skill [Foresight LV 2] has become [Foresight LV 3].>

The eel moves as if in time with the Divine Voice (temp.).

Body unfurling, it lashes at me with its tail.

I dodge it, of course, but the beast's attack doesn't end there.

The tail sweeps sideways, zeroing in on me again.

I edge farther back to avoid it.

This time, the eel's head comes at me instead, swapping places with the tail.

That's exactly what I was waiting for.

As the world moves around me somewhat slowly thanks to Thought Acceleration, I fix my eyes on the eel's approaching mouth.

Just as I judge that it's about to get too close for me to dodge, I activate Poison Synthesis.

Then I immediately evacuate.

It's the same strategy I used against the catfish. However, it has a huge effect.

The poison goes down the eel's throat, just as I planned.

Its HP rapidly decreases.

In agony, the eel's body whips around violently.

I retreat beyond the reach of its writhing.

In the end, if both sides are strong enough to kill the other with a single blow, the winner will be whoever lands an attack first.

Which means the one who comes up with the better strategy to land that blow wins.

That, and my evasive ability surpasses the eel's accuracy.

Even with level-10 Hit and Probability Correction, it couldn't outdo my combination of Evasion, Thought Acceleration, and Foresight.

So as soon as the eel was lured ashore, my odds of winning skyrocketed.

Still, it's not over yet.

Despite all my talk about a single deathblow, that one attack probably won't be enough to kill it.

Even the catfish didn't die after one attack, so there's no way that would work on an even stronger species.

Besides, the eel still has another skill on its side.

Its HP is rapidly recovering right before my eyes.

<Life Exchange: Recovers HP by consuming SP>

It's a level-3 ability from the Fire Wyrm skill.

It consumes SP, and HP is recovered by a corresponding amount.

Although it can't recover fully because of the amount of SP it has, it's still enough to resist my Deadly Poison.

On top of that, as I evaluate the eel's Appraisal results, it gains Poison Resistance level 1 and HP Auto-Recovery level 1.

The poison in its body is still eating away its HP little by little, but the peak of the damage has passed already.

Still, it's not like I'm just gonna stand here and watch the thing revive itself.

I make the sturdiest thread I can and wrap it around the eel's body.

It'll burn up right away, but that doesn't matter.

All I need is to immobilize it for even a moment.

Luckily, I manage to do exactly that.

In that instant, I target the eel's face and activate Poison Synthesis in rapid succession.

Globs of poison strike liberally.

The eel tears through the restraints and thrashes wildly.

But the poison has already seeped into its eyes and mouth, draining its HP mercilessly.

The rate of damage is far too high for its new Auto-Recovery skill to counteract.

And it's far too powerful for its new Poison Resistance skill to combat, either.

A shield whipped up on a moment's notice can hardly withstand weaponry I've been perfecting my entire life as a spider.

Without enough SP left to spend on recovery, the attack proves too much for the eel.

<Experience has reached the required level. Individual small poison tara-
tect has increased from LV 7 to LV 8.>

<All basic attributes have increased.>
<Skill proficiency level-up bonus acquired.>
<Proficiency has reached the required level.
  Skill [Parallel Thinking LV 4] has become [Parallel Thinking LV 5].>
<Proficiency has reached the required level.
  Skill [SP Recovery Speed LV 2] has become [SP Recovery Speed LV 3].>
<Skill points acquired.>

<Experience has reached the required level. Individual small poison tara-
  tect has increased from LV 8 to LV 9.>
<All basic attributes have increased.>
<Skill proficiency level-up bonus acquired.>
<Proficiency has reached the required level.
  Skill [Instantaneous LV 8] has become [Instantaneous LV 9].>
<Proficiency has reached the required level.
  Skill [Persistent LV 8] has become [Persistent LV 9].>
<Skill points acquired.>

<Experience has reached the required level. Individual small poison tara-
  tect has increased from LV 9 to LV 10.>
<All basic attributes have increased.>
<Skill proficiency level-up bonus acquired.>
<Proficiency has reached the required level.
  Skill [Arithmetic Processing LV 6] has become [Arithmetic Processing LV 7].>
<Proficiency has reached the required level.
  Skill [Vision Enhancement LV 8] has become [Vision Enhancement LV 9].>
<Proficiency has reached the required level.
  Skill [Life LV 8] has become [Life LV 9].>
<Skill points acquired.>
<Condition satisfied. Individual small poison taratect can now evolve.>
<There are multiple options for evolution. Please choose from the following.

  • Poison taratect
  • Zoa Ele

>

Ooh, evolution.

Wait, evolution?! Already?! Isn't this a little soon?! Last time with the monkeys seemed really fast, too!

Well, I can worry about that later.

For the moment, I want to savor my victory.

I wooon!

Whoo-hoooo! I won, I won! That eel was super-strong, and I beat it!

Amazing, right?! Am I hella strong or what?!

Heh. Heh-heh.

I fought head-on, barely even used my thread, but I still won.

That means I'm not weak anymore, right? I'm sooo strong!

Yahoooo!

That eel was a formidable enemy. It was no joke. A real fight to the death.

But in the end, victory is mine!

I'm number one! Heh-heh-heh-heh.

I did it! The winner is me! Ha-ha-ha!

file.08

ELROE GUNERAVE

LV.01

status

Average Offensive
Ability : 881

Average Defensive
Ability : 809

Average Magic
Ability : 444

Average Resistance
Ability : 421

Average Speed
Ability : 573

HP 980 / 980

MP 490 / 490

SP 880 / 880

950 / 950

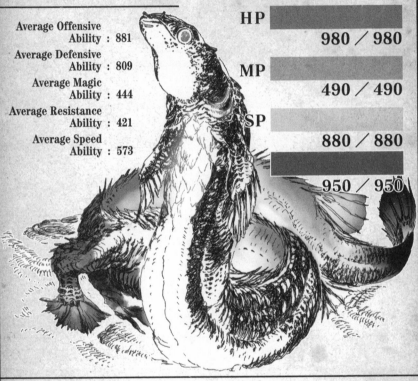

skill

[Fire Wyrm LV 4] [Dragon Scales LV 5] [Fire Enhancement LV 1]
[Hit LV 10] [Evasion LV 1] [Probability Correction LV 1]
[High-Speed Swimming LV 2] [Overeating LV 5] [Heat Nullification]
[Life LV 3] [Instantaneous LV 1] [Persistent LV 3]
[Strength LV 1] [Solidity LV 1]

Also known as an eel. A midranking wyrm monster that looks like an eel with limbs. Evolved form of the catfish. Its fire attacks are far more powerful than those of any lower-class wyrm. In addition, its high physical strength makes it strong on a practical level, and it is intelligent enough to make decisions based on its situation. It isn't as cowardly as the catfish but has still been known to flee if it meets a much stronger opponent. Danger level B.

S3   Fei's Training Diary

We have to raise Fei's level soon. Because she's a fledgling earth dragon.

Since she's a kind of monster, if she doesn't evolve by leveling up, she'll die before reaching adulthood.

In order to grow, she has to defeat monsters and level up.

She's reached the point where her life is in jeopardy if she doesn't evolve soon.

Unfortunately, I'm not allowed to leave the academy.

So instead, I talked to my maid, Anna, and asked her to help raise Fei's level.

"Very well. We shall return."

Anna leaves the school grounds with Fei in her arms.

There are several men accompanying her who seem to be soldiers, but since Anna is a half elf, she's not as young as she looks.

She's among the most talented magic users in the entire kingdom.

I'm sure she'll be able to help Fei grow and come back safely.

By the way, Anna doesn't know Fei is a reincarnation.

As far as I know, she just thinks of her as a somewhat clever baby earth dragon.

The only people who know the truth are me and the other reincarnations.

I haven't even told Sue about it.

I always thought she was pretty close to Hugo in the past, but when I asked her, she just said, "Natsume? Did anybody actually like him?"

So I guess I was wrong about their relationship.

Hugo burst out laughing when he saw what Fei looked like, too, so they might've actually been pretty incompatible from the start.

Within a few days, Fei evolved without a problem and returned.

Leveling up means fighting monsters.

Considering this, I had been a little worried since it seems dangerous, but apparently, my concern was unfounded.

Which is good and all, but the real problem is how Fei looked when she got back.

"You got a lot bigger, huh?"

"It's called a growth spurt, duh."

Fei's body has gotten quite a bit larger.

Initially, she'd been about the size of a chameleon, able to ride on my head or shoulder without a problem, but now her body is about three feet long.

If you include the length of her tail, she might even be almost as long as I am tall.

She went from being the size of my hand to the size of a large dog.

"This is still small for a dragon, you know. Once I evolve again, I'll get even larger."

"You probably won't be able to go indoors anymore when that happens, then."

She's able to live in my dorm room with me for now, but if she gets any bigger, she may not fit.

"That is a bit of an issue..."

She might've been reincarnated as a monster, but she was still originally a high school girl from Japan.

It's no surprise that she wouldn't want to sleep outside like other monsters.

"Well, now that I've evolved once, my life expectancy should be significantly longer. No need to worry just yet."

If she says so, I guess that's fine.

Hopefully, she's not just saying it to avoid getting kicked out of my room.

I also got her permission to Appraise her and see how her stats have grown after evolving.

Turns out she's stronger than me now.

"Well, monsters' stats grow a lot more rapidly than humans' do."

I mean, sure, but still—isn't this an awfully drastic departure from her stats prior to evolving?

"What's the big deal? Your stats are pretty broken for a human as it is. I risked my life for this, you know! I don't see why I shouldn't be allowed to get a little stronger as a reward. Not that it feels like much of a prize for me anyway."

"Oh, right. Girls don't care about being strong anyway, huh?"

"This one certainly doesn't. I don't have much of a choice but to get stronger, but don't think for a second that I enjoy fighting for my life. Besides, you saw my skills, didn't you? Overeating..."

I know all about it. Overeating is a skill that saves extra SP based on how much you eat.

If a human being gets the Overeating skill, they'll still gain weight for the extra food they consume, but for whatever reason, this doesn't apply to monsters.

"Since I have that stupid skill, that Anna keeps feeding me monster meat. She has some ridiculous idea that eating the flesh of strong monsters will make your stats go up more easily. Isn't that just awful?"

Yikes. I'll pass on that, thanks.

Monster meat... I guess it depends on what kind, but on the whole, I wouldn't want to eat it at all.

"I'll definitely make that maid pay for this someday! She shoved that monster meat down my throat even though I clearly didn't want it! Disgusting!"

I, uh...my condolences.

Still, when I think about it, monsters have awfully high stats.

Mine were higher than hers before she evolved, but Fei's have definitely surpassed mine now.

She's averaging around 700 in each stat at the moment.

As far as I know, only a handful of supremely accomplished humans have obtained that.

And Fei is still a lesser dragon, too.

If she keeps evolving like this, those numbers may even exceed 1,000.

In terms of stats alone, she could even catch up to my brother Julius, the hero.

On top of that, even though her skills are still developing, they're already quite strong.

The main reason humans are able to fight monsters whose stats outrank theirs is that our skills give us an advantage.

Monsters don't generally train their skills, after all.

An ordinary monster usually only has a small amount of skills to boot, but that doesn't apply to Fei.

It's like she has the advantages of both a monster and a human.

If all the monsters in the world were like Fei, humans and demons would probably be extinct by now.

I mean, she was born much later than I was, and she's already this strong.

Not to mention, this is all the result of training hard for just a few days.

If she had been born earlier than me and spent more time leveling up...

For example, if she had hatched in the Great Elroe Labyrinth where she was originally found and had been fighting to survive in there all this time, I doubt anybody could have defeated her.

That, or if there was another monster with the intelligence of a human in similar circumstances...

Well, I guess there's no use worrying about a hypothetical like that. I doubt there are any other exceptional cases like Fei.

Interlude The Duke's Daughter and the Earth Wyrm

"Boy, you got big."

"You're telling me! If I get any bigger, I'll end up having to live outside."

"So does that mean you'd rather not evolve any more?"

"You've got that right. Why, is that a problem?"

"I wouldn't say that, but...you live in Shun's room right now, don't you? I know you're a dragon now and all, but are you really okay sleeping in the same room as a boy?"

"Do you really think that matters to me now that I'm in this form? Frankly, I'm a different species now, so that sort of feeling wouldn't even occur to me. You don't have some kind of weird thing for reptiles, do you?"

"'Course not!"

"If you do, keep it to yourself. But it's the same way for me. I'm not really interested in human men anymore."

"Oh really?"

"Certainly. I can recognize good looks and all, since I used to be human myself, but a normal earth dragon wouldn't even be able to distinguish between human faces, you know?"

"Ah, I guess I get that. I can't tell the difference between animals' faces and stuff, either."

"Well, I've never met any other earth dragons, so I don't know what would make one attractive or not, but my point still stands."

"Yeah, I can't really picture that myself."

"Although I'll admit, I got excited for a minute after I was born when I saw that princely Shun."

"Huh?"

"I mean, he totally looks like a handsome prince in this world. And I still felt a bit like a human being back then."

"Hey now..."

"What're you getting worked up about? Well anyway, once I found out who was inside, I changed my mind about that in a hurry."

"Oh, did you?"

"I mean, it's Yamada, you know? He never really had much going for him."

"Hey. Isn't that a little harsh?"

"Oh, don't be angry. I respect him now, in a way. I mean, he managed to stay thoroughly average even after being reborn in a new world. That's got to take some real dedication."

"Wow, I can't tell if you're complimenting or insulting him."

"It's a compliment, more or less. Man, aren't you overprotective, though! Sensitive much?"

"I am not."

Well, he doesn't like me living with Shun, got all worked up when I mentioned possibly having feelings for him, and was totally relieved when I said I don't. It's obvious what's going on here, isn't it? But it'll be more fun if I don't say anything about that.

Huff… Wheeze…

I'm so excited, I can barely breathe. Guess I got a little carried away celebrating my victory over that tough opponent.

Whew. All right, that's enough of that. What should I do now?

First of all, I leveled up a whole bunch at once.

Thanks, eel. I guess you aren't considered a dragon species for nothing.

By stats alone, it was way out of my league. Combine that with the effects of Pride, and it's no wonder I maxed out my level in one go.

My skills grew quite a bit in this battle, too. What a windfall of experience points.

Although honestly, I wasn't sure if I was gonna win for a minute there.

If I'd made a single mistake or misstep, I'd probably be cinders by now.

That's how strong that eel was.

Really, strictly judging by our stats, no one would think I had a chance in hell of winning.

Between that and those monkeys, I think I might get in over my head in battle a little too often…

Anyway, I think the skills I'm happiest about leveling up are HP Auto-Recovery and Fire Resistance.

So far, my recovery rate has been just enough to cancel out the damage from this scorching-hot terrain, but now it should exceed it enough to heal me at least a little.

I can't check right now, though, since my HP fully recovered when I leveled up.

Hopefully, though, I'll be able to recover with time if I take a bit of damage from now on.

It was pretty rough avoiding even the tiniest injury this whole time, but now I should be able to relax a little.

Although, I'll still probably bite the dust if I take a direct hit from a single attack.

Also, I'm level 10.

That means I can evolve again.

But should I? Is it really safe to evolve in a place like this?

I mean, evolving comes with a bit of risk in itself.

For one thing, when I evolve, I totally pass out.

That leaves me completely unprotected for a while, so if another monster attacks me or something, I'll be screwed.

Last time—and the time before that—I spun myself a web to give myself a safe place to evolve, but that's not an option this time.

I can't use my silk here, after all.

If I try to construct a web in this magma-drenched hellscape, it'll burn up before I can even finish it.

Evolve in the middle of a fire? No thank you.

That's not all, either.

Since evolution requires a lot of energy, my MP and SP will be totally drained.

MP's not that big of a deal, but if I run out of SP, I might be too hungry to even move.

Worst-case scenario, I could starve to death.

So far, I've always had a big stockpile of food to pig out on after I evolved, but my current situation is a bit different.

Well, there is the eel, but I don't think even this monstrosity would be enough to fully recover my SP.

I don't have to worry about starving, but I think I'd have to actively hunt for prey for a while.

Oh, but what happens to my stock from Overeating?

I didn't have any Overeating stores the first two times I evolved…

I did use some in the battle with the eel, but there's still a good amount left over.

If I can use that stock to fuel my evolution, maybe I won't be running on empty afterward.

Hmm. But I probably shouldn't act based on wishful thinking, huh?

On a purely emotional level, I definitely want to evolve—but from a safety perspective, maybe it's better not to just yet?

But I'm worried that if I don't, I won't level up anymore.

Are small creatures limited to level 10?

If that's the case, all the experience I gain in this form will go to waste, and I'm pretty sure I still have a ways to go in the Middle Stratum.

Yeah, I really don't like that.

In which case, maybe I should just evolve after all? Hmm.

At any rate, it looks like I have multiple options for evolution again, so maybe I'll investigate first.

All right, Appraisal, I'm counting on you.

‹Available Evolutions: Poison taratect OR Zoa Ele›

Hmm? Poison taratect is no surprise, but what's this Zoa Ele thing?

It's not even a taratect?

‹Zoa Ele: Evolution Requirements: Small spider-type monster with stats above a certain amount, [Assassin] title. Description: A small spider-type monster that is feared as an ill omen. Has high combat and stealth capabilities.›

Ooh, Appraisal!

You added evolution requirements, too! For me?

That's my Appraisal for you! Never misses a beat!

Hmm. So I can evolve into this because my stats exceed the requirements.

Which means they were lower than the requirements until now, probably.

And wait, titles are involved in evolution?

I wonder if I was able to evolve into a small poison taratect because I had the Poison Technique User title?

That definitely seems like a possibility.

‹Poison taratect: Evolution Requirements: Small poison taratect LV 10. Description: A rare young species of the spider-type monster species taratect. Has extremely powerful poison.›

So that's my other option: poison taratect.

But if I'm going to evolve, I'd probably have to go with door number one.

Zoa Ele. The conditions for evolving into that are pretty tough, and as my precious Appraisal informed me, it has high combat capabilities to boot.

The fact that it's apparently "small" is a big plus, too.

Although I guess I am a little nervous about it, since judging by the name and description, it seems to be a different line from the taratect species.

If I keep evolving as a taratect, I'll definitely get stronger.

I know this because I witnessed that evolved form with my own however-many eyes.

The gigantic spider presumed to be my mother, the one I saw in the Lower Stratum: the greater taratect.

It's hard to imagine judging from how weak I've been so far, but I know for sure that if I keep evolving, I'll reach that level eventually.

I know that, but at the same time, it also means I'll get bigger.

I know bigger is better and all, but in the end, I think all cutting-edge technology aims for miniaturization.

Small size, but high performance. That's what I desire!

And more importantly, if I get too big, I won't even be able to move anymore.

I mean, how far can my mother really get around at that size?

I'd rather not suddenly lose the ability to maneuver in passages that never posed an issue before.

Besides, can you imagine being that big here in the Middle Stratum?

It'd be way too easy to miss a step on a narrow passage and stick your foot right into the magma!

It's not like stepping in a puddle, you know! I'd die!

I don't know how big I'd get as an adult, but in my case, there are some major downsides to getting too big.

Not only in terms of ability to move, but also with regard to battle.

I mean, dodging is my specialty, here. Being bigger just means being a bigger target.

For someone who relies on evasion, being small is a good thing.

Besides, if I get bigger, I'll get heavier, too.

Being heavy would only slow me down.

You're telling me, a speed demon, that I have to slow down? Yeah, right.

All of this adds up to me not wanting to evolve along the taratect line anymore.

So if I have a choice now that looks like a different path, of course I wanna take it.

It's not that I'm without reservations, of course.

The evolved forms of the taratect line are definitely strong, but I can't say that for sure about the Zoa Ele.

In the worst-case scenario, Zoa Ele might even be the end of that evolutionary line.

If that's the case, I'd have been better off sticking with the taratect species.

But if that happens, well, so be it, I suppose.

I can still increase my stats by leveling up and train my other skills and stuff, too.

Even the weakest monsters can be strong if they're raised with care. Take me, for example.

I mean, really, compared with where I started, I've gotten pretty damn strong.

When I remember what it was like to be so weak that anything could kill me with a little shove, most other problems seem a lot more manageable.

So I guess I'll evolve into a Zoa Ele.

The problem here is how to do so safely, but I think I have an idea.

I can't quite say for sure it's totally safe, but it's better than nothing.

So... C'mere, Mr. Dead Eel!

It's time for today's three-minute recipe.

What I have here is the corpse of an eel. Only the highest quality.

First, we're going to stretch this out.

Next, we'll coil it around, starting from the tail.

Be sure to make a nice, even coil all the way around.

Now, we're gonna want to leave some space in the center here.

Once you have a basic circle, pile the eel on top of itself and make another coil.

Instead of from the outside in, we'll work from the inside of the coil out.

Repeat this process a few more times, then place the head over the middle.

Voilà! Our eel shelter is done.

Wow, this is looking great!

All right. Since the eel has Dragon Scales, it should be pretty sturdy.

It may not be as nice as a web, but I think it'll do pretty nicely as defense goes.
I should be safe if I evolve in here, I think.

All right, let's give it a shot.

<Individual small poison taratect will evolve into Zoa Ele.>

Yep. And with that, my consciousness slips away.

Good morning.

Although I don't know if it's actually morning.

Well, looks like I managed to wake safely again. That's good, at least.

I think this round of evolution was a record high for riskiness.

I'm glad I didn't wake up in heaven or anything like that.

Huh? What do you mean, hell?

As if an honest, upstanding citizen like me would ever go to hell! Ha-ha-ha.

Anyway, time for my usual self-Appraisal... Er, after I ensure my own safety, that is.

The eel shelter seems to be intact, but it's possible that I've been surrounded by monsters outside or something.

All right, let's take a liiiittle peek outside.

Sweet. Looks like we're all clear. Nice, nice.

All right, let's just snack on this eel while I... Aw, man, wait.

Just like the time with the snake, I can't eat the eel until I pull its scales off. Damn. Oh well.

I'm not so hungry that I can't move or anything. Maybe Overeating had my back like I hoped?

All right, guess I'll do some de-scaling while I check my status.

<Zoa Ele	LV 1		Nameless	
Status:	HP: 195/195 (green) 100UP		MP: 1/291 (blue) 100UP	
	SP: 195/195 (yellow) 100UP)		: 195/195 (red) +43 100UP	
	Average Offensive Ability: 251 118UP		Average Defensive Ability: 251 118UP	
	Average Magical Ability: 245 100UP		Average Resistance Ability: 280 101UP	
	Average Speed Ability: 1,272 100UP			

Skills:

[HP Auto-Recovery LV 6]

[MP Recovery Speed LV 4 1UP]

[MP Lessened Consumption LV 3]

[SP Recovery Speed LV 3]

[SP Lessened Consumption LV 3]

[Destruction Enhancement LV 2 1UP]

[Cutting Enhancement LV 2 1UP]

[Poison Enhancement LV 4 1UP]

[Mental Warfare LV 2 1UP]

[Energy Conferment LV 2]

[Deadly Poison Attack LV 3]

[Rot Attack LV 1 NEW]

[Poison Synthesis LV 8 1UP]

[Threadsmanship LV 3]

[Utility Thread LV 1 NEW]

[Thread Control LV 8]

[Throw LV 7]

[Spatial Maneuvering LV 5]

[Stealth LV 7 1UP]

[Silence LV 1 NEW]

[Concentration LV 10]

[Thought Acceleration LV 3]

[Foresight LV 3]

[Parallel Thinking LV 5]

[Arithmetic Processing LV 7]

[Hit LV 8]

[Evasion LV 7]

[Appraisal LV 9]

[Detection LV 6]

[Heretic Magic LV 3]

[Shadow Magic LV 3 1UP]

[Poison Magic LV 3 1UP]

[Abyss Magic LV 10]

[Destruction Resistance LV 2 1UP]

[Impact Resistance LV 2]

[Cutting Resistance LV 3]

[Fire Resistance LV 2]

[Dark Resistance LV 2 1UP]

[Deadly Poison Resistance LV 2]

[Paralysis Resistance LV 4 1UP]

[Petrification Resistance LV 3]

[Acid Resistance LV 4]

[Rot Resistance LV 3]

[Faint Resistance LV 3 1UP]

[Fear Resistance LV 7]

[Heresy Resistance LV 3]

[Pain Nullification]

[Pain Mitigation LV 7]

[Vision Enhancement LV 9]

[Night Vision LV 10]

[Vision Expansion LV 2]

[Poison Resistance LV 8]

[Olfactory Enhancement LV 7]

[Taste Enhancement LV 7]

[Tactile Enhancement LV 7 1UP]

[Life LV 9]

[Magic Mass LV 8]

[Instantaneous LV 9]

[Persistent LV 9]

[Herculean Strength LV 4 1UP]

[Sturdy	[Protection	[Skanda	[Pride]
LV 4 1UP]	LV 4 1UP]	LV 3]	

[Overeating	[Hades]	[Taboo	[n% I = W]
LV 8]		LV 5 1UP]	

Skill Points: 500

Titles:

[Foul Feeder]	[Kin Eater]	[Assassin]	[Monster Slayer]

[Poison Technique User]	[Thread User]	[Merciless]	[Monster Slaughterer]

[Ruler of Pride]

>

Huh? Hmm? Wait a sec.

Let me look at this again. Maybe my eyes are playing tricks on me.

I carefully review my status numbers.

Huh? Wha—?! Wh-whaaaaaat?! Wh-wh…what?

They went way up. WAY, waaay up!

Is this for real? Did my stats improve that much?

Wow. That description wasn't kidding around when it said "high combat capabilities"…

Uh, can I really get away with this?

Is it really okay for me to get so strong so fast?

You know I'm gonna get really cocky if I get this powerful, right?

That's okay, yeah? It is?

…Heh, heh-heh-heh. I'm in the prime of my liiiiife!

This solves the conundrum of my once-terrible stats all in one go!

They're still low compared with big game like the eel, but now I'm finally strong enough that a lone poke from the local small-fry won't be enough to do me in!

All this time, I've had to assume that a blow from a single attack would be the end of me.

But now, finally, FINALLY I have respectable stats!

Heh, heh-heh-heh. Hee-hee-hee-hee.

This means I'm stronger than the sea horses in terms of stats—and even the monkeys—doesn't it?

My skill levels increased a lot, too. Looking good, looking good.

Wait, Taboo went up again?!

Hey! What do you mean, level 5?!

Does that mean I'm halfway to maxing it out?!

If my prediction is correct, I'm pretty sure something big's gonna happen if it reaches level 10.

Crap.

Well, it's still only halfway. I'm okay for now. I think.

Let's see, what else? I also gained a few new skills.

Rot Attack? Seriously?

By "Rot," you mean that attribute, right?

The one that was way scarier than I expected when I Appraised it?

I can use that now? Damn, I'm talented.

The next unfamiliar skill is Silence.

I feel like I can more or less guess what that does, but maybe I'll Appraise it just to be sure.

<Silence: Suppresses the creation of sound>

Yep. That's what I thought.

Awesome! My ninja skills are on the rise!

Maybe I'll be able to defeat things with a single ambush now?

There's also a very strange skill situation here.

Spider Thread and Cutting Thread have disappeared. Instead, there's a new skill called Utility Thread.

It's probably an evolved form of Spider Thread, but where did Cutting Thread go?

<Utility Thread: Generate customizable threads. Customizable Qualities: Viscosity; Elasticity; Resilience; Texture; Strength; Size; Attribute Confer- ment including "Cutting," "Impact," "Shock"; Attribute Resistance.>

Now I can add more attributes and stuff than with Spider Thread.

It looks like Cutting probably has the same effect as Cutting Thread, Impact adds the Impact attribute, and Shock adds the Shock attribute.

Impact just means a normal strike.

And apparently, Shock can briefly generate some sort of shock wave in the thread.

If an enemy touches the thread while it's in that state, it'll get shocked and take damage.

Man, if I weren't in the Middle Stratum, this would be super-useful!

Ugh, I really wanna get outta here fast so I can try it out!

Anyway, I finished de-scaling the eel while I was checking all that.

Okay, time to see if this eel meal is the real deal.

Let's take a little bite.

…It's delicious.

The flavor is totally different from the catfish.

I'll say it again: Delicious!

This time, when I evolved, I didn't lose my SP.

Instead, it drained most of my Overeating stock.

That just proves that Overeating functioned perfectly.

Given that, as long as I keep building stores with Overeating, I'll be fine even if I don't have a bunch of food on hand when I evolve.

So I'll just have to eat a ton so I can save as much as I can.

Judging by my previous amounts, it seems like I can stock about 100 SP per skill level, so right now I should be able to stock about 800.

<Proficiency has reached the required level.

  Skill [Overeating LV 8] has become [Overeating LV 9].>

Well, speak of the devil.

Now I can stock up even more!

Speaking of stocking, I suddenly have way more skill points than before.

I thought they rose by 20 per level, but I have 280 more than last time I looked.

If 60 of those came from leveling up three times, what's the deal with the other 220?

Does evolution come with a bonus or something?

If so, that would explain why my skill point calculations didn't make sense before.

Well, I'll certainly take however many I can get.

I've got a whole 500 now, so maybe I can find a really good skill.

I'll have to take a good look at the list of acquirable skills later.

Before that, though, there's something else that concerns me.

My body shape has changed a little. I noticed as I was pulling off the eel's scales.

The two legs in front, which used to be shaped like sharp claws, are more like thin scythes now.

And these sickle things happen to cut extreeemely well.

It took me forever to get the scales off that snake a while back, but this time, I made quick work of it.

I can't cut the scales themselves, but I was able to slice between the scales and the skin.

Is it because my attack power went up or because these scythes are so sharp?

In addition, my body is black now. It was always pretty dark, but now it's black for sure.

I'm telling you, it's pitch-black! The kind of black that doesn't reflect light at all.

I can't see the rest of me, since I don't have a mirror, but I'm guessing those are the biggest changes.

I don't feel like my size is any different or anything.

But I bet there are some little details that have changed that I'm just not aware of.

So far, since I was sticking with the taratect species, my shape didn't seem to change at all when I evolved.

But with this evolution, my species has changed.

If I could get a good look, I'd be willing to bet that there are lots of differences.

At times like these, I really wish I had a mirror. I can't even find out what I look like.

As far as I can tell from moving around, though, nothing feels particularly off.

The overall makeup of my basic parts doesn't seem to have changed much, so I should be able to move as usual without a problem.

I never really felt any bodily changes before evolving anyway.

So it's a relief that I don't seem to have changed much this time.

I guess these scythes are a pretty big change, though.

They kinda look like they'd make a noise like *ka-shing!* or something when you swing them around.

Come to think of it, they definitely bring the grim reaper to mind, huh?

The description of this species did say something about an "ill omen" or whatever, and now I have Rot Attack and stuff, so that makes sense.

I definitely still have a ninja-style thing going on, but in extreme cases, I could probably pull off the grim reaper image, too.

I'd better check in on the skills that leveled up, as well.

I'm always glad to see Herculean Strength and Sturdy improve.

That'll add a bonus to related stat growth from now on, too.

My stats have definitely gotten a lot stronger, but they're still pretty low compared with an opponent like the eel.

Let's see… Poison Synthesis, Poison Magic, and Shadow Magic all leveled up, too.

I still can't use the magic skills, but I do want to check if I gained anything for Poison Synthesis.

<Attribute Conferment "Paralysis": Adds Paralysis attribute>

What? Wh-wh-wh-what's this, now?!

I think I might've just gotten something really wild!

Poison Synthesis, the skill that's worked so wonderfully for me here in the Middle Stratum, just took another huge step forward!

Oh man. I've gotta try this out right away.

So, I want to experiment with adding the Paralysis attribute to my Deadly Spider Poison.

I'll see what kind of effect it has as soon as I get a chance to test it out.

Ah, but Deadly Spider Poison will probably kill most enemies instantly…

Okay, let's add the attribute to Weak Poison, too.

Next time I find an enemy, I'll have to start by using this Paralysis-infused Weak Poison on them.

Aah, I can't wait!

As for magic… Well, who cares? Not like I can use it anyway.

Huh? No, wait a minute. Can I really still not use magic?

My Parallel Thinking and Arithmetic Processing skills both rose quite a bit.

Doesn't that mean I might be able to use Detection right about now?

It's been a while since my last attempt, so I guess I'll give it a try.

Huff… Whew. All right!

Detection on!

Gah! Hnnnngh! Oof!

<Proficiency has reached the required level.

Skill [Arithmetic Processing LV 7] has become [Arithmetic Processing LV 8].>

<Proficiency has reached the required level.

Skill [Parallel Thinking LV 5] has become [Parallel Thinking LV 6].>

<Proficiency has reached the required level.

Skill [Detection LV 6] has become [Detection LV 7].>

<Proficiency has reached the required level.

Skill [Heresy Resistance LV 3] has become [Heresy Resistance LV 4].>

Off!

Whew. That was rough.

But I was definitely able to endure it longer than before.

It takes all my concentration just to deal with it, but that's still a big step forward.

So it looks like my approach wasn't wrong.

It may be a while yet until I can really master it, but I think I can see the light at the end of the tunnel, maybe?

I've been wandering around in the Middle Stratum.

I'm pretty full after eating the eel, so it looks like I don't need to worry about passing out from hunger or anything.

Since I don't need to actively hunt for more prey right now, I can proceed at my leisure.

I'm feeling pretty good right at the moment. I can even deal with this stupid heat.

Ugh. The climate still sucks, though.

There aren't any monsters around just now, so maybe I'll check in on my skill point situation.

I got quite a few points with this evolution, so maybe I'll discover a cool skill or two.

All the skills I've acquired so far have been killer except for Detection, so hopefully, I'll keep lucking out.

So far, aside from increasing the level of Taboo, Pride doesn't seem to have any drawbacks.

And even Taboo isn't doing any harm at the moment, so really, it's like there are no downsides at all, right?

Considering how crazy its effects are, the positives vastly outweigh any negatives.

Why I was able to get this skill for 100 points is a total mystery to me.

With these effects, I wouldn't be surprised if it was worth 1,000 points, easy.

It's probably too much to expect to find another awesome bargain like Pride, but if there are any skills that look good, I might as well take 'em.

There's no point in trying to save skill points too much, after all.

These things really burn a hole in your pocket.

Saving up even more and waiting for the bigger skills to be unlocked seems incredibly inefficient anyway.

All right, Appraisal, do your thing!

First, I double-Appraise my skill points.

Then I take a look at the list.

Hmm. There are still lots of skills I can get for 100 points.

I haven't taken any of them because they don't look particularly important, but maybe I should try to raise my proficiency for some of them when I have some free time?

But I guess if I have time for that, I should spend it improving more-useful skills.

Ah, but wait, there may be some skills like Prediction that suddenly turn into something more useful when they evolve...

Hmm. I dunno.

Oh, but first, I should really take a look at the skills that cost more than 200 points, since I couldn't see them last time.

Whoa, whoa, whoa. I found one. A broken skill like Pride.

<Perseverance (500): n% of the power to reach godhood. Expands the user's divinity field. As long as MP is maintained, the user will survive with 1 HP regardless of the amount of damage taken. In addition, the user will gain the ability to surpass the W system and interfere with the MA field.>

Another skill chock-full of mysterious terminology...

And then there's that ridiculous, almost laughable ability.

Does this work by constantly consuming MP, or what?

I don't know how much MP it uses, but does that mean you can keep attacking like a zombie as long as you have MP left?

I don't get it. Sounds pretty freaky.

Well, I'm not gonna hesitate this time. Boop.

<Number of skill points currently in possession: 500. Number of skill points required to acquire skill [Perseverance]: 500. Acquire skill?>

Yes, please.

<[Perseverance] acquired. Remaining skill points: 0.>

With Pride already under my belt, I no longer know the meaning of the word "retreat"!

I'll take every one of these skills I can get!

Come on, Taboo or whatever it might be, do your worst!

<Proficiency has reached the required level.
  Skill [Taboo LV 5] has become [Taboo LV 7].>

Okay, I'm sorry. I definitely didn't want you to do that much.

<Condition satisfied. Acquired title [Ruler of Perseverance].>
<Acquired skills [Heresy Nullification LV 1] [Conviction] as a result of title [Ruler of Perseverance].>
<Skill [Heresy Resistance LV 4] has been integrated into [Heresy Nullification].>

Man, so Taboo rose, just like I figured. Two times, even. Well, what're you gonna do?

Letting it level up this way doesn't seem like a good thing, but it's not like I have any means of countering it.

So don't insta-kill me or strike me with lightning or anything, okay?

Ugh, the worst part about not knowing is that it makes my imagination run wild, know what I mean?

More importantly, take a look at that title.

I've got no time to be standing around worrying! I gotta check out this title right away!

‹Ruler of Perseverance: Acquires skills [Heresy Nullification] [Conviction]. Acquisition conditions: Obtain [Perseverance] skill. Effect: Increases defense and resistance stats. Lifts ban on Evil Eye-type skills. +Correction to resistance skill proficiencies. Grants ruling-class privileges. Description: A title granted to one who has conquered perseverance.›

Uh-huh. I knew it. This is another one of those cheat titles.

My defense and resistance increased!

Both went up 100 points, so now my defense is 351 and my resistance is 380.

Man, really, what's going on here? Isn't this a little too much like cheating?

The fact that my resistance-type skills will improve more easily now is huge, too.

Since I specialize in evasion, I hardly ever get hit by attacks, which means my resistance skills don't really change much.

But now this'll compensate for that weak point. I'm pretty psyched.

How did I earn proficiency for the resistance skills I gained during my training, you ask?

My theory is that the proficiency of resistance skills for attributes that I possess get better every time I level, or something like that.

I mean, I gained Dark Tolerance without doing anything, so that pretty much proves it.

Yep. It makes sense, since I have Abyss Magic and all.

The other resistances I gained by using threads and stuff to injure myself.

I mean, if you knew you could gain a skill just by whipping yourself a little, anyone would do it. So that's what I did.

Huh? What do you mean, that's just me? C'mon, that's not true. It's totally normal.

I'm also intrigued by this "Evil Eye" stuff.

I waaant it.

I mean, with an Evil Eye–type skill or whatever, wouldn't you get to say lines like "My right eye…it burns!" or "You're already trapped in my illusion!" or whatever?

Man, I'd be like some kind of badass video game villain.

Ugh, I want it, but now I'm out of skill points!

Oh well. I'll just have to hurry and level up so I can save more skill points for it.

Last but not least, I got the skills Heresy Nullification and Conviction.

Heresy Nullification seems to be the highest form of Heresy Resistance.

Heresy Resistance increases your defense against attacks that directly influence the soul, so I guess Heresy Nullification must cancel them out entirely.

So now, even if I run into an enemy that uses Heretic Magic or something like it, I should be just fine.

‹Conviction: Against targets that have in-system sins in their souls, deals nonresistable damage in proportion to the total amount of guilt›

Wow. So it's an attack that does more damage against guilty parties? The "nonresistable" part is pretty scary.

Hmm? Wait a sec.

Is this maybe connected to Taboo?

Like, the higher the Taboo level, the more damage you take?

That's gotta be it!

Yikes, if anyone else has this Conviction skill, I'll be in it deep.

Hmm, but this wasn't on the list of skills obtainable with skill points, so…

If it's a special skill that can only be obtained with a ruler title, maybe there're only a few others besides me who have it.

This is all wishful thinking, but I hope it's true.

If so, then I've got a pretty valuable skill here.

But this reminds me of that Hades skill. I bet I can't even use it.

I give it a shot, but nothing happens.

It might've just misfired because I didn't have a target, but I get the feeling that I just can't use it at all.

Well, even if I can't use Conviction, this was still a net positive.

Sure, Taboo went up again, but I don't see any way around that at this point.

As long as I don't die instantly or run into any "game over"–type scenarios like that, I'll just have to accept whatever the penalty is.

Man, though. My stats improved a ton, and so did my skills.

Am I totally strong now or what?

file.09

ZOA ELE

LV.01

status

HP

200 / 200

MP

200 / 200

SP

200 / 200

200 / 200

Average Offensive
Ability : 100

Average Defensive
Ability : 100

Average Magic
Ability : 100

Average Resistance
Ability : 100

Average Speed
Ability : 100

skill

[Spider Thread LV 1]   [Poison Fang LV 1]   [Rot Attack LV 1]
[Cutting Enhancement LV 1] [Stealth LV 1]   [Silence LV 1]
[Shadow Magic LV 1]   [Poison Resistance LV 1]

A small spider-type monster that is feared as an ill omen. Because few witnesses have ever seen it, it's said that anyone who merely encounters one will die within the next few days. Legend says that it will often suddenly appear behind its victims and use Rot Attack to decapitate them with its scythes. Its danger level varies depending on its stats, but its basic abilities as listed above would be ranked C.

S4 SCHOOL LIFE

My school life is going well.

I already know most of the stuff they're teaching in our classes, but I play close attention anyway as a way of reviewing it.

When it gets too boring to bear, I can always pass the time by discreetly working on raising my skill levels.

If you were to look just at my classes, it'd seem like everything's going great, but I'm having quite a few problems with my interpersonal relationships.

This has a lot to do with my social status and that incident during the magic lesson from the other day.

Since I am technically royalty and all, even though that shouldn't have any impact on my standing at the school I attend as a student, it's still a bit of a problem.

No matter how hard I encourage them to relax, people from this kingdom can't seem to help acting reserved around me.

Even nobles from other countries have a hard time speaking to me casually.

Seems like only royalty or a close equivalent, like a duke's heir, can approach me on even footing.

Among those, there were a few who were just trying to curry favor with me, but Katia took care of them in no time.

Honestly, since I tend to be a bit of a pushover in situations like that, I'm grateful to have someone like Katia around.

That said, between that and the magic lesson incident, I've been feeling a bit lonely.

Hugo, on the other hand, has picked up quite a few followers since that lesson.

Already, nearly half the boys in our year are supporters of his. He's becoming their self-appointed leader, just like in his previous life.

And just like in *my* previous life, I'm doing my best to avoid getting involved with that group.

It's obvious that Hugo regards me as an enemy ever since the magic incident.

I don't see any reason to try and get close to someone who already hates me. Why make more trouble for myself?

So right now, I mostly spend my time with Katia, Sue, Fei, and now Yuri.

Katia and Sue understand me, and while Fei can be a little much, we've spent a lot of time together.

As for Yuri, well, I don't know.

Sure, we're fellow reincarnations and all, but sometimes I have a hard time dealing with her, albeit in a different way from Natsume.

Hasebe's new name is Yurin Ullen.

Apparently, her surname is the name of the church that took her in instead of an orphanage.

Hasebe, or Yuri, was left to fend for herself as a child.

As it turns out, that's commonplace in this world.

Of course, orphans existed in our old world, but here, where civilization hasn't developed as much and monsters run rampant, it happens all the more frequently.

Lots of children end up being abandoned as babies and raised in a church.

However, Yuri's circumstances are different from those of other orphans.

She's had her memories of her previous life since shortly after birth, so she was fully aware of what was happening around her.

Imagine suddenly waking as a baby.

It happened to me, too. It was pretty shocking.

It's completely confusing and, most of all, frightening.

Did I die? What's going to happen to me now?

And what happened to my previous life?

That alone was enough anxiety to last a lifetime.

But on top of that, Yuri was abandoned in that state. The shock I experienced can't possibly come close.

To be honest, I can't even begin to imagine how Yuri felt at the time.

In the midst of all that distress, Yuri had only one thing to rely on.

That was the Word of God.

The Followers of the Word of God are the religious group that took Yuri in, and it is one of the most widespread religions among humans.

To give a rough explanation, their basic creed is "improve our skills so that we might hear the Word of God."

The Word of God. I still don't really know what it means.

It's sort of like system messages in a video game, but in this world, everyone is accustomed to hearing it.

We reincarnations are probably the only people who find it strange.

It's natural to hear this voice. Having skills is normal, too. Here, that's just commonplace.

The Followers of the Word of God preach that the voice is truly God's and that raising one's skills and level so that the voice speaks to you more often brings one closer to God.

From my point of view, it sounds like a load of nonsense, but for whatever reason, it's common wisdom in this world.

And Yuri, despite being a reincarnation just like me, is totally hooked.

"Shun, your skills are quite high, are they not? I think that's just wonderful. Let us continue to raise our skills that we might hear the Word of God in plenty."

"Shun, you aren't raising your level? That just won't do! When you raise your level, the Word of God speaks to you at great length, you know. We must keep leveling up to listen to God's voice."

"Shun, you can use Appraisal, can you not? Well then, if you should ever see someone with a skill called Taboo, please tell me at once. It's simply unthinkable to have a skill that God has dubbed Taboo. You must not let it pass, no matter what, for the Taboo skill means that the holder has committed some act that even God dares not to name. There is no reason to let such an individual live. It is our holy duty to slay them. So be sure to tell me, okay? Promise me."

"Shun, today one of my skills leveled up, and I heard God's voice! Ah, the divine voice of God has spoken to me. Today is sure to be a blessed day."

I can't do it. I just can't.

I mean, I'm sure Yuri can't help the fact that her eyes glaze over when she talks about this "God."

But I don't think she was like this before.

She was just an ordinary high school girl.

It must have been her unique circumstances that changed her so much.

The terror of being reincarnated. The despair of being abandoned by her parents.

The anxiety of being forced to live in a new world.

Given all that, it's not surprising that the Word of God, speaking in our dearly missed language of Japanese, would bring her comfort.

Not to mention that she was surrounded by people who worship that voice.

It might've even been inevitable that she would latch on to the teachings of the Followers of the Word of God.

Though, I'm not sure I understand getting obsessed to the point of becoming a candidate for sainthood.

Also, I wish she'd stop harassing others about converting.

I mean, her way of saying hello is asking, "Have you opened your heart to the Word of God?"

Sorry, but I'm not really the religious type.

No matter how often I politely turn her down, though, Yuri shows no signs of surrender.

If anything, she just comes at me even more aggressively.

This has been going on for so long that I've gotten used to the sight of Sue swooping in furiously to fend her off, then Katia arriving to mediate.

Speaking of Sue, she's been acting pretty strange herself.

It seems like she wants to ask me something but doesn't know how to bring it up.

That being said, I do have an inkling of what her question might be.

Or rather, I'm pretty sure I know, because Katia told me all about it.

"Sue tried to ask me about our relationship."

"Huh? What do you mean?"

"You know...our past lives. She probably guessed something was strange when she saw us talking with Ms. Oka."

"Ahh... I guess we were speaking Japanese in front of her, huh?"

"Yeah, exactly. I mean, if you had an older brother who you've been together with basically since birth and one day he suddenly started speaking to total strangers in some unfamiliar language, of course you'd be weirded out."

"Right... Crap."

"Well, if she asks you, it's up to you whether to tell her the truth or think of a convincing lie."

"Huh? I can't tell her the truth, can I?"

"I'm saying that's up to you. Do you want to keep lying to your little sister or be forthcoming? Whatever you decide, you'd better be ready to fully commit to your response. It's the least you can do for her, don't you think?"

"Urk… All right, I got it."

So I guess Sue wants to ask me about my relationship with the others.

To be honest, I'm not ready at all.

Tell Sue the truth?

We may only be half siblings, but we're still siblings.

But my previous life had nothing to do with Sue. The old me is a total stranger to her.

I've always seen Sue as my real sister, but once she knows the truth, will she still see me as her older brother?

On top of that, I've had the advantage of my memories and experiences from my previous life while maturing in this one.

For Sue, who's come all this way without any such advantage, it might seem like cheating.

Will she look down on me when she finds out about that?

I don't think she's that kind of person, but…just imagining it makes me afraid to tell her.

Which leaves the option of making up some excuse, but the idea of deceiving her like that hurts, too.

Considering how much my younger sister is struggling to ask me about it, it wouldn't be right to just lie to her when she finally works up the courage to approach me.

If I'm going to lie to her now, I have to be prepared to keep lying for the rest of my life.

I still haven't decided what I'm going to do.

But I know that if and when she does ask me, I have to consider my answer very seriously.

If it weren't for what Katia said to me, I might've just played it off without thinking too deeply about it.

I have to thank her for giving me advice beforehand.

So basically, I have all kinds of problems to worry about right now.

Hugo despises me, Yuri is trying to indoctrinate me, and I have to figure out what I'm going to tell Sue.

On top of all that, Ms. Oka is still as mysterious as ever.

At times, she'll be absent for so long that we assume she went off somewhere, and that's exactly when she casually attends class.

When I try to ask her about it, she usually just dodges my questions.

I feel this is especially the case when I ask her about Kyouya's whereabouts.

Kyouya is a friend with whom Katia and I were particularly close in our past lives.

But Ms. Oka won't tell me a thing about him.

It definitely seems like she knows something, but he doesn't seem to be in her care.

I want to know where he is and what he's doing, but it doesn't look like she's going to tell me anytime soon.

Everyone's changed so much in this world.

Yuri's become a religious fanatic.

Hugo's already strong ego has gotten even more intense, and his desire for the spotlight seems to be running unchecked.

Ms. Oka has lost her grip on things.

Maybe this was inevitable.

It's a very different environment from Japan, and we've been here for a long time now.

In fact, it might be harder to stay the same. But I'm afraid to change.

I mean, look at what happened to Yuri and Hugo. It's almost like they've gone mad.

"Katia, promise me you won't change."

Preoccupied with these thoughts, I accidentally made a weird comment to Katia.

But when I imagine even Katia changing from the Kanata I know, it scares me.

Honestly, I think having Katia here to keep me connected to my previous life has played a huge role in my ability to remain stable.

So it's only natural that I don't want Katia to change, either.

Interlude THE DUKE'S DAUGHTER AND THE FUTURE SAINT

"Ooshima, why are you changing clothes with the girls?"

"Huh? ...Oh, right. Sorry. It's been so long, I don't even think about it anymore. But if it bothers you, Hasebe, I can wait until after everyone else is done or change somewhere else?"

"Oh, um, well..."

"C'mon, what's up?"

"Oh, well... I guess I didn't expect you to respond so calmly. Wouldn't you normally panic and apologize in this kind of situation?"

"I dunno... I don't really feel anything about girls' bodies since being reincarnated. It's hard to believe I was so crazy about them when I was a guy, honestly. But I don't feel a thing when I see girls now, so I don't really feel guilty or anything."

"Really? You don't find it embarrassing at all?"

"I mean, since I was reborn into a duke's family, I've had maids helping me change clothes and bathe since I was a baby, y'know? I got over being embarrassed pretty quickly."

"I...see... That sounds hard, in its own way."

"I guess. I certainly feel a lot better living in a dorm where I don't have to deal with that. If anything, I find it hard to believe the other girls complain so much about not having their maids."

"Oh yes. I agree."

"Right, 'cause you grew up in an orphanage, huh...? Between that and having memories from Japan, doesn't that make it hard to hit it off with all the nobles here?"

"Well, yes, to be honest."

"Yeah, I figured. Even I have trouble dealing with it at times."

"Ha-ha. Sounds like we've both had it tough, albeit in different ways."

"Uh-huh. But I don't think my struggles are a big deal compared with what you've been through."

"No?"

"'Course not. I mean, it was hard, but it's not like my life was in danger."

"I suppose that's true. But nonetheless, I'm happy with how my life has gone."

"Oh yeah?"

"Very much so. That's how I learned the importance of God's voice!"

"O-oh yeah."

"Don't you agree? God sees everything, you know. The Word of God is omnipotent and all knowing. The fact that the voice has chosen to speak to us in Japanese is proof of that. As long as you follow God's voice, all will be well!"

"R…riiight. I guess so."

"Of course it is! That's why you should join the Followers of the Word of God, Ooshima!"

"Ah… Uh… Sorry. I can't choose my religion because of my family circumstances."

"Is that so? What a shame. But if you change your mind, please do let me know."

"Yeah, sure. Oh, right, what did you want me to do? Should I change clothes somewhere else?"

"Ah, well, let's see. I think perhaps talking with you has made me feel a bit better about it. I'm sure I'll get used to it in time."

"You sure?"

"Of course. In fact, when I think about it, seeing you here doesn't make me uncomfortable in the least."

"What d'you mean?"

"Well, you don't seem like a man. You're perfectly feminine in just about every way."

"I dunno if I should be happy about that or not..."

"I'd say it's a good thing, no? After all, you'll have to keep living as a woman from here on out."

"It's complicated."

"Well, it's my mission in life to guide others. So if you have any issues with womanly matters, feel free to come to me about it!"

"...Thanks. I'll keep that in mind."

"So Shun doesn't want me to change... That's asking way too much. How am I supposed to stay the same in this situation? ...And Yuri thinks I'm feminine... I wonder if Shun doesn't see me as a woman, then. Huh? Wait, what am I saying? That doesn't mean anything... Right?"

7   The Administrator's Shadow

Oh, since Heresy Resistance turned into Heresy Nullification, maybe using Detection won't hurt my head anymore?

It is a Heresy Attribute attack, isn't it? Is it cool if I call it an attack?

I mean, there's no way that pain so strong it busts right through my Pain Mitigation could be a normal headache, right?

So if I can cancel out the Heresy attack that normally accompanies Detection, maybe it won't hurt my head anymore?

It's worth a try.

Huff... Whew. Here goes!

Detection on!

...Whoa. This...this is seriously incredible.

I could never tell before, since I was too busy dealing with the pain, but...is this what Detection is like when it doesn't cause a headache?

This time, my head didn't split wide open when I activated it.

Well, technically, I guess there's a little throbbing, but thanks to Pain Mitigation, it's hardly even worth mentioning.

I think what I'm feeling now is just a normal headache from using my brain too much.

That's how much information Detection provides all at once.

<Proficiency has reached the required level.

Skill [Arithmetic Processing LV 8] has become [Arithmetic Processing LV 9].>

<Proficiency has reached the required level.

 Skill [Parallel Thinking LV 6] has become [Parallel Thinking LV 7].>

<Proficiency has reached the required level.

 Skill [Detection LV 7] has become [Detection LV 8].>

<Proficiency has reached the required level. Acquired skill [Divinity Expansion LV 1].>

Looks like I got some new skill. I'll check it out later, though.

Right now, I want to relish this feeling for a bit.

I'm psyched that I finally succeeded at using Detection.

But even more than that, I'm overwhelmed by the amount of information Detection provides.

It's like it gathers all the data available on everything within my present range of perception.

The flow of magic, the material makeup of things, the flow of air... All of this streams through my brain.

It almost feels like I'm omniscient.

I understand everything around me.

Even information I wouldn't normally be able to understand makes sense to a certain extent when I use this skill.

But even that in itself feels like a sea of information. Like I've stolen a glimpse at some cosmic truth.

And this is all just from the tiny space I'm currently aware of.

It feels like I've learned anew the vast scope and grandeur of the world around me.

Oh man, I even feel like I'm gonna cry for some reason. Although, I don't know if spiders can actually cry.

Okay. Let's turn Detection off for a minute.

Whew. That was crazy. I don't even know where this feeling is coming from.

If I had to compare it to something, I'd say it was kinda like getting emotional from looking up at a starry sky. That sorta thing.

Ah, I wanted to stay immersed in those feelings for a little longer. I'd better get a move on, though.

So. Detection is a success.

Does that mean I should keep it active all the time from here on in?

Hmm. The thing is, I'm worried that it's so high-performance that it might actually be inconvenient.

I mean, it's so much input at once that it might distract me and make it harder focusing in battles or something.

But maybe I can just get used to it?

Sure, it's overwhelming when I activate it right now, but I used to feel a little drunk from using Appraisal at first, too. If I got acclimated to that, I'm sure I could adapt to this easily enough.

So I think I'll keep Detection active all the time, even if it might be a bit dangerous at first.

It'll raise my other skill levels, too, so I think it's for the best.

All right, then. Detection on.

Whoa. This really is crazy.

But I can't get emotional again.

Guess I'll start by checking out the skill I just acquired.

<Proficiency has reached the required level.
  Skill [Parallel Thinking LV 7] has become [Parallel Thinking LV 8].>
<Proficiency has reached the required level.
  Skill [Divinity Expansion LV 1] has become [Divinity Expansion LV 2].>

...Or maybe it'll level up first...

What is this skill, exactly?

The description of Perseverance said something about a divinity field.

I think Perseverance expands that, too, doesn't it? So this is on top of that?

Does that mean my divinity field or whatever is spreading out all over the place now?

At any rate, I'd better Appraise it.

<Divinity Expansion: Expands divinity field>

You don't say? Thanks a lot.

This is where you really get to strut your stuff, Appraisal! Double-Appraisal, puh-leeeze!

<Divinity Field: The depths of a living thing's soul. It is the foundation of every life, as well as the self's final field of dependence.>

Hmm? I still don't get it.

Well, I get that it's an important part of the soul or whatever, but what happens when you expand that?

Hmm. So I still don't know what it does.

More is usually better, but it doesn't have any actual effects so far as I can tell...

<Proficiency has reached the required level.

Skill [Arithmetic Processing LV 9] has become [Arithmetic Processing LV 10].>
<Condition satisfied.

Skill [Arithmetic Processing LV 10] has evolved into skill [High-Speed Processing LV 1].>
<Proficiency has reached the required level.

Skill [Detection LV 8] has become [Detection LV 9].>

Whoa, they really go up so fast!

I already maxed out Arithmetic Processing, huh?

And now it's evolved into High-Speed Processing. Definitely sounds like an upgrade to me.

Anyway, I originally got Detection in the hopes of perceiving enemies, didn't I?

But my natural ability to identify threats is high enough that I've managed pretty well without Detection so far.

I gotta say, combining that innate ability with the power of Detection will make my enemy-spotting skills pretty much perfect.

No one's ever going to get the jump on me now! I'd like to see them try!

Okay, so next, I'd hoped Detection would give me Magic Power Perception.

If my predictions are correct, then if I combine this with the Magic Power Operation skill, I should be able to finally use magic. I think.

That means I'll finally be able to bust out the skills I've been sitting on for so long, like Abyss Magic and Heretic Magic!

But...I don't have any skill points! Dammit!

I don't regret picking up Perseverance, but it still sucks that I'm out of skill points.

Aw, man, and I was hoping to use my next batch for Evil Eye!

What am I gonna do? I want them both! Aaargh!

I know this is kind of a dumb problem, but even so, which should I get first?!

<Proficiency has reached the required level.

Skill [Detection LV 9] has become [Detection LV 10].>

<Proficiency has reached the required level.

Skill [Parallel Thinking LV 8] has become [Parallel Thinking LV 9].>

Huh? For real? Detection's maxed out already?

Huh? But it doesn't evolve or add new skills or anything?

Aw, come on. What's up with that?

After all the trouble I went through to get it to work...

I mean, it definitely paid off, but to be honest, I kinda wanted even more.

Even if I can't get strong enough to defeat an earth dragon, I wanna at least be able to run away safely!

I really don't get anything?

<Fzzt......fzzzt...>

Hmm? What was that?

...Maybe I'm just imagining things?

Well anyway, no use whining about it.

The simplest solution is to keep getting stronger.

If I just keep working on that, I might at least reach the point where I can escape from exceptionally strong enemies. So I've decided: I'll make a sincere effort to get stronger.

Step one is leveling up.

I'll start actively hunting monsters from now on.

Step two is skills.

I seem to be able to level up skills just by moving around.

Like Appraisal, Detection, Foresight, and Thought Acceleration.

I did max out Detection, but using it trains other skills, too.

So I'll keep it active until all those skills are maxed out.

At the same time, I should start working on other skills that I can level up as I move.

The safest bet is probably the five sense-enhancement skills.

If I squint my eyes or sniff around a bit or whatever as I walk, they'll probably go up in no time.

I have a few skills that seem close to the max, so I'll start with those.

And there's one other thing.

I don't want to do this while I walk. I want to stop somewhere and devote my full attention to it.

That would be practicing Magic Power Operation.

Thinking about it, it's definitely possible for me to get skills without paying skill points if I just build enough proficiency.

In which case, I should save my skill points for Evil Eye, since I have no idea how I'd go about increasing proficiency for that, and try to practice Magic Power Operation on my own.

Thanks to Mr. Detection, I can perceive magic now.

If I concentrate on it enough, I can grasp the flow of magic power.

As long as I can figure out a way to manipulate that somehow (or at least try to for long enough), I should be able to acquire the skill by naturally accumulating proficiency. I hope.

Once I accomplish that, I can finally start practicing magic.

All that being said, I have to remember that my main goal is still to get through the Middle Stratum and return to the Upper Stratum.

Leveling up and improving skills and stuff are just things I'm doing along the way.

So I shouldn't actually stop moving just to work on that stuff.

Whatever I do, it has to be something I can do on the go.

I'm not putting down roots in the Middle Stratum. I'm just passing through.

I can't forget that.

<Proficiency has reached the required level.
  Skill [Thought Acceleration LV 3] has become [Thought Acceleration LV 4].>
<Proficiency has reached the required level.
  Skill [Foresight LV 3] has become [Foresight LV 4].>

Nice, nice. Thanks to my Ruler of Pride title, my mental skills are leveling up really quickly.

Just gotta keep it up.

Since I have the Ruler of Perseverance title, too, my resistance skills should also improve relatively easily, but most of them aren't the kind of thing I can level up on the move.

Technically, I'm sure I could gain proficiency in a lot of them with self-inflicted attacks: Deadly Poison Resistance and Paralysis Resistance with Poison Synthesis, and Cutting Resistance, Impact Resistance, Destruction Resistance, Rot Resistance, and Shock Resistance (which I'm sure also exists) using Utility Thread. But I should probably save that until I've settled down somewhere for a while.

The Middle Stratum, where my recovery is slow and there's no decent place to rest, is no place for that sort of thing.

I'd like to raise my stat-enhancement skills as quickly as possible, but that's something else better done when I can stop someplace.

They'll probably level up in battle, but other than that, I'd have to do muscle training and the like if I want to level them up on my own.

If I have the time and strength to do that, I'd be better off using it to keep moving.

For the time being, better to focus on those five sense skills that I can raise passively.

Vision Enhancement is at level 9, almost the max, so I'll start with that.

It's been a while since I evolved and started making my way through the Middle Stratum.

I've been wiping out every monster I lay eyes on, so my level's skyrocketed.

No one would believe how quickly my stats grow now.

The description really wasn't kidding when it said I have "high battle capabilities."

On average, they rise about twenty points apiece each time.

Even if you take into account the growth rate enhancement from Pride and the individual stat-raising skills, the rate at which my stats are increasing is still wild.

If I keep improving like this, my low stats will be a total thing of the past.

Besides my level and stats, my skills have also been progressing quite a bit.

That said, I've been trying to focus my eyes on various things, but my Vision Enhancement skill still hasn't budged.

I guess raising a level-9 skill is bound to take some time.

I've been killing it on my other skills, though!

First of all, Silence is level 3 now. Ninja power up!

Thought Acceleration and Foresight both reached level 5, so my evasiveness gets a power up, too!

Even Fire Resistance finally made progress, putting it at level 3.

In theory, Perseverance should be making it easier to gain proficiency for resistance skills, but it still feels like it's taken ages.

Just how weak am I to fire anyway? Actually, is that still the case, since I'm a different species now?

I wonder if my other resistances besides fire have changed...

But I have no way of finding out, so there's no point speculating.

Anyway, since I'm not exactly a defensive tank to begin with, my resistances changing a little probably wouldn't make much of a difference.

Still, since my defense is starting to improve, it might be good to know my resistances well.

After all, it's possible I have other weaknesses besides fire. Not that I have any way of finding that out...

Last but certainly not least is Parallel Thinking.

This one reached level 10 and evolved.

Its new form is called Parallel Minds!

Now this is a super-convenient skill.

As the name implies, it's basically like I have multiple minds now.

With Parallel Thought, it was like I was using one brain to think about several different things at the same time, but with Parallel Minds, it's like my brain actually split into segments. Almost like split personalities.

Both of them are me, but each is a separate body of consciousness with its own set of thoughts.

And that's on top of what Parallel Thinking already allowed me to do.

It's functionally doubled my cognitive ability. Super-convenient.

This skill is like a partial realization of the wish kids often make, the same one adults do when they're really pressed for time: "I wish there was another me..."

You know, so one "me" can work and study and stuff while the other plays.

Though since they're both equally me, whenever one wants to slack off and play, the other's gonna get mad.

Still, that means I can divide the work I was gonna do alone between two of me, so it's still way better.

As the skill level rises, it's possible I'll be able to make more, too.

However, only one of them can control my body at any given time.

That's why I've decided one half will be in charge of my body while the other half processes information from Appraisal and Detection and so on.

By delegating like this, I can reduce the amount of work each half has to do, so each can concentrate on its responsibilities that much more.

You know how, when you're fighting, your vision gets a whole lot narrower? People who've done martial arts know what I mean, right?

Personally, I think that's a consequence of extreme tension and concentration.

However, now that I have a separate mind for processing information, I no longer have to deal with it.

That way, I can focus on picking up information and leave the hard work to the body brain.

I'm counting on ya, body brain!

【You got it, information brain!】

See? Now I can even have conversations with myself.

And since they're both me, we've got data sharing on lock.

There's no main unit or subunit in this setup. Both of them are me. I'm me, therefore I'm me!

Yeah, I know. It makes no sense.

Like, I'm getting by all right, but I bet some people would start questioning their definition of the self if they did something like this.

You know, like losing track of which is the real them and going crazy or whatever.

I can totally see that happening. If anything, maybe that makes me super-special for being able to handle it normally? Okay, probably not.

Wow. While my information brain was thinking about all that stuff, my body brain beat a monster.

Good job, me.

【No biggie, me!】

This time, I tried out my new Rot Attack, but I can't really use it.

I mean, it wasn't useless. The attack power itself was amazing.

Like, way too strong for level 1.

It was excessive. I mean, it turned the monster to dust in a single hit! Isn't that freaky?

Is that really what "rot" means? It's not, like, corrosion or whatever?

This goes past food going bad, straight into disintegration territory. No way do I want to mess with an attribute that "regulates the decay of death."

It's already overkill at level 1.

What in the world happens when it levels up more?

Anyway, there are two reasons why I can't use it.

First, it doesn't leave behind any remains. In other words, no food.

Sure, I can still gain experience like this, but it totally renders half my motivation for hunting monsters moot.

It doesn't feed the beast. Literally and figuratively.

The other problem is even worse.

I take damage from it, too.

Take a look at the scythe-leg I used for the Rot Attack. The blade is falling to pieces! And I've lost HP...

This attack is like a suicide bomb!

So while its power is really high, so's the backlash.

If I ever get into a situation where I'd be in big trouble if I don't go all out, maybe I'll use it, but beyond that, it doesn't make much sense to waste it on small-fry.

Especially while I'm in the Middle Stratum, where my automatic recovery is slower.

Ugh, I wonder when this scythe will heal?

I'll probably level up soon, so I'm sure it'll fix itself then, but in the meantime, I won't be able to use this leg in my next battle.

I do still have Poison Synthesis, at least, so it's no big deal as long as I don't run into some big game like the eel.

I only started using my scythe-arms recently anyway. My main weapon in the Middle Stratum remains Poison Synthesis.

After all, just making contact with Middle Stratum monsters injures me.

If I use my scythes, I can raise skills like Cutting Enhancement, but that still means taking damage.

Besides, when I cut monsters with the scythes, their insides fall out, making them harder to eat.

So, body brain, make sure you use Poison Synthesis for the next prey, all right?

【Yep, roger that, information brain.】

Man, Parallel Minds sure is convenient.

If I had two bodies to go with it, I could even have a shadow clone! Now that's the dream.

Oh, but since they'd both be my main body, it'd hurt if either got destroyed. Aw, man, that sucks.

As long as one was left, I'd still survive, but wouldn't that mean I'd basically experience death?

Hmm. That's not something I really want to try.

Actually, I guess I technically have experienced it once already, but as I have no memory of it, that doesn't count.

So don't do anything that's gonna get us killed, okay, body brain?

【Come on, information brain. You know I wouldn't do that!】

You're right, you're right.

<Proficiency has reached the required level.

   Skill [Vision Enhancement LV 9] has become [Vision Enhancement LV 10].>

<Condition satisfied.

   Skill [Telescopic Sight LV 1] has been derived from skill [Vision Enhancement LV 10].>

All right! I finally maxed out the Vision Enhancement skill.

So the reward was a new skill, huh?

May as well Appraise it right away to see what it does.

<Telescopic Sight: Allows user to magnify view of distant sights>

Okay, so pretty much what the name says, then?

Hmm. Not sure if I get it.

The five sense-enhancement skills are pretty basic improvements, but the derived skills seem pretty plain, too.

Well, I guess I'll try it out.

Okay, body brain, activate Telescopic Sight!

【Request received. Telescopic Sight activated!】

Oh? Ooh? Ooooh?!

Whoa, this is amazing. I'm sorry for calling it plain before.

My field of vision now displays a magnified telescopic image as well as my original range of vision at the same time.

I was expecting my entire field of vision to be enlarged, like looking through a telescope, but it seems like I can activate it in just one eye.

Normally, it'd be pretty confusing to get two completely different views at once, but who do you think you're talking to? I'm basically a two-in-one package deal already.

If I split the work between the two units, it's not confusing at all.

Since it's still only level 1, the range and extent of magnification is pretty low, but it could be pretty useful once it levels up some.

For example, I could use Detection to figure out where an enemy is hiding, then use Telescopic Sight to zoom in on that location while still keeping my other eyes on what's in front of me.

Yep, yep. And this seems to be another passive skill, 'cause it's not consuming MP or anything.

I'll keep it active all the time to level it up, then, since it may have a lot of potential in the future.

【Hey, information brain, sorry to interrupt while you're on a roll, but...】

What is it, body brain?

【Spotted some prey in the Telescopic Sight view.】

Would you look at that! The newbie's already earning its keep.

【Wanna take it down?】

Doesn't that go without saying?

【Aye, aye, sir!】

I sneak up on the enemy right away.

Since I can't use one of my sickles after the suicidal Rot Attack, I'll just drench it in Deadly Spider Poison using Poison Synthesis.

The monster's HP drains in an instant. As usual, my poison is terrifyingly strong.

<Experience has reached the required level. Individual Zoa Ele has increased from LV 2 to LV 3.>
<All basic attributes have increased.>
<Skill proficiency level-up bonus acquired.>
<Proficiency has reached the required level.
    Skill [Vision Expansion LV 2] has become [Vision Expansion LV 3].>

<Proficiency has reached the required level.
  Skill [Life LV 9] has become [Life LV 10].>
<Condition satisfied.
  Skill [Life LV 10] has evolved into skill [Longevity LV 1].>
<Skill points acquired.>

Oh, perfect, I leveled up.

Which means I get to molt, so now my scythe is back to normal!

Plus, one of my stat-increasing skills finally evolved.

Do your thing, Appraisal.

<Longevity: Raises HP by 10x the number of the skill level. Also, growth of this stat at each level-up increases by the number of the skill level.>

Just as I figured, it's in the same category as Herculean Strength.

So if the rest of my stat skills evolve, their growth rates increase, too?

That really makes me want to level them up right away, but it'll just have to wait until I get through the Middle Stratum.

I definitely want to get somewhere secure as soon as possible.

And hey, wait a minute!

Leveling up means I have 100 skill points now! Yay!

Since I evolved, the number of skill points I gain per level increased to 50.

It was only 20 before, so that's a big upgrade.

That means that after evolving just twice, I already have 100 points.

Now then, I wonder if those Evil Eye skills I've heard so much about have been added to the list?

<Cursed Evil Eye [100]: Deals curse attribute damage to anything in the user's field of vision>

<Annihilating Evil Eye [100]: Deals rot attribute damage to anything in the user's field of vision>

<Paralyzing Evil Eye [100]: Deals paralysis attribute damage to anything in the user's field of vision>

<Petrifying Evil Eye [100]: Deals petrification attribute damage to anything in the user's field of vision>

<Discomfiting Evil Eye [100]: Inflicts the heresy attribute effect "Discomfort" on anything in the user's field of vision>

<Phantom Pain Evil Eye [100]: Inflicts the heresy attribute effect "Phantom Pain" on anything in the user's field of vision>

<Maddening Evil Eye [100]: Inflicts the heresy attribute effect "Madness" on anything in the user's field of vision>

<Charming Evil Eye [100]: Inflicts the heresy attribute effect "Charmed" on anything in the user's field of vision>

<Hypnotizing Evil Eye [100]: Inflicts the heresy attribute effect "Hypnotized" on anything in the user's field of vision>

<Fearful Evil Eye [100]: Inflicts the heresy attribute effect "Fear" on anything in the user's field of vision>

Whoa. I really can get them now.

These skills definitely weren't on the list before.

There are a bunch of different kinds, too. How am I supposed to choose just one? This is gonna be tough.

【Hey, information brain.】

What is it, body brain?

【Wouldn't it be better to get more than one?】

Huh? What do you mean?

【I mean, you know I have eight eyes, right?】

What about it?

【Well, doesn't that mean we can use Evil Eye in up to eight eyes at once?】

?! What are you, some kinda genius?!

【Heh-heh-heh. Yep, I'm a genius all right.】

Oh man. So I am a genius! That means I can get away with just about anything!

【That's right. Wouldn't it be amazing to use eight different Evil Eyes at the same time?】

Yooo. This is crazy. It's like a whole new world of possibilities.

【Although, one eye is using Telescopic Sight, so that only leaves seven.】

We should probably make sure we still have normal vision, too, so wouldn't it be six?

【I guess so. So we'll pick one for now, then get five more as we get more skill points?】

Sounds good. Then, body brain, which Evil Eye should we get first?

【I'd say we should go for one of the attributes we don't have, so either Curse or Petrification. The Heretic kinds seem more like they're meant for use on people than for fighting monsters.】

That's a good point. I think I'd go with Curse, then. Petrification seems to take a while, judging by our experiences with that stupid lizard in the Upper Stratum.

【It's that much more powerful for the time it takes, though. But you're probably right. Curse would be safer.】

Good ol' me. I really know what I'm talking about.

I'll take the Cursed Evil Eye, then.

<Curse: Weakens all stat values and causes damage to HP, MP, and SP>

Cursed Evil Eye level 1, get! Sweet.

Obviously, I have to find a monster to test it out on tout suite!

Maybe the info from Mr. Detection can help me here.

Hmm. Hmm, hmm, hmm. Looks like there's something over there.

It's still too far away to get detailed intel, but whatever it is, it seems to be on land.

Perfect. I've found my lab rat.

Oh, it's an evolved frog.

Boy, that brings back memories. This guy looks like the upgraded form of those frogs I used to eat.

Doesn't seem like it's that much stronger than they were, but I think it probably evolved to adapt to the Middle Stratum. It even has Heat Nullification.

Between that and the fact that it has Night Vision despite the constant glow from the magma, I have to assume it came from the Upper Stratum.

It's pitch-dark in the Upper and Lower Stratum, after all.

Maybe it got lost and couldn't find its way back, so it evolved out of necessity.

I hope there aren't any Lower Stratum monsters that wandered in here like that.

If one of those things evolved to adapt to the Middle Stratum environment… Yeaaaah, no.

Also, now that I can see the frog's skills, it looks like those "spit attacks" were actually Poison Synthesis, the same mine.

Apparently, it uses the Expel skill to shoot the poison through the air. Ooh… I'd like to get my hands on that myself.

Then I could fire globs of poison that would put the frog's wimpy attacks to shame.

I wonder if I can get proficiency for it by shooting threads out of my butt or something?

【Hey, information brain. Since you seemed busy with some stupid thoughts, I went ahead and synthesized paralysis poison and immobilized the frog.】

Ooh, good one, body brain.

Now we can try out the Cursed Evil Eye.

All right, Evil Eye activate!

Yep. It seems to be working just fine.

So how's this thing work? Oh… Ooh!

The frog's HP, MP, and SP are slowly decreasing.

Since it's still only level 1, it makes sense that it'd be slow, I suppose.

Both its yellow and red SP are going down, but the yellow bar recovers faster than the damage can reduce it, so no effect there.

Maybe once the skill levels up, the damage will outmatch the recovery?

Then I can keep my opponents in a constant state of hyperventilation? Ooh, creepy.

But I guess it'd run out of HP and die before then.

HP and SP are usually around the same amount, after all.

Oh, its stats are going down, too.

There's a little box next to the numerical values that says "decreasing."

It displays the normal max value of each stat in parentheses next to their current numbers, too.

Oh-ho-ho. So this is what it looks like when you hit something with a stat-lowering attack.

Sure makes it easy to tell the curse is working.

Good old Appraisal always has my back.

Anyway, it looks like Evil Eye isn't a passive skill, which I guess would've been too much to hope for. My MP is decreasing.

But it's not particularly fast. About 1 point every ten seconds.

And the frog seems to take 1 damage every five seconds or so, so I suppose it's fairly efficient?

With my current MP, I could keep it active for about fifty minutes, so that seems cost-effective to me.

Plus, once it advances, I'm sure it'll deal damage more quickly.

Oh, looks like the paralysis is wearing off.

…No, wait, body brain's already on it with another round of Poison Synthesis. Great job, me. Always quick on the draw.

Hmm. Its HP and stuff are still going down nicely, but the rate has slowed.

The stats were all decreasing at the same pace as its HP and so on until they hit the halfway point, but now they won't go much lower.

Is there a limit on how much stats can be reduced, then?

Well, guess that makes sense, now that I think about it.

If it kept going, you could end up with 0 defense or something.

Talk about paper-thin. Actually, that'd be so weak that paper would seem strong in comparison.

Still, just bringing its stats down by half is a pretty big deal in itself.

It's not that big of a difference on small-fry like this frog, but if I could cut the stats of strong monsters like that eel in half…

Monsters sometimes depend on stats even more than skills in battle, so weakening their stats means a significant drop in their combat abilities.

If the eel's stats were cut in half, for instance, it wouldn't be much stronger than a catfish.

This could be a real trump card against powerful monsters.

I'll have to make raising its level my top priority.

Hmm? Huh? The frog died?!

What the hell? I thought it still had some HP left…

The rest of its HP drained in a flash. But why?

Ahh, it ran out of red SP before it ran out of HP.

So that's why. Guess when you run out of red SP, your HP starts decreasing really quickly.

WHAAAT?!

Yikes. I've had some pretty close calls after evolving and stuff, then.

Good thing I had food at the time.

Thanks to Overeating, my red SP hardly ever goes down, but I'll have to be extra-careful from now on.

At any rate, Cursed Evil Eye seems pretty useful.

Maybe when I have MP to spare, I'll activate it to earn more proficiency.

Yeah. I'll make sure I keep at least half of my MP in case of emergencies, then use the rest to work on Evil Eye.

That should be easy, since I can keep it active while I'm walking.

Okay, but this Evil Eye is totally magic, isn't it?

I mean, it drains MP, and it's clearly some kind of supernatural phenomenon that ignores the laws of physics.

Although, that seems true of a lot of other skills, too...

So what's the difference between magic and those other skills?

I don't know. Appearance, maybe?

Guess Evil Eye is pretty subtle in that you can't see its effects unless you use the all-knowing Appraisal.

When you think of magic, you think of something a little louder and flashier, right?

Yep. It's important to have some flair. I really wanna learn magic.

Sure, Cursed Evil Eye is technically a long-range attack, but it isn't the immediate impact I'd originally expected.

What I really want is a straightforward, easy-to-understand, ready-aim-fire-boom, long-range attack.

Cursed Evil Eye is useful in its own way, but can you imagine how strong it'd be combined with magic missiles or something?

Damn, wouldn't that be nice.

Hmm. My quest to learn magic continues, I suppose.

I am a body brain.

As yet, I have no name.

Listen, I gotta vent about the information brain for a moment, okay?

What an idiot.

Take a little while ago, for instance. She wanted to learn some shooting skill or other, so she was all, "Shoot thread out of my butt!" So I tried, but it shot out with more force than I expected, and— *Splat!* Went right into the magma.

It caught fire immediately, of course.

If I hadn't severed the thread in time, we'd have gone up in flames by now.

So basically, she's always making these stupid suggestions, and I'm the one who has to deal with the consequences.

I don't think a single one of her ideas has worked out yet.

Although, I guess I'm also the one who goes along with them every time...

Still, I wish she'd come up with some better ideas.

Couldn't you think these things through a little?

Why is the one who's supposedly the brains of this operation so damn clueless?

Are you stupid or what?

Yeah, I think she must be.

That's why I, the body brain, have to keep things together.

My actions mean life or death for both of us, after all.

Body brain, body brain!

【What is it, information brain?】

Do you think we can combine Evil Eye with Telescopic Sight?

【?! What are you, some kinda genius?!】

Heh-heh-heh. Yep, I'm a genius all right.

【Oh man. So I am a genius! That means I can get away with just about anything!】

That's right. Would using Evil Eye from a long distance be wicked or what?

【Yooo. This is crazy. It's like a whole new world of possibilities.】

Okay, then let's find some prey!

【Whoo-hoo!】

I am an information brain.

As yet, I have no name.

So using Telescopic Sight and Evil Eye together didn't work. Hrmph.

I guess it really was too good to be true, huh?

At least keeping Telescopic Sight active all the time has raised it to level 5.

The distance and amount of magnification it can do has risen quite a lot compared with level 1.

If I could just apply Evil Eye to this, I could attack from a pretty fair distance, but seems like that isn't actually an option.

Oh well. Evil Eye is still pretty useful.

Since I've been using it whenever I have the MP to spare, it's level 3 now.

It seems to level up pretty slowly.

But I haven't been using my MP much in the Middle Stratum anyway, so that's fine.

At some point, I noticed using Evil Eye doesn't affect my vision.

I couldn't combine it with Telescopic Sight, but it seems to be perfectly compatible with Vision Enhancement and such.

If I can see just fine while using it, there's no reason to make sure I keep one eye free for it.

Now I'm one step closer to my dream of having eight different evil eyes at once.

Also, it seems like you can't use any of the attribute-adding skills on Evil Eye.

I tried it with Poison Attack, but it didn't work. So be it.

Just like combining it with Telescopic Sight, that probably would've been too overpowered anyway.

If I could combine my deadly poison with Evil Eye, I'd be like some anime character who can kill with a glance.

Just being able to weaken things *and* inflict damage simply by looking at an enemy seems broken enough as it is, so it'd be greedy to ask for even more.

I thought maybe I wouldn't be able to activate these skills in all eight eyes at the same time, but it looks like that actually works.

However, it doesn't change the effect.

Since I'm using it in eight eyes simultaneously, I'd hoped it would multiply the effects eightfold, but no such luck.

However, the several-eyes-at-once thing turned out to be pretty useful for Telescopic Sight.

Depending on how I use it, I can monitor several locations concurrently and zoom in as needed.

Anyway, on a different note, can we talk about the body brain for a second? What an idiot.

Take a little while ago, for instance. I wanted to try to get the Expel skill, so I suggested we try shooting thread out of my butt. So she was all, "Great idea! Let's try it right now!" and proceeded to fire it on the spot. Toward the magma.

She said it was "more force than I expected" or whatever, but what kind of idiot does that in the direction of magma in the first place?

Of course, the thread went straight into the inferno with a *splat* and ignited.

The flames were coming at me like a fuse! It was awful.

Luckily, the body brain cut the thread in the nick of time, but we were this close to my butt getting set on fire.

Essentially, she jumps at my suggestions like an idiot and takes them too far.

Or should I say takes them in the completely wrong direction?

I mean, what good is it making genius proposals if my body brain is too incompetent to enact them?

Couldn't you think these things through a little?

Has operating the body all this time turned you into a meathead?

Are you stupid or what?

Yeah, I think she must be.

That's why I, the information brain, have to keep things together.

My instructions mean life or death for both of us, after all.

【Information brain, information brain!】

What is it, body brain?

【I was playing with Telescopic Sight and found a monster.】

For real? It's not in range of my Detection yet.

【Heh-heh. Maybe you're becoming obsolete, information brain?】

Shut up, body brain. You couldn't provide more information than me if you had a hundred eyes.

【Bwa-ha-ha, enjoy that while it lasts! You'd better watch your back, pal!】

Pfft, I'm not holding my breath on that threat. Go ahead and try to catch up with me!

【Heh-heh-heh.】

Ba-ha-ha.

【So what should we do?】

We'll hunt it, of course.

【Aye, aye, sir. Come on, guys! Battle stations!】

Whoo-hoo!

Another day of roaming the Middle Stratum.

Hmm. I've been here quite a while now, but there's still no end in sight.

Guess this really is the biggest labyrinth in the world.

If a human tried traversing it, they'd probably have to be prepared to devote their entire life to the endeavor, wouldn't they?

But it's a piece of cake for me, of course!

Yep, I'm the best!

Evolving made my stats a lot better, and my skills are coming along nicely, too.

Is there any enemy in the Middle Stratum capable of challenging me anymore?

And if not, doesn't that mean I'll totally dominate once I get back to the Upper Stratum?

Heh-heh-heh. I've spent a lot of time struggling just to survive, but things are really going my way now!

Once you're not constantly one blow away from death, this gamelike world is actually kinda fun.

<Proficiency has reached the required level.
  Skill [Appraisal LV 9] has become [Appraisal LV 10].>

Oh? Ooh? Ooooh?!

Finally. I finally maxed out Appraisal!

Oh man, I'm so pumped!

Appraisal, the first skill I ever picked up, the skill that's been with me through thick and thin, has reached its final form at long last!

I still remember how incredibly useless it was at first.

Then, each time it leveled up, there were subtle improvements.

What joy I felt as it gradually became more useful!

Especially when it shed its veneer of mere adequacy and became truly fantastic.

My dear Appraisal. No matter how much I complained about you, you kept working hard and growing.

And now, you've developed into a skill that anyone would be proud to call their own.

You finally made it! Waaah!

At last. At long last. I'm so emotional!

Thanks for everything, Appraisal! You and I are just getting started!

…Still, no evolution or derivative skills, huh?

No, no, it's fine.

Just the fact that Appraisal hit its level cap is amazing enough.

I guess I was just kinda expecting some kind of wisdom-granting evolution or something.

No dice, huh? Since it's you, Appraisal, I don't mind either way, but... nothing at all?

I'm shocked.

...There's seriously nothing?

<Fzzzt...ʃzzt, ʃzzt, ʃzzt......>

...What's that sound? It's like radio static...

<Fzzt, request, ʃzzt...upper administration authority limit, ʃzzt...>

Huh? What's going on?

<Fzzt......nistrator Sari...ʃzzzt...rejected, ʃzzt...>

Okay, this is bad.
I don't know what's bad or why, but this is definitely bad.

<Fzzt...*ping!*>

Compared with the other sounds, the *ping!* is so clear that I flinch.

<Upper Administrator D has accepted the request.>
<Now constructing skill [Wisdom].>
<Construction completed.>
<Condition satisfied. Acquired skill [Wisdom].>
<Skill [Appraisal LV 10] has been integrated into [Wisdom].>
<Skill [Detection LV 10] has been integrated into [Wisdom].>
<Proficiency has reached the required level.
  Skill [Taboo LV 7] has become [Taboo LV 8].>
<Condition satisfied. Acquired title [Ruler of Wisdom].>
<Acquired skills [Height of Evil] [Celestial Power] as a result of title [Ruler of Wisdom].>

<Skill [MP Recovery Speed LV 4] has been integrated into [Height of Occultism].>
<Skill [MP Lessened Consumption LV 3] has been integrated into [Height of Occultism].>
<Skill [Magic Mass LV 9] has been integrated into [Celestial Power].>
<Skill [Protection LV 4] has been integrated into [Celestial Power].>

What? What? Whaaaaaaat?

Okay, hold on a second. Something's wrong. Something is very wrong here.

What's going on? How did this happen? What do I do?

I've gotta calm down. Body brain, let's take a deep breath.

Huff... Whew.

Okay. Let's go through this step-by-step.

First, I started hearing that weird noise.

What was that? I have no idea.

Normally, I'd just say there's no point in racking my brains over things I can't understand, but this is a little too much to just let it slide.

I mean, this is clearly an abnormal situation here.

Yeah. Abnormal.

Here I've been going along all this time acquiring skills and stuff under the assumption that that's just how this world works.

If this were still Japan, of course, their very existence would be abnormal.

Was it really all right to just blithely accept that skills exist here because "that's just how it is in this world"?

Up until recently, I thought it was fine. But now I'm not so sure.

I definitely heard the Divine Voice (temp.) say this:

<Upper Administrator D has accepted the request.>
<Now constructing skill [Wisdom].>
<Construction completed.>

It's like someone was watching me and made a new skill in direct response to my complaints.

If that's true, the culprit must be this Administrator D.

And the term "upper" means that this D isn't the only administrator.

So what exactly do these "administrators" manage?

That's obvious. Skills.

It's the only explanation I can think of.

The point is, the skills in this world are granted by a group who call themselves administrators.

But how? And why?

Naturally, I have no idea.

But I do know this much.

There's something wrong with this world.

A shiver runs down my spine.

I'm overwhelmed with fear, a different sort from what I felt when I ran afoul of the dragon.

Are those administrators laughing at me right now, watching me panic like this?

Terrifying.

The skills I've relied on all this time seem like a disturbing mystery to me now.

Am I wrong?

If my skills were given to me by these administrators, then I've been dancing in the palms of their hands.

Because the whole time I've depended on these skills to survive.

"Gamelike"? "Kinda fun"? I'm a fool.

How could I say that so lightly, when clearly the whole system was deliberately constructed this way by so-called administrators?

If these administrators really do manage the skill system, does that mean they're watching the goings-on of this world as if it really is just a game to them?

And if so, doesn't that make me just another character?

That makes them sound almost like gods.

What am I supposed to do now, knowing all this?

What do I do now?

S5 RULING CLASS

Today we have extracurricular activities.

My activity, the exploration class, convenes on a small mountain close to the academy.

Though, "close" is relative, since it takes half a day just to walk there and just as long to get back.

Only students who have passed an exam administered by the academy can participate.

Among us first-years, a total of twelve people received permission to take the exploration class.

We leave the school early in the morning and arrive at the foot of the mountain just before noon.

There we have a final briefing session in the cabin at the base and eat lunch.

After lunch, we get divided into groups and start the ascent.

We'll spend the whole day exploring the mountain, camp there overnight, and head back down the following morning.

In terms of danger levels, only the weakest, lowest-class monsters live in the area.

Before the exploration, the high school sent some personnel to investigate, confirming that no strong monsters had turned up.

Even weak monsters sometimes evolve and become strong, so apparently, they check before each lesson.

There are several objectives for these outings:

To learn basic survival skills.

To experience an environment inhabited by actual monsters.

To collect medicinal herbs and gain more knowledge about mountains.

The overall goal is to accumulate all these experiences.

Ideally, we're supposed to do that by remaining safe throughout the trip.

There's even a penalty if anyone tries to confront monsters directly.

If you are attacked, you can gain points based on how you deal with it, but going out of your way to attack monsters is strictly forbidden.

The class is divided into parties, each consisting of four students and one teacher.

The makeup of these parties is decided by lots, and unless there's a major balance issue, there's no switching places.

Unfortunately, Sue, Katia, and Yuri ended up on separate teams from me.

Even more unfortunately, I'm on the same team as Hugo.

Our party consists of myself, Hugo, Ms. Oka (aka Filimøs), and Parton, a knight's son. The teacher in charge is Professor Oriza, our magic instructor.

Parton and I are more than just acquaintances, but we don't quite have a proper friendship.

Parton's father was a former baron, but he worked his way up to the peerage rank of count through his military accomplishments.

He also trained his son quite rigorously, so Parton specializes in physical-based skills.

His strength is also on the higher end in our grade.

Apparently, that's still not enough to satisfy him, so he devotes himself very seriously to daily training.

He tends to act very deferential toward me, so while we talk sometimes, I don't think we're particularly close.

Professor Oriza is a middle-aged magic teacher.

He seems fairly unmotivated compared with the other teachers. That he's only here because it's his job is pretty transparent.

Clearly, he's not a fan of dealing with trouble, so when Hugo and I were assigned to his party, he made no effort to disguise his irritation.

Seems like the fact that Hugo despises me is common knowledge.

However, since Professor Oriza is a teacher and all, his combat abilities are definitely high enough to deal with any issues.

Though he specializes in magic, he also has the skills for close-range combat, and his attributes are certainly high compared with any student's.

If anything unexpected happens, the teacher has to protect the students, so it wouldn't make sense for a weak teacher to accompany us on this field trip.

What does surprise me is Filimøs, formerly Ms. Oka, actually participating. She often vanishes without warning.

It seems to me she's working behind the scenes, but she won't tell us what she's doing.

If it requires her to skip class without permission, she must be pretty busy.

So I wasn't expecting her to show up for a class that lasts almost two full days.

That said, considering my situation with Hugo, I'm pretty glad to have her around.

This way, if Hugo tries to pick a fight with me, Ms. Oka is sure to intervene.

"All right, that's it for now. After you've all finished lunch, please break up into your groups and set out."

The teacher in charge of the excursion concludes the briefing.

Once we've eaten, we'll be heading out with our parties.

"Well, my dear brother, we must part for a short while. It'll be terribly lonely."

"Sue, it's only for one day."

"Even one day is too much to bear. When I consider what could happen to you while I'm not around, I doubt I'll be able to sleep at night."

"It'll be fine, okay? They've already confirmed the mountain's safe. Nothing's going to happen."

I pat Sue on the head reassuringly.

"Shun, be careful of Hugo, all right? He seems to have gone completely crazy in this world."

"…Got it."

Katia's quiet warning before we part ways keeps echoing in my mind.

Crazy, huh…?

He certainly does seem more fixated on gaining power than ever.

By gathering so many promising young men as his followers, he's basically building a base for a future army.

I'm sorry, but he's like a kid playing king of the mountain.

He was always a bit self-centered and childish, but since he reincarnated, it's only gotten worse.

Well, I'll just have to be careful to avoid pissing him off with some minor misstep.

Apart from my own private worries, our exploration has been going smoothly.

We arrive in the designated camping area without running into any monsters.

"Sir Schlain, is this the camping point?"

"I think so. Looks like we got here earlier than planned."

"Oh, young boys have sooo much energy. A little lady like me had suuuch a hard time keeping up, you knooow!"

"Yeah, right. Your stats're pretty high, aren't they, Oka? You should have no problem with this crap."

"If you ask meee, a gentleman would pretend not to know that and treat a lady with kindness anywaaay!"

"I ain't wastin' my time fawnin' over chicks, thanks."

"Aah, I suppose some girls go for the bad-boy type anywaaay."

While Hugo argues with Ms. Oka, Parton and I start setting up camp.

Professor Oriza simply watches us in silence.

"Sir Schlain, could I ask you to hold that, please?"

"Yeah, sure. Like this?"

"Precisely. Then if we just do this and this…"

"Gotcha. Hey, it's done. Thanks, Parton."

"Not at all. In fact, I apologize for troubling you to help. I ought to have done it on my own, but…"

"Parton. Social status doesn't matter at the academy. So you don't need to worry about it so much, all right?"

"That's certainly part of it, but, Sir Schlain, I respect you on a personal level as well. I do these things of my own free will. If anything, there's no need for you to be so apologetic about it."

I'm taken aback by Parton's frank gaze.

Why do he and other people—like my sister, Sue—feel compelled to fawn over me so much?

I don't understand it.

After we finish establishing our camp, we're still ahead of schedule, so we have a bit of time to kill.

We decide to check out our surroundings a bit.

Each of us will act independently, exploring in a small area without straying too far.

I'm somewhat opposed to the idea, but we agree to stay within hearing range of each other's voices.

That way, if anything happens, the other members will be close enough to come running.

And that's how I wind up alone on the mountain.

If you collect medicinal herbs and other edibles on your own, you can get extra points.

So I activate Appraisal, and now I'm looking for herbs.

Suddenly, I hear the sound of swords clashing.

It's coming from nearby, where Parton should be exploring.

The sound is muffled, as if one of the swords is either specially forged or the wielder is using the Silence skill.

But with Auditory Enhancement, my ears pick it out clearly.

I make to dash toward Parton only to find someone blocking my path.

It's Hugo.

"Yo."

"What are you doing, Hugo...no, Natsume?"

Hugo greets me pleasantly enough, but it does little to ease my nerves.

"Oh, you know, I was just thinkin' that now would be as good a time as any to get rid of you."

Hugo's voice is calm, but I can barely believe my ears.

I can't help but gulp.

"You're joking, right?"

"Do I look like I'm joking? You're an eyesore, and I'm sick of it."

At that moment, the light smirk vanishes from Hugo's face.

"See, this world exists just for me... I'm gonna be the strongest guy alive and take over this whole place. So it don't make sense for someone to be on the same level as me, or maybe even stronger, now does it?"

"What the hell are you saying? This world doesn't belong to anyone. Come back to your senses already."

"My senses, huh? But you can do anything in this world if you have the right skills. It's like a dream! Obviously, it exists only for me. But a world like that doesn't need losers like you in it. So die."

Hugo draws his sword. I have no choice but to do the same.

I don't believe this. Is he insane?

I knew he hated me, so I thought something might happen during this trip, but I never would have guessed he'd try to kill me, especially for such a ridiculous reason.

He's serious, isn't he?

I mean, I know this isn't a joke, but…

It still doesn't seem real.

And yet, I can hear my heart pounding like a drum in my ears clearly, and my hands tremble as I clutch my sword.

I try to swallow the confusion and panic and check Hugo's status.

<Human Status:	LV 31		Name: Hugo Baint Renxandt
	HP: 628/628 (green)		MP: 566/566 (blue)
	SP: 609/609 (yellow)		: 502/611 (red)
	Average Offensive Ability: 608		Average Defensive Ability: 599
	Average Magical Ability: 546		Average Resistance Ability: 522
	Average Speed Ability: 583		

Skills:

[HP Auto-Recovery LV 4]	[MP Recovery Speed LV 4]	[MP Lessened Consumption LV 4]	[SP Recovery Speed LV 8]
[SP Lessened Consumption LV 8]	[Destruction Enhancement LV 7]	[Cutting Enhancement LV 7]	[Impact Enhancement LV 4]
[Flame Enhancement LV 4]	[Magic Power Perception LV 8]	[Magic Power Operation LV 5]	[Magic Warfare LV 5]
[Magic Power Conferment LV 4]	[Magic Power Attack LV 2]	[Mental Warfare LV 7]	[Energy Conferment LV 7]
[Energy Attack LV 7]	[Flame Attack LV 3]	[Paralysis Attack LV 2]	[Swordsmanship LV 6]

[Throw LV 5]	[Spatial Maneuvering LV 6]	[Hit LV 8]	[Evasion LV 8]
[Stealth LV 3]	[Silence LV 1]	[Emperor]	[Concentration LV 9]
[Prediction LV 3]	[Arithmetic Processing LV 3]	[Fire Magic LV 5]	[Destruction Resistance LV 2]
[Impact Resistance LV 2]	[Cutting Resistance LV 3]	[Fire Resistance LV 3]	[Poison Resistance LV 2]
[Paralysis Resistance LV 1]	[Pain Resistance LV 1]	[Vision Enhancement 10]	[Telescopic Sight LV 1]
[Auditory Enhancement LV 10]	[Auditory Expansion LV 1]	[Olfactory Enhancement LV 8]	[Taste Enhancement LV 7]
[Tactile Enhancement LV 8]	[Longevity LV 5]	[Magic Hoard LV 4]	[Instant Body LV 5]
[Endurance LV 5]	[Herculean Strength LV 5]	[Sturdy LV 5]	[Monk LV 4]
[Talisman LV 3]	[Acceleration LV 5]	[n% I = W]	

Skill Points: 350

Titles:

[Monster Slayer]

>

He's strong. Unlike mine, his stats lean a little heavily toward the physical side.

And unlike me, he's been actively acquiring skills with his skill points.

The most concerning is the Emperor skill.

‹Emperor: Increases the effects of skills. Additionally, can inflict the heresy attribute effect "Fear" on an opponent through intimidation.›

I can resist the Fear effect.

But increasing the effect of all his other skills is a big problem.

Hugo swings his sword at me.

I meet his blade with my own.

Oof, so heavy!

"Hey, guess what? I know you haven't used your skill points at all. You haven't even leveled up. Points exist to be used, you know! Just like this!"

Hugo's sword starts gushing flames.

I just barely manage to avoid it.

"Make it quick and die, will ya? If this gets too out of hand, the other groups might notice."

"You really think you can get away with doing something like this?"

"Sure, why not? I'm the future ruler of this world. Obviously, I can do whatever I want! Besides, I've got it all planned out. My lackeys should've made short work of the others by now. Once I finish you off, we'll just release the monsters we brought along. Strong ones that wouldn't normally show up around here. Then we'll just say they suddenly appeared and devoured a bunch of poor students and teachers, get it? And that I defeated them and survived."

"You don't think anyone will suspect you with a half-baked plan like that?"

"Who will? What're they gonna say? This ain't Japan, you know. I'm the future sword-king! Who would dare speak against me just 'cause something's a little fishy? You think they wanna start an international incident? Yeah, right. That's how things work here. There's no goody-goody justice system to stop me!"

His words shock me. He doesn't think like a Japanese person at all anymore.

And he's accepted that like it's totally natural.

"See ya. Don't worry. I'll remember you in some tiny fraction of my memories."

His sword gathers huge flames as it swings downward.

However, it doesn't reach me.

Hugo's body is suddenly blown backward.

"Natsume. You've gone way too far."

A cold, intimidating tone with no trace of the usual drawl.

An overwhelming presence unsuited to such a tiny elf.

Ms. Oka.

"Your plan's failed, Natsume. All of your subordinates have been arrested. And I took the liberty of disposing of the monsters you brought."

"Wh-what?!"

"It seems you were so preoccupied with Shun that you wrote me off far too lightly. I'm sorry, but I can't let your little rampage go unchecked anymore."

Our teacher walks over to the fallen Hugo.

He tries launching a surprise attack at her, but—

"Guh?!"

—something invisible knocks him back down to the ground.

It must be the same force that blew him away a minute ago.

I'm guessing it's some kind of wind magic.

Ms. Oka's hand grasps the top of Hugo's head. Then, I sense the flow of magic power.

She seems to have cast some kind of spell on him.

"Activate ruler's authority. Activating ruler-exclusive skill at the ruler's request. Consent to activation?"

"Consent granted."

A flat voice emerges from Hugo's mouth. It doesn't sound like him.

Is she hypnotizing him using forbidden Heretic Magic?!

My surprise doesn't end there. In fact, that's only the beginning.

Before my eyes, Appraisal shows Hugo's stats rapidly decreasing.

On top of that, his skills are disappearing.

In a matter of seconds, all of Hugo's skills are gone except for the mysterious one with the garbled letters.

"What?! What did you do to me?!"

Hugo bellows as soon as he returns to his senses.

"I lowered your stats and revoked your skills."

"Huh?! That's impossible!"

"Shun, what does Appraisal say?"

"…Just as you said, ma'am. All his stats have dropped to thirty. Plus, his skills are gone."

"Wh…? How…?"

"This world does not belong to you. I would strongly advise you to reflect on your actions and start trying to live a normal life. Nothing good will come of you acquiring skills and getting stronger anyway…"

Hugo is absolutely dumbfounded. I'm confused, too.

After that, the exploration class is suspended.

Parton, Professor Oriza, and the others are all safe.

It seems to have been a close call, but thanks to Ms. Oka's intervention, no one was seriously injured.

All of Hugo's minions who'd attempted to attack people were captured.

However, none of them would admit to their connection with Hugo, and he cut ties with them as well.

Apparently, a more detailed inquisition will be initiated at the academy, but judging by how it's gone so far, I doubt much will happen.

Hugo is confident he can talk his way out of it, so he may already have some sort of contingency plan.

Everyone, including me, is completely focused on Hugo right now.

So no one notices the monster, released surreptitiously, quietly following us back.

8   Wisdom

<Perseverance (500): n% of the power to reach godhood. Enables acquisition of browsing level-1 information regarding anything in the user's range of perception. In addition, the user will gain the ability to surpass the W system and interfere with the MA field.>

<Ruler of Wisdom: Acquires skills [Height of Occultism] [Celestial Power]. Acquisition conditions: Obtain [Wisdom] skill. Effect: Increases MP, magic, and resistance stats. +Correction to magic skill proficiencies. Grants ruling-class privileges. Description: A title granted to one who has conquered wisdom.>

<Height of Occultism: Increases support for controlling magic power within the system, as well as maximizing all rune-related stats. Also, maxes out MP recovery speed while minimizing MP consumption.>

<Celestial Power: Adds a +1,000 correction to MP, magic, and resistance stats. Also, growth of these stats at each level-up increases by 100.>

...Not long ago, I would've thought these were crazy good.

Well, to be honest, I still think that, but it doesn't feel like something to celebrate.

Ugh. Uugh. Uuugh. Aaargh!!

Enough already! I don't wanna think about it! What's the point of getting hung up on it anyway?

Even if these administrators or whatever do exist, what am I supposed to do about it?

I'm just a spider.

What can one spider do against a bunch of godlike freaks?

Nothing, of course.

So why shouldn't I just keep living my life as I please?

Stalkers? Peeping toms? Do your worst.

I don't care if you're an administrator or a god or what. Go ahead and watch. I'll show you a life you won't soon forget!

I'll shine like a comet until I burn into nothing!

Feast your eyes on my glorious life!

【Information braiiin!】

What is it, body brain?

【We're on fire!】

I know—I'm totally fired up right now!

【No! I mean we're physically on fire!】

Huh?

【The thread, the thread!】

Wh-whaaa…?!

【You were spacing out, so we forgot to cut it off, and now we're on fire!】

What's wrong with you?! Don't just report to me about it—put it out!

<Proficiency has reached the required level.

　Skill [Fire Resistance LV 3] has become [Fire Resistance LV 4].>

Hot! Hot! Synthesize some poison! Hurry!

【All right, Weak Poison comin' up!】

Geh?! Now I feel numb!

【Oh nooo! I forgot Weak Poison still had paralysis attached!】

Seriously, what's WRONG with you?!

<Proficiency has reached the required level.

　Skill [Paralysis Resistance LV 4] has become [Paralysis Resistance LV 5].>

So hot! So numb!

【I-I-I-I've become so numb!! I can't f… Aaaah! Our HP!】

No more jokes! We're gonna die!

【Oh, our HP reached 0.】

Wha—?!

【Activate Perseverance! As long as we have MP to sacrifice, we'll be revived with 1 HP!】

Ooh!

【But if we don't put the fire out, it's gonna run out again! Are we still paralyzed?!】

Almost... There, it wore off!

【Okay, this time I'm synthesizing Weak Poison sans Paralysis! And we'll set it to the max amount, while we're at it!】

Whoa?! That's a huge glob of poison!

【Ouch. It crushed us. Our HP's down again.】

Ugh. But at least it put the fire out.

【Oh, you're right. Well, now we know Perseverance works, so I guess it worked out all right?】

How is any of this remotely all right?

【Look, just don't worry about it.】

I mean, what kind of first KO is this?

【Don't worry about it.】

Right...

【Our MP's down to about half now.】

If we didn't have Wisdom, that would've meant death.

【Good thing we got Wisdom, then.】

But it was because of Wisdom that this happened in the first place...

【Don't worry about it.】

Skills really are handy, aren't they?

【They sure are.】

I don't know why someone would make skills and distribute them, but I guess since they're there, we might as well use 'em, right?

【Guess so. Yeah. Let's go with that.】

So Wisdom functions sort of like a somewhat powered-up combination of Appraisal and Detection.

I might as well just start calling it Professor Wisdom at this point.

For one thing, it's added details to status Appraisal results for powered-up items.

If I double-Appraise these details, I can access even more information about them. It's wonderful.

Attack and defense, for instance, give detailed numerical values for each part of the body.

Thanks to that, I learned that my scythes are the strongest attack area on my body, and my defense is pretty much even throughout.

The defense power of the main trunk of my body is a little low, but since I specialize in evasion anyway, I just have to make sure I don't mess up and get hit there.

My speed is also broken down into reflex speed, instantaneous speed, persistent speed, and so on.

They're mostly around consistent, but instantaneous speed is a little higher than the others.

And then there's magic. Where do I even begin?

There are a lot of different entries—magic attack power, rune speed, rune stability, rune strength, and so on—but every one of them aside from attack power is maxed out.

99,999, apparently. That's not average at all!!

I suppose this must be thanks to the Height of Occultism skill.

It did say something about maximizing rune stats, so this must be what it meant.

So. This must mean that I can use magic now, right?

Fwa-ha-ha. Finally! Finally, I'll get to use magic!

Oh man. I'm so hyped for this.

But first, I'd better finish going over the results of Professor Wisdom's assessment.

No need to get ahead of myself.

Last but definitely not least, resistance contained the most important revelation of all.

It shows all of my attribute resistance stats. Now I know what my weaknesses are.

My biggest weakness, of course, is fire.

Even with the Fire Resistance skill, it's still the lowest number.

Oh, by the way, turns out that having a resistance skill raises your resistance stat for the corresponding attribute.

Aside from fire, I'm also pretty weak to water, ice, and light.

Ice, especially, is almost as low as fire.

I doubt I'm gonna run into any ice attacks while I'm in the Middle Stratum, but it's still good info to tuck away in the back of my mind.

My highest resistance, on the other hand, is heresy. I do have Heresy Nullification, after all.

My heresy resistance stat is 99,999.

The next highest is my poison resistance.

And surprisingly, the one after that is dark.

So now I know my strengths and weaknesses as far as resistance goes, but you know, I think this may actually apply to my attack capabilities, too.

For instance, if I use fire magic when it's my weakest attribute, the effect probably wouldn't be very strong.

On the other hand, the high ones like heresy and dark would probably be really powerful.

I mean, this is still just speculation, but I'm pretty sure I'm onto something.

Moving on, I can see more details about my skills now, too.

Specifically, I can see the proficiency values of all my skills.

It shows how much proficiency I need to get to the next level, too, which will help me level up skills even more efficiently from now on.

I can even see the proficiency amounts for skills I haven't acquired yet.

Guess what: Now I can look at the skill list even if I don't have any skill points.

That really caught me by surprise. And all the skills are unlocked, too.

I could definitely waste a whole day just looking at this list.

For one thing, there are some skills that require such a stupidly high amount of points that there's no way I'm ever gonna get them.

In exchange, of course, they're incredibly powerful, but I don't think it's gonna happen.

Hmm. I wonder if I should stop jokingly calling it the Divine Voice (temp.).

Nah, might as well stick with that.

Oh, right… Where was I?

Yeah, so it turns out there really is an Immortality skill, you know? So I asked the Divine Voice (temp.) how much it costs as a joke, and the answer was…1,000,000 points.

Unreal. I'm never getting that.

But unattainable skills aside, there were some good ones that actually seem achievable if I try hard enough, so I think I'll save up and get them.

I'll be using points for Evil Eye skills for a while, but once I'm finished with that and have some to spare, I think I'll expand my repertoire.

As for the new and improved Detection, turns out that now I can Appraise information I sense with Detection.

However, because the information provided by Mr. Detection is already pretty detailed, there's usually no need to Appraise it further.

So while it doesn't seem particularly useful at the moment, there's certainly no harm having it, and it might still come in handy someday.

Finally, and most important of all, an auto-mapping function was added! OMG.

And I can even view maps of everywhere I've been since I was born, even before I had Professor Wisdom!

This is amazing. Seriously.

The parts of the Great Elroe Labyrinth where I've just been wandering around randomly all this time are now totally clear to me on this map!

This labyrinth is way too big...

There's a partial map of the Upper Stratum where I started, the Lower Stratum where I fell, and the Middle Stratum where I'm currently traveling.

When I tried putting them all together to get an idea of the scale, that alone was easily the size of Hokkaido. And that's just a fraction of this place?

Anyway, based on my estimation of the distance from the Middle to the Upper Stratum, I think I still have a long way to go.

It's only an estimate—and maybe I'll get lucky and find a shaft leading upward or something—but I think I'm better off assuming this is gonna be a long trip.

Oh, and that mysterious garbled skill is still impossible to Appraise.

Man, though, I thought I was gonna die back there. In fact, speaking in terms of HP, I'm pretty sure I actually did.

Without Perseverance, I would've died for real. Imagine actually suffering such a stupid death. So much for a glorious life.

Mr. Administrator, if you saw all that, could you please delete it from your log? Thanks a lot.

Anyway, I did unintentionally confirm the effects of Perseverance, at least.

Rather than being resurrected if my HP runs out, it's more like once my HP hits 0, my MP starts getting used up instead.

Judging by how much my MP went down when I was on fire earlier, I think that basically my MP temporarily serves as my HP.

So whatever damage that would have affected my HP gets subtracted from my MP instead.

It's sorta like my HP and MP are stuck together.

So if I get hit with a really big overkill attack, my MP could all get drained at once, too.

But thanks to Celestial Power, my MP is crazy high now, so I guess I've actually become pretty tough.

However, since I also have to use MP for its original purpose, it's probably better to only think of that as emergency insurance.

So. Thanks to Celestial Power, my magic stats are all crazy high now. It'd be a waste not to use it, right?

That's where Height of Occultism comes in! Oh yes.

This skill is like the ultimate version of Magic Power Operation, the skill I've wanted for so long—the last piece of the puzzle that is using magic!

Wonderful!

On top of that, it's a package deal that includes all kinds of convenient MP-related skills!

What a bargain!

If you act now, thanks to our friend Professor Wisdom, you can even get it absolutely free!

H-how can that be?!

Don't worry, we've already put it in your cart and purchased it for you!

Congratulations to me!

So yeah, Height of Occultism. This skill is seriously crazy.

It's like I got maxed-out versions of [Magic Power Operation], [MP Recovery Speed], and [MP Reduced Consumption] all at once.

My MP, which was down to half after I effectively died a little while ago, is already fully recovered.

It recovers at a rate of two or three points per second, so it only took about ten minutes.

Can you believe that? It's like an all-you-can-use MP buffet.

And since I have MP Lessened Consumption, it should go down way more slowly when it's not being used for Perseverance.

As long as I don't mess anything up majorly, I can pretty much use it as often as I want.

Like, I can keep Evil Eye activated all the time, and it recovers so fast, it's like it doesn't use any MP at all.

That being the case, I might as well leave it on nonstop.

So, now that the stage is set, I definitely want to use magic for real.

But I still don't know how.

At least, I didn't until now! Yes, I've finally learned how to use magic!

Once again, this discovery was made possible by Professor Wisdom, which came with a new search feature.

It's no Spoogle, mind you, but if you look up a word related to the skill system, it'll display an explanation.

Yes, I finally have a user manual, kinda. Better late than never, right?

And so I research how to use magic.

According to the search, there are several steps you have to complete in order to use magic.

First, you have to recognize magic power. This corresponds to the so-called Magic Power Perception skill.

If you can't sense the existence of magic power, you can't use it as fuel to activate any magic spells. So it's a major building block in the whole process.

Thanks to Professor Wisdom, I've got Magic Power Perception on lock.

Next, you have to manipulate that magic power.

You picture the magic power inside as a dense liquid. Then you will that liquid to move as you desire.

In essence, this is Magic Power Operation. It's even better if you can move it quickly or in complicated patterns.

Usually, you'd go through lots of training and gradually learn how to manage it, but thanks to Height of Occultism, I can manipulate mine however I want.

Then comes constructing the rune.

Each variety of magic has its own set, so you choose the corresponding rune, which is then automatically formed for you.

Once it's constructed, you picture it sort of like a pipe, I guess?

The construction speed also varies based on your stats.

Again, since all my rune stats are maxed out, the rune gets generated the instant I select it. Seriously, it's like I'm using a cheat code.

Finally, you pour some magic power into the completed rune, and the magic is complete.

It sort of feels like liquid flowing through a pipe.

When the liquid reaches the end, it finally becomes a phenomenon that affects the physical world.

At that point, if you increase the amount of liquid flowing into the pipe, the attack power of the magic increases, and if you increase the speed, it shortens the amount of time it takes to activate.

However, that also applies an extra load to the pipe.

Depending on its thickness, there's a limit to the amount of liquid the pipe can hold at a given moment. Therefore, it has to be made sturdily, or it can burst under the pressure.

If that happens, the rune can't bear the load, so the spell might misfire or even backfire.

More advanced magic has longer and more complicated runes, so the chances of accidents become higher.

To stabilize the rune, you have to build a bigger, stouter pipe.

This is no problem for me, either, thanks to Height of Occultism.

You have to go through this whole process just to activate a single spell.

But here's the thing! Since I have Height of Occultism, I don't have to bother worrying about any of that junk!

I can operate my magic power as easily as I move my body, and as soon as I select a spell, an optimal rune is forged instantly.

I can activate magic as easily as pouring water into a glass!

Since there aren't any monsters handy at the moment, let's try out a spell with easy-to-test results.

Guess I'll start with the level-2 Poison Magic spell, Poison Shot.

Heretic Magic is no good without a target, and frankly, Shadow Magic doesn't seem like it'd be that impressive.

As for Abyss Magic… Yeah, I feel like that's a tad too advanced for my first try.

All right, here goes! Construct rune! Fill it with magic power! Poison Shot, activate!

Almost instantaneously, something black and round appears before my eyes and streaks forward.

Oh, whoa!

It was so easy it was almost anticlimactic, but still. I used magic.

Awesome. I'm kinda moved.

Poison Shot doesn't seem very powerful, though.

It doesn't utilize my Deadly Spider Poison after all.

Apparently, instead of using my poison, this Poison Magic spell generates and fires its own.

As opposed to my Deadly Spider Poison, it employs a blend developed exclusively for this spell.

Yet even with my crazy magic attack power, it still isn't as strong as my Deadly Spider Poison.

If I use more magic power, I could make it stronger, but in that case, I'm better off just using Poison Synthesis.

So even though I have this magic, it might not come in handy very often…

Well, next up, I'll test out the level-1 Poison Magic spell, Poison Touch.

It's supposed to be a spell that causes poison damage to anything you touch, but I should've known there'd be a catch.

At first, I thought it was pretty strong for a level-1 spell, but go figure—it also hurts me.

It's another suicide-bomber technique. Is it just me, or do I have way too many of those?

It might be handy for deliberately raising my own resistance, but otherwise, I'm not gonna use it.

Oh, but what if I combine it with the level-3 spell, Poison Resist?

Poison Resist is a spell that temporarily increases your poison resistance, so if I use them both at once, I might be able to use Poison Touch.

Still, since I have Poison Synthesis, there's no real reason to do that.

Why would I go out of my way to activate this sad, weak, self-destructive power?

Since it's so ineffective, it wouldn't even help much with proficiency.

I can probably still find a use for Poison Shot, but Poison Touch seems totally worthless.

Next, I'll try out Shadow Magic.

It's, well...yeah. Pretty unimpressive. I could probably make some great shadow puppets now, but that's about it.

I can't test Heretic Magic without a target, so I'll have to try it next time I run into a monster.

Although, since it's a kind of mental attack, I don't know if I'll be able to tell whether it's working just by looking.

Lastly, there's the final boss lurking in the back. Abyss Magic.

The thought of trying this makes my heart pound. For various reasons.

I mean, it's gotta be pretty crazy, right?

When I got Professor Wisdom, I tried Appraising it one more time, but the description was unchanged.

I still have no idea what the spells actually do.

Obviously, it's some kind of advanced Dark Magic, but that's pretty much all I know.

It could be a really powerful asset if I learn how to use it, but not knowing what it might pop out is pretty disturbing.

Thanks to Height of Occultism, I'm not too worried about failing, but it still scares me.

However, out of all the magic skills I have, this is the most magical-seeming magic of all.

I mean, it's got that sinister, "dark arts" kinda ring to it.

How could I not get excited?!

All right, let's start by trying the level-1 spell, Hell Gate.

Here goes! Construct rune!

...Huh?

W-wait a second! Even with Height of Occultism, I still can't control it?!

Why is this construction so ridiculously difficult?! Ugh. I can't do it.

The stupid rune slipped out of my control and fell apart while it was still being formed.

Like, how could that happen?

Height of Occultism is supposed to be the best magic skill there is, just like the name implies.

And even with that skill, I still can't do it?

If it won't work for me, then how could anyone in the world use Abyss Magic?

And if it's this hard to construct, what kind of crazy effects does it have?

What's the point if even the level-1 spell is too hard for anyone to do?

So if you used the level-10 spell, Hell of Treachery, would it end the world or what?

Ha-ha, I'm sure that's not the case. Right? It can't be...right?

Well, if the level-1 spell is this hard, I guess I'd never be able to use the higher ones anyway.

No, wait. I can't give up so easily.

Sure, it was hard. But I only just started using magic. I'm still a beginner.

Other magic users probably work really hard, practicing and raising their skill levels and stuff, but I skipped all that by getting these cheat skills.

In other words, I'm not used to it yet.

That's why I can use simple magic thanks to my skills, but I'm too inexperienced to use the really advanced stuff yet. I bet that's all it is.

In which case, the answer is simple. Practice makes perfect!

So hey. Body brain.

【Hey, information brain. I know what you're getting at, but...】

Oh good, you already know?

【Mm-hmm. What are we gonna do about information if you do that, though?】

I dunno, can't you pick up my slack a little?

【In theory, sure, but if I'm doing twice the work, I probably won't be as efficient...】

Hmm.

<Proficiency has reached the required level.

Skill [Parallel Minds LV 1] has become [Parallel Minds LV 2].>

Wow, perfect timing!

Hello, me number three.

〚Hellooo. Don't worry—I heard everything. Now that I'm here, it'll be fine!〛

Great! All right, number three. You're gonna be magic brain!

〖Okay, I'm on it.〗

So, with Parallel Minds leveled up, I can have three different minds going at once.

The body brain and information brain will stay the same.

And the new magic brain will practice magic, focusing on Abyss Magic, as we go.

Thanks to the Ruler of Wisdom title, my magic proficiency should improve easily, meaning that if I level up Poison Magic and Shadow Magic, too, they should be useful eventually.

On top of that, if we're in battle, the magic brain can independently assist with magic.

Poison Shot doesn't have much going for it on its own, but if used in co-operation with the body brain, its utility value would skyrocket big-time.

It could be used for all sorts of things, like diversions or sudden attacks.

And information brain's role in assessing the situation is important, too.

We're like the Holy Trinity here.

Man, I'm impressed with myself all over again.

My stats have gotten way higher, and now I can move around and shoot magic at the same time.

I know I wouldn't wanna fight me, would you?

Wow. Am I super-strong or what?

All things considered, my Middle Stratum campaign is going pretty well.

I've defeated a ton of monsters, leveled up a bunch, and my skills are growing, too.

In the meantime, Overeating finally reached level 10.

I braced myself, wondering if Gluttony would be next, but instead I got:

‹Gorge: Allows the user to ingest food beyond normal limitations. HP, MP, and SP will recover accordingly. In addition, the excess can be stocked as surplus. Surplus is stored as pure energy, so the user will not gain weight. The amount that can be stocked increases with higher skill levels.›

Well, it's not Gluttony, but it's still pretty amazing.

Basically, instead of just being stocked as SP like with Overeating, it'll also be applied to HP and MP.

The amount that can be stored for those is lower than for SP, but that doesn't make it any less impressive.

Really, any increase to my low HP is enough to make me happy.

And with the effect of Perseverance, when my HP and MP improve, so do my chances for survival.

I already have an excessive amount of MP, but if I can stock on top of that now, so much the better.

I don't really benefit from the not-gaining-weight part, though.

I mean, I didn't gain weight before, either. I wonder why?

The description of Overeating said the user gains weight in proportion to how much they stock, but even when I stuffed myself as much as I could, I never gained any weight.

I don't know if it's some special predisposition because I'm a spider or something, but since now it's more certain that I won't gain weight, I guess there's no reason to worry about it.

That's right. Before the skill leveled up, I had reached the max amount of possible Overeating stock.

The max increased by 100 with each level, stopping at 900.

Now that it's evolved into Gorge, the upper limit's risen a bit more, but I'm guessing it'll stop again at 1,000.

It's probably my anti-wasteful nature as a Japanese person to feel like I need to use my SP once I can't stock any more.

Which is why I've been trying to consume as much SP as possible with my normal movements.

Specifically, by jumping or running as I move forward.

By doing this, I also earn proficiency for skills like Skanda.

As a result, both that skill and some others have leveled up.

Instantaneous and Persistent advanced that way, too, and finally maxed out.

They evolved into Acceleration and Durability, respectively, adding a multiplier to the growth rate of the corresponding stats.

With that, I now have plus corrections on all my stats whenever I level up.

Although my magic-related ones already progressed insanely quickly thanks to Wisdom, and I'm already plenty fast thanks to Skanda.

Hmm. I'm supposed to be a high-speed physical type, but looking at my stats, I seem more like a high-speed magic type.

Professor Wisdom is the main reason for that, but I can't say for sure whether I've actually become a magic specialist now.

I mean, even though my magic-related skills have all gotten better…

…they're still not as strong as Deadly Spider Poison.

So when I'm in a serious scrap, Deadly Spider Poison is my main trump card while magic is more like a support skill.

There really isn't much I can do about that.

My Spider Poison and Spider Thread are the two main reasons I've come this far in the first place, after all.

If magic appeared out of nowhere and surpassed them just like that, it'd feel like all that hard work had been for nothing.

Ugh, I wanna use my threads agaaain. Get me out of here alreadyyy.

When I reach the Upper Stratum, I'm gonna build a home right away and spend some time doing skill research there for a while.

After that, I'm honestly not sure what's next.

I know I'm not supposed to worry about it, but I can't quite put it out of my mind.

Administrators. Skills.

If I want to know more about all that, I'd have to ask someone with more information.

But what do the people in this world think of the administrators anyway? I have no idea.

Really, if you think about it, I can't communicate with anyone here, huh?

【You've got me!】

〖And me!〗

Yeah, but you guys are just me! I'm talking about other people, like actual OTHER people!

Whew. Man, now that there're enough idiots on board, it's extra-hard for me as the information brain, aka the only smart one.

Anyway, yeah, communication.

I didn't do a lot of communicating in my past life, either, but I was able to get data just fine thanks to the Internet.

But not anymore. I have Professor Wisdom, but I can really only look up information about skills.

Besides, even if I could check it, I wouldn't be able to get to the bottom of things.

Any information that might be connected to the administrators can't be Appraised.

Really, from a global perspective, I'm just some homebody who's never once been outside.

I've been in the Great Elroe Labyrinth all my life.

Can you blame me for not knowing anything about the state of the world when I've been trapped inside without any input?

If I want to know more about the administrators, I need to get out of this labyrinth and interact with the various people who live in this world.

But I'm a monster, and I can't talk. How am I supposed to carry on a normal conversation?

Well...I can't do anything about being a monster, but maybe I can find a way to talk after all.

One option is to gain the Telepathy skill.

The other is to evolve into a certain monster.

See? There's another new tool Professor Wisdom gave me: an evolution tree.

Studying it, I can see at a glimpse what kind of monsters I can evolve into in the future.

Whenever I evolved up until now, I just picked mostly going by my gut, but apparently, I had the right idea.

Looking at my evolution tree now, I can see that I've been choosing poison types and relatively rare species. Including my current species, Zoa Ele.

But that's not the point right now.

The real matter at hand is the intel I found about a certain monster that appears further down the line of my evolutionary tree.

Arachne. A monster with the lower body of a spider and the upper body of a human.

As a concept, it's pretty well known even back in Japan.

If I want to evolve into that form, it'll be a bit of a long haul, but I can do it.

And if I have a human upper body, I'll probably be able to talk.

The problem is I'll still be a monster, so I don't know if humans will be willing to talk to me.

Either way, though, being able to have a human body—even just half of one—would be huge.

Sure, I've gotten used to my spider body and all, but what kind of healthy former human girl would want to spend the rest of her life this way?

You wouldn't, would you?

If I have the opportunity to become even partially human, of course I'm gonna go for it.

But there's no point dwelling on that now.

It'll be a long time before I have to decide whether to go that route.

I have to get out of the Middle Stratum before I can even consider leaving the labyrinth in the first place.

I'll worry about the rest later.

S6 EARTH WYRM ATTACK

Shortly after we get back to the school, it suddenly appears.

To be precise, it must have been following us the whole time.

"Wh...what...?"

I hear someone groan in disbelief.

That's how terrifying its presence is.

The earth wyrm.

An incredibly high-powered monster that should never be in a place like this.

And yet, here it is, baring its teeth at us on academy grounds.

"Natsume! Is this another part of your scheme?!"

Ms. Oka confronts Hugo in a rage.

"D-don't look at me! If they planned anything like this, nobody told me!"

Hugo looks genuinely panicked. I don't think he's lying.

"Hey, guys, what the hell is this thing?!"

Hugo turns on the group of criminals arrested for working with him.

"It was supposed to be the ace in the hole for our plan."

"So you guys prepared this?!"

"That's right. A summoner contracted it. But apparently, it's no longer under his influence."

"What? Who was it?!"

"It's me, but I can't stop it now. It was too strong for me to control in the first place. It was docile enough when I first captured and contracted it, but now it won't obey me at all!"

The criminals, all similarly hysterical, rush to answer Hugo's questions.

I barely resist the urge to slap a palm to my forehead.

What kind of idiot summons a monster they can't control?

In my time with Fei, I also acquired Creature Training, a skill necessary for summoners.

But it only lets me handle monsters weaker than myself.

It is possible to form a contract with a stronger monster if they agree to it.

But that only works if there's mutual trust between both parties.

Otherwise, it's entirely possible for the monster to betray the summoner. Like what's happening right now.

The wyrm flexes its sharp nails and beats its huge, log-sized tail.

The students and their seniors who were participating in the exercise are trying to intercept the beast, but the difference in power is clear.

It's no wonder. Appraising it, I can see its stats are all around 2,000. It's incredibly powerful, even for a wyrm.

"Well, doesn't this look great!"

Fei, who'd come out to greet me, communicates her unease through Telepathy.

"At this rate, we'll all be killed. I have to help!"

"Wait just a minute! I won't allow that. It's too dangerous!"

Ms. Oka tries to hold us back.

But I can't just ignore all the people being injured right before my eyes!

I shake Ms. Oka off and run toward the wyrm.

"Well, if that's how it is!"

"I'll come with you, Brother!"

"Let me heal you!"

Katia, Sue, and Yuri follow.

I start preparing magic as I run—the water spell I learned in class.

Activate! A sphere of water flies toward the wyrm.

Just before it hits, though, the attack disappears as if it evaporated.

"It has Imperial Scales!"

Imperial Scales, an advanced version of Dragon Scales possessed by upper-class wyrms.

In addition to a simple increase in defense power, it interferes with the composition of magic spells.

This nasty skill makes landing both magic and physical attacks difficult.

"Students, get back!"

One of the teachers yells at us, but we can't stop now!

I rank among some of the strongest people here.

I can't back down just because I'm a student.

"Sue! Back me up!"

"Right!"

Sue and I release more water magic simultaneously.

The spells combine in midair.

Like me, Sue's highest aptitude is water magic.

If we combine our powers, it might be enough…!

This time, the Water Shot hits the wyrm's body without scattering.

The wyrm roars in discomfort.

This could work! It's not a lot of damage, but at least we can penetrate its defense!

Following our lead, the other teachers and students start combining their spells.

Katia and Professor Oriza work together to shower the wyrm in fire magic.

Then, when it shrinks away, the people who specialize in close combat push in for the attack.

The damage still isn't much, but it's not nothing.

But just as I start feeling hopeful, the earth wyrm stretches its neck.

It's preparing a breath attack.

"Retreat!"

Someone shouts, but there's no time!

Instead, I take a step forward and activate Magic Warfare and Mental Warfare at full power.

At the same time, I use skill points to pick up Light Attack.

Filled with light, my sword intercepts the wyrm's breath.

"Aaaargh!"

Hang in there, body! Come on!

"Honestly! You're so reckless!"

I hear Fei.

At the same time, the breath attack abruptly stops.

My sword swings toward the wyrm's exposed neck and slices right through.

*   *   *

"Don't move, okay? I'll treat you in just a moment."

As the Word of God informs me that I've leveled up, Yuri uses recovery magic to heal my body.

My arms are in particularly bad shape. If the breath attack had lasted any longer, they might've been blown right off.

The thought makes my body tremble belatedly.

Sue and Katia wanted to come check on me, but before they had the chance, they were pulled away to help care for the others who'd been injured.

I don't want them seeing me like this anyway.

When it happened, I was just focused on the battle.

But now that it's over, the terrifying realization that I could've died is sinking in.

At the same time, the sword still clutched in my hand as if frozen in my grip looks terrifying to me now.

The feeling I experienced when severing the earth wyrm's head remains vivid.

This is what it means to take a life. This is a real battle.

I was confident I could fight because of my high stats and skills.

And in theory, that's exactly what I did.

But now that the battle's over, I've realized something.

I didn't have a clue what combat really means.

Is fighting always this scary?

Killing…?

Slowly, I release the sword.

My fingers move stiffly, as if they're numb with cold.

Only when Yuri finishes healing me do they finally let go completely.

Assuring me that everything's okay now, Yuri is dispatched to heal others.

My injury is all right now. But I can't say the same for my mental state.

Honestly, it's pathetic.

Sure, I didn't expect to fight something so huge in my first battle, but I shouldn't be freaking out this much.

Especially when the fight's already over.

My older brother Julius fights battles like this practically every day.

If I want to catch up to him, I should be able to get over something like this without a problem.

And look—now a few people are eyeing me worriedly.

I have to smile and reassure them I'm okay.

I'm sure that's what my brother would do. Come on. Smile!

...I can't do it.

I'm scared. Scared that I could have been killed. Scared that I killed a living thing.

How can my brother, or any of the inhabitants of this world, do such a terrible thing so easily?

How could Hugo try to kill me like that?

If it's this upsetting just slaying a monster that had to be defeated anyway, how could anyone stay sane after killing another person?

Why would anyone even consider such a thing?

Or is it just that Hugo had already gone mad a long time ago?

That's definitely possible.

Hugo had the title Monster Slayer.

It's something you receive after defeating a host of monsters.

Which means Hugo's already killed tons.

That he's done what I just did over and over.

Maybe he grew accustomed to it somewhere along the way.

Numb to the act of killing.

Will that happen to me, too, someday?

I'm terrified. Just imagining it makes it hard to breathe.

I inhale deeply and try to calm down.

I still can't sort out my feelings about all this.

But if the person who's supposed to lead the way to victory is in such a sorry state, it'll be hard for everyone else to celebrate.

I don't think I can smile just yet, but I should at least try to put on a dignified air.

Even if it feels like it's a little late for that.

Just then, I notice Fei nearby, looking at the fallen earth wyrm.

Fei was the one who saved me.

At that crucial moment, she bit the wyrm's neck, interrupting its breath attack.

If she hadn't, I might have been killed.

"Fei, you saved my life. Thank you."

I push down the fear threatening to rise again as I offer a belated thank-you.

"Sure. Don't mention it."

Fei continues staring distractedly at the dead wyrm.

"What's the matter?"

"Take a look at my status."

Puzzled, I obediently Appraise my vaguely depressed-looking companion. Then I notice her new title.

[Kin Eater]

As its name suggests, it's a terrible title conferred on those who have eaten the flesh of a blood relative.

"It...can't be..."

"I don't see any other explanation, do you?"

Fei must have bitten right through the wyrm's neck.

If so, her grant of this title would make sense.

In fact, that's the only way it could have happened.

"I wonder if that wyrm came here...looking for me?"

It's...not impossible.

Fei's egg was found in the Great Elroe Labyrinth, a dungeon far from here. If that wyrm wasn't one of Fei's parents, I can't see any other reason why it would have come all the way here.

In which case, a parent who'd come looking for its kidnapped offspring might have been killed at the hands of that very child.

Which means I decapitated one of her parents right in front of her...

"Ugh...*bleegh!*"

I empty my stomach.

My first real battle has become a truly bitter memory that will be forever seared into my mind.

Interlude DESPAIR OF THE DEFEATED

"Shit! I won't let it end like this! This is my world! It exists for me, only for me! Like I'd accept this ending?! Not a chance in hell! It's not over until everything is mine!"

<Proficiency has reached the required level. Acquired skill [Desire LV 1].>

"Damn that elf! I'll have my revenge! She'll goddamn well rue the day she messed with me!"

<Proficiency has reached the required level. Acquired skill [Wrath LV 1].>

"I'll take everything from her someday! Just like she did to me!"

<Proficiency has reached the required level. Acquired skill [Usurp LV 1].>

"Just you wait! I'll destroy all she holds dear! Then I'll beat her to a pulp while she wails and cries over their remains!"

<Proficiency has reached the required level. Acquired skill [Crude LV 1].>

"You watch! I'm gonna take this world back for myself!"

THE DUKE'S DAUGHTER AND THE
NOISY REINCARNATIONS

"Fei, are you okay?"

"I'm fiiine. Sure, it was a bit of a surprise, but...even if that was one of my parents, it's not like we ever met, right?"

"Gotcha. Make sure Yuri doesn't find out about this, all right?"

"Good point. If she found out I have Taboo now, she'd probably kill me."

"Hmm? Did someone say my name?"

"Huh?! I definitely didn't!"

"Don't pop up out of nowhere like that! It's bad for my heart."

"What do you mean? I just walked over here quite normally."

"It's all right. I'll just have to scare you as compensation for the year I just lost off my life."

"What?! Why?!"

"Oh hey, so are you giving Shun a pass on your missionary work today?"

"Oh, I already did it earlier."

"You did, huh...?"

"Why, I couldn't possibly abandon my mission to convey God's greatness to others! Even if you don't understand it now, I'm sure the time will come when you all recognize God's glory!"

"Can't wait."

"I just realized, this whole blind faith thing is a bit like those ridiculous siblings."

"Oh yeah, I think I know what you mean. Shun is a Follower of Julius, and Sue is a Follower of Shun."

"Quite so! He treats me like a religious fanatic, but he doesn't realize that he's a hero fanatic himself! Isn't that just awful?!"

"That's rich coming from you."

"I guess I kinda get what you mean, though. When it comes to Julius, that guy never shuts up."

"Yeah, I've heard enough tales of the hero's bravery to teach a class on it myself."

"Like the one where a poor village couldn't afford to pay for monster extermination, so he saved them free of charge?"

"How do you feel about that, as part of the Church the hero is supposed to work for?"

"Well, he isn't supposed to do things like that, but...he makes up for it by donating to the Church himself, so the higher-ups can't really complain."

"That's royalty for you. Is he loaded or what?"

"Yeah, he's got the support of the whole kingdom behind him. If the hero were just a commoner, he'd probably be wielded like a weapon and sent out on all kinds of dangerous missions. But if anyone tries to force Julius to do too much, they risk making him an enemy of the Church."

"Seems complicated."

"Yeah, and apparently, Julius takes it upon himself to do dangerous work like that anyway."

"He's quite the hero!"

"I've actually met him, too, and he totally lives up to the hype. His existence itself is a miracle."

"I guess with an older brother like that, you'd either rebel or end up worshipping him."

"Maybe it's better this than rebelling, then?"

"Sure, I think so. Wanting to follow in his brother's footsteps is the manly thing to do."

"I'm not sure how convincing that is, coming from a former man."

"I'm pretty sure I'm still a man on the inside, thanks."

"No you're not." "Yeah, right."

"What's with the instant rebuttals?!"

"Ah-ha-ha. Still, I'd love to meet Sir Julius for myself."

"You haven't? Aren't you the future saint?"

"I'm still just a candidate for now. As long as the current saint, Lady Yaana, still lives, it's strictly hypothetical. As a mere future saint, I have no relation to the hero. A new saint is only born when the current saint or the current hero passes away."

"So if the hero dies, the saint gets replaced even if she's still alive?"

"Of course. A saint only serves one hero. So if Sir Julius died, a new saint would be chosen even if Lady Yaana lived... Ah, but it's improper to speak of such things."

"It's all right. Shun may be blinded by admiration when it comes to Julius, but nobody's invincible. There was even a time when he fell into a demon's trap and was poisoned. If a full-blown war with demons breaks out, there's no guarantee even Julius would survive."

"That's true. We can't talk about it in front of Shun, but apparently, fighting a real demon is quite difficult."

"Yes, and the long-silent demon lord has started moving again."

"Yeah. According to the rumors, it might've been right around when we were babies."

"It seems like a lot happened around that time, doesn't it? The religious war between the Word of God and the Goddess, the appearance of the Nightmare of the Labyrinth, and so on."

"The goddess is a false idol!"

"Ah, sure, sure. The Nightmare of the Labyrinth... That was the spider monster that dealt Julius his first and only defeat, right?"

"I overheard him talking about it with Shun. It sounds almost like the demon lord!"

"What if it really was?"

"How could a spider be the lord of demons? I thought all demons were humanoid."

"Yeah, but maybe it had a Humanification skill, like what you're after, Fei."

"You know there's no such skill as Humanification, right?"

"Oh, so there isn't..."

"There's not. Although, I suppose it's possible there are skills that could do something similar."

"Well, they say demons look exactly like humans, so if a monster could disguise itself as human, it could probably mingle with demons."

"That's misleading. Demons really ought to at least have horns or something."

"Wouldn't that make it a devil, not a demon?"

"I've never heard any such distinction."

"Hmm. Say, this is just a thought, but…a new demon lord took over right around when we were born, right? Could you imagine if the demon lord was one of us reincarnations?"

"Yo, don't even joke about that. Besides, that'd mean the demon lord was a baby at the time, too."

"Oh dear. I'm sorry."

"I doubt a baby could become a demon lord so quickly unless it spent every waking moment from the time it was born moving around and leveling up."

"Wow, talk about a horror story."

Wow. This sucks.

A lake of magma stretches in front of me as far as I can see. And this time, there's no path through it.

Did I take a wrong turn somewhere?

I don't think that's possible. The layout of the Middle Stratum is pretty much just a single, fairly expansive passage stretching ahead.

It's more than half a mile wide, though, so I don't know if "passage" is really the right word.

Anyway, that means I have to cross this magma lake to advance.

Luckily, while there's no path, there are at least some small islands dotted throughout.

With my jumping strength, I can leap from island to island, or even go by way of the ceiling if I have to.

Man, how would a human ever get past this, though?

I bet they can only survive in the Upper Stratum.

I mean, logically speaking, how could anyone conquer a labyrinth that's bigger than Hokkaido?

They'd have to be a hero or have some legendary power or something.

I don't know if that sort of thing even exists here.

Maybe if an administrator took a liking to a beautiful youth and gave them a special ability or something?

Wow, that'd be unfair.

You should give it to me instead!

No dice, huh? Okay, I guess that makes sense.

Whoops. I got a little off track for a second there.

Anyway, yeah, technically, I can get past this, but there's a problem.

There are tons of monsters lurking inside.

On top of being enormously wide, this magma lake is pretty deep, too.

At its deepest, it can go as deep as six hundred feet.

If there's that much magma, shouldn't it cool down and harden or something?

Apparently not. It forms a huge freaking lake.

And in this expansive, deep lake, there are tons of monsters.

I'm supposed to cross this?

Man, what's up with this labyrinth?

I don't see how anyone's supposed to beat it.

Ugh. Well, it's not like I have any other choice, so I'll just have to cross it.

I'm sure it'll work out somehow, right?

Besides, I was able to beat that eel, so I doubt anything else would pose much of a threat. I doubt there are too many monsters around as strong as that.

Even if there are, I'll just beat them at their own game.

I've evolved since I fought the eel, literally and figuratively. My stats have gotten crazy good, my skills have improved, and most importantly, I can use magic now!

Heh-heh-heh, I couldn't touch monsters while they were in the magma before, but now that I know magic, no hole-up-at-home strategy will work against me!

I'll snipe you with my magic! Bwa-ha-ha!

I have new skills besides magic, too.

First of all, Evil Eye.

I got my second Evil Eye skill, too. This time, I chose Paralyzing Evil Eye.

Petrification was tempting, too, but it takes a long time for its effects to kick in, and worse, I can't eat something that's been petrified.

So instead, I chose paralysis, which renders things immobile much more quickly while keeping them perfectly edible.

I also learned a skill called Magic Warfare.

You can use it to consume MP in exchange for raising stats. I happened to pick it up just by focusing on cycling magical power through my body.

So basically, this is the MP-consumption version of Mental Warfare, which uses SP. But thanks to Height of Occultism, I don't need to worry about spending my MP.

Even if I keep it active all the time, it recovers more quickly than the rate of consumption.

So at the moment, I'm keeping it active all the time.

As a result, now my stats are even higher.

I've also been occasionally activating Mental Warfare with an eye for my amount of Satiation stock, slowly raising its skill level.

If I activate both at once, my stats improve drastically, so I can use that as a trump card for sure.

Satiation is a pretty amazing skill, as it turns out.

I mean, it even stocks automatic recovery.

So my HP and MP stocks have been bolstered in no time.

My MP, especially, is getting to the point where I can't possibly use it all.

I can activate Magic Warfare, keep both Evil Eyes on nonstop—and even practice magic—and still have plenty of MP to spare.

Height of Occultism is crazy powerful. So is Satiation, which stocks any excess.

Although, I haven't been able to save as much MP because of the magma damage.

So now that I have magic as a long-range-attack method and my stats are vastly improved, I'm sure I could take down an eel without breaking a sweat.

Which means there's no reason to be afraid of a little magma lake!

If any small-fry attack me, I'll just bring 'em down and eat 'em.

Time for my first jump!

I leap over the magma and land on a little island.

It's a little scary, but I can always retreat to the ceiling if I have to, so I think I can make it work.

I'm still hopping my way across.

Hmm. It's going so smoothly that it's actually a little boring.

I haven't been attacked by a single monster.

Honestly, I was so prepared for a fight that it's almost more of a letdown than a relief.

No, it's fine, though. Peace is a good thing.

But if it's too peaceful, I could run out of SP, so it'd be nice if a monster would attack once in a while. Purely as a food source, of course.

If it's a tasty monster, so much the better. Like catfish, or catfish, or maybe catfish.

C'mon, can't one poke its little head out of the magma for me?

Sploosh.

<Elroe gunesohka   LV 17

Status:

HP: 2,331/2,331 (green) (details)	MP: 1,894/1,894 (blue) (details)
SP: 2,119/2,119 (yellow) (details)	: 2,315/2,315 (red) +264 (details)
Average Offensive Ability: 1,999 (details)	Average Defensive Ability: 1,876 (details)
Average Magical Ability: 1,551 (details)	Average Resistance Ability: 1,528 (details)
Average Speed Ability: 1,657 (details)	

Skills:

[Fire Wyrm LV 9]	[Imperial Scales LV 2]	[HP Auto-Recovery LV 2]	[MP Auto-Recovery LV 1]
[MP Lessened Consumption LV 1]	[SP Recovery Speed LV 3]	[SP Lessened Consumption LV 3]	[Flame Attack LV 5]
[Flame Enhancement LV 3]	[Destruction Enhancement LV 2]	[Impact Enhancement LV 4]	[Cooperation LV 5]
[Leadership LV 7]	[Hit LV 10]	[Evasion LV 10]	[Probability Correction LV 8]
[Presence Perception LV 4]	[Danger Perception LV 7]	[High-Speed Swimming LV 7]	[Overeating LV 8]
[Impact Resistance LV 6]	[Heat Nullification]	[Longevity LV 1]	[Instantaneous LV 8]
[Persistent LV 9]	[Herculean Strength LV 1]	[Sturdy LV 1]	[Technique User LV 4]
[Protection LV 4]	[Running LV 5]		

Skill Points: 11,250

Titles:

[Monster Slayer]	[Monster Slaughterer]	[Commander]

>

Something came out?!

It's a wyrm.

It's way more legit than the eel. A real, 100 percent genuine wyrm.

Judging by its skill set and such, it may be an even-further-evolved form of the eel.

You couldn't even call this thing a fish. It's a fire wyrm, plain and simple.

Aah, this is not good!

Imperial Scales is a superior version of Dragon Scales, with a much higher effect.

I didn't care about its effect of interfering with magic construction and weakening magic's power, but now it poses a big problem.

The eel's Dragon Scales probably wouldn't have been strong enough to dissolve my Height of Occultism–enhanced magic, but this fire wyrm's Imperial Scales may just do the trick.

Plus the Hit / Probability Correction combo that gave me so much trouble when I fought the eel is still going strong.

Not to mention, now it even has Evasion.

And it's fully loaded with fire-attribute attacks, my biggest weakness.

But the most dangerous thing of all might be its Cooperation and Leadership skills.

My Detection skill is alerting me about monsters popping out of the magma, one after the other.

Cooperation and Leadership have effects that absolutely live up to their names.

Cooperation improves the ability to work together, and Leadership makes subordinates follow commands.

They're both skills you get with the title Leader, which is an extra layer of trickiness.

This title has the effect of slightly raising the subordinates' stats.

I'm completely surrounded by a swarm of monsters.

And the fire wyrm is their boss.

I know I said I could beat an eel no problem, but no one told me something this strong was gonna show!

Body brain!

【Yeah, let's run for it!】

Our decision is immediate. I don't think I could even beat this freak one-on-one, never mind with a whole army of flunkies.

In that case, running is my only shot.

The footing here is bad—no, it's the worst—but it's still my best option.

I jump over to an island opposite the fire wyrm.

Immediately after making the move, Detection informs me the island I was standing on before has gone up in flames.

Oh, geez! I know it was tiny, but still, it got swallowed whole!

I don't think I can escape across these things.

The fireballs that wyrm spits out are too huge and too powerful.

Even with my new and improved stats, if I get hit with one of those, there'll be nothing left.

I land on the next island, then immediately leap toward the following.

But while I'm in the air, a bunch of sea horses pop out of the magma and pepper fireballs at me.

It's like antiaircraft fire.

Countless projectiles fly in a beeline toward me with pinpoint accuracy, as if the sea horses had trained together for this moment.

I've seen sea horses in groups before but never working together like this. Thanks to the leadership of the fire wyrm, though, they're attacking in perfect sync.

I feel like I'm fighting a whole army.

No sense holding anything back.

On top of Magic Warfare, I also invoke Mental Warfare.

Then I shoot an Energy Conferment–enhanced thread toward the ceiling, using it to escape to the ceiling before my modified silk catches fire.

Tons of fireballs pass by directly below me, almost grazing my feet.

But already, a much bigger fireball is zeroing in on my spot on the ceiling. It's one of the fire wyrm's.

I race along the ceiling and manage to avoid the missile.

When it connects, the fireball destroys a portion of the cavern, scattering flames and debris everywhere.

If that hit me in the air, even if I still had HP left, I'd plunge into the magma.

The sea horses put up another fusillade.

I avoid most of them and douse the rest with Poison Shot.

Poison Shot has some degree of physical attack power.

If it hits something flying through the air, it can cancel it out.

And since Poison Shot is a simple spell and I have Height of Occultism and a portion of my mind dedicated purely to magic, I can even use it rapid-fire.

Of course, I can't produce them fast enough to counter every single fireball this army of sea horses chucks at me, but I can at least use it to offset the ones I can't dodge.

Until a fireball that I can't dispel comes barreling toward me.

A really, really humongous one.

And it's from the direction I was headed.

I can't avoid it on the ceiling, so I let myself fall, landing on a nearby island.

Immediately, a bright-red flower blooms on the ceiling.

I look forward.

That wasn't the wyrm's fireball.

Instead, my way forward is blocked by eels.

Not just one, but three.

I'm in checkmate.

Eels at the front gate. A fire wyrm at the rear.

If it were just one eel, I might be able to break through, but getting past a group of three will be virtually impossible.

So I turn back toward the fire wyrm, since there's only one of those, but it's closing on me with its army of countless sea horses.

On top of that, it's accompanied by a fourth eel.

This is bad.

The only way I can survive is by avoiding the enemies' attacks and reducing their numbers.

Even small-fry like the sea horse can be big trouble in such large numbers.

I have to bring those numbers down if I want to stand a chance.

There's nothing funny about being assailed by a wall of fireballs!

Right now, the only saving grace is that the fire wyrm's leadership is actually too perfect.

Basically, the attacks aimed at me are a little too accurate.

There are so many of them that it would be a simple matter to carpet the whole area, leaving me with nowhere to go, but instead, they all target me directly.

As long as I have somewhere to run, I can avoid them.

I sprint off to the side, trying to break through the siege of the fire wyrm and the eels.

As I run, I activate magic.

Poison Magic level 6: Poison Fog.

As the name suggests, it's a spell that generates a toxic cloud.

It'd be great if I had a spell that would directly attack a wide range in one shot, but this is the only weapon in my arsenal capable of affecting multiple enemies at once.

It's not as strong as my Deadly Spider Poison, so it won't drain their HP in an instant, but if they keep breathing it in, the poison will gradually eat away at them.

If I can just keep escaping, this fog should reduce their numbers significantly!

But of course things won't be so easy.

Some of the sea horses come on land to block my path.

Grr, out of my way!

I swing my scythes toward the standing sea horses.

Each of the scythes bisects a sea horse to my left and the right.

That's how strong my scythe attack has become with my improved stats.

Swinging my forelegs back, I cut down two more sea horses.

At the same time, I jump straight into the air!

A fireball smashes into the ground where I was standing less than a second ago.

The blast accelerates my body all the more, and I reach the ceiling without using any thread.

But the aftershock alone was enough to decrease my HP significantly.

Catching sight of an eel getting ready to unleash a fireball, I synthesize some Deadly Spider Poison half out of desperation.

Paying no attention to how much MP it consumes, I maximize the amount.

Instantly, a huge ball of poison far bigger than I am appears and drops.

The giant glob of poison collides with the eel's fireball and bursts in midair.

The majority is evaporated, but what's left falls down like rain.

There may not be much, but it's still my Deadly Spider Poison.

Even that tiny amount manages to bring down several of the weakling sea horses.

Perfect.

I scurry along the ceiling before the next fireball arrives.

As I move, I synthesize more Deadly Spider Poison, spraying it everywhere.

The fire wyrm and the eels hesitate. Maybe they're afraid to disperse the lethal concoction with their fireballs.

They frantically scramble to avoid the falling poison.

The Poison Fog is taking effect, too; one by one, more of the sea horses fall.

Hey, this is going pretty well. If I just keep scattering poison as I run, maybe I can get away.

<Experience has reached the required level. Individual Zoa Ele has increased from LV 6 to LV 7.>
<All basic attributes have increased.>
<Skill proficiency level-up bonus acquired.>
<Proficiency has reached the required level.
    Skill [Threadsmanship LV 3] has become [Threadsmanship LV 4].>
<Skill points acquired.>

Wha...?!

Shoot. I'm molting.

If this happens while I'm on the ceiling, it'll slow me way down.

Sure enough, as soon as the peeling husk stops me in my tracks, an eel lands a direct hit on me with a fireball.

Ow! Hot! I'm gonna die!

I'm falling.

Luckily, there's an island directly beneath me.

Safe! I managed to avoid landing in the magma. Lucky me.

Good thing that shot came from an eel and not the fire wyrm. Otherwise, I'd have gone up in smoke on the spot.

Still, one hit from the eel's fireball has me living on Perseverance.

It's already drained my usually excessive stock of MP in half.

I never imagined that molting, after helping me out so many times, would screw me over like that.

But I survived!

A giant figure approaches, interrupting my relief.

One of the eels is charging me, its body covered in flames.

I'd escape, but there's no time.

I use Rot Attack on one of my scythes.

Immediately, intense pain runs through the leg, but I ignore it.

Just barely dodging to the side of the charging eel, I raise my Rot-infused scythe and chop away.

Despite the eel's Dragon Scales, the scythe slices through with no resistance.

Rot Attack really is terrifying.

<Experience has reached the required level. Individual Zoa Ele has increased from LV 7 to LV 8.>

<All basic attributes have increased.>

<Skill proficiency level-up bonus acquired.>

<Skill points acquired.>

<Experience has reached the required level. Individual Zoa Ele has increased from LV 8 to LV 9.>

<All basic attributes have increased.>

<Skill proficiency level-up bonus acquired.>

<Proficiency has reached the required level.

Skill [Mental Warfare LV 3] has become [Mental Warfare LV 4].>

<Skill points acquired.>

I can't believe I killed an eel in one blow.

Pieces of its body sink into the magma.

Part of it stays intact, of course, but the areas where it was cut collapse as if they've turned to sand.

Meanwhile, thanks to my molting, my self-destructed scythe is fully recovered.

Now there are three eels and the fire wyrm left.

Thanks to the Poison Fog, most of the sea horses have been downed.

<Experience has reached the required level. Individual Zoa Ele has increased from LV 9 to LV 10.>

<All basic attributes have increased.>

<Skill proficiency level-up bonus acquired.>
<Proficiency has reached the required level.
    Skill [Poison Magic LV 6] has become [Poison Magic LV 7].>
<Proficiency has reached the required level.
    Skill [Poison Enhancement LV 6] has become [Poison Enhancement LV 7].>
<Skill points acquired.>

<Condition satisfied. Acquired title [Wyrm Slayer].>
<Acquired skills [Life LV 1] [Wyrm Power LV 1] as a result of title [Wyrm Slayer].>
<Skill [Life LV 1] has been integrated into [Longevity LV 1].>

Oh. When the last sea horse went down, I leveled up and gained some kind of title.

Maybe I can do this?

I activate Cursed Evil Eye and Paralyzing Evil Eye in four eyes each.

Matching the number of remaining opponents perfectly.

Apparently, this makes the fire dragon and the eels uncomfortable as they start frantically shooting fireballs at me.

I run.

Two of the eels pursue.

It's like a pincer attack, with one on either side.

That's not gonna work on me now!

I dodge with a vertical leap.

But it seems the fire dragon anticipated that.

A fireball homes in on me while I'm in midair.

Guess my patterns were getting predictable.

That sucks, but nobody said I can't move while airborne!

I create some shock-enhanced thread and smack myself with it before it burns up.

The shock runs through my body.

The resultant impact sends me soaring.

Ha! With this little trick, I can practically fly—

—as long as I don't mind taking a chunk out of my own HP anyway!

Its target gone, the fireball lobs uselessly through empty space.

I watch it with satisfaction even as I tailspin, then use some thread to land properly on the ceiling this time.

By now, the eels have fallen victim to my Paralyzing Evil Eye, floating totally stiff in the water.

All that's left now is the fire dragon.

Possibly in a last-ditch effort, the fire dragon's body erupts in flames as it charges.

I counter with more magic.

My newly acquired Poison Magic level-7 spell, Paralysis Shot.

Game, set, match.

Once the effects of Paralyzing Evil Eye have set in, the victim will remain paralyzed as long as you keep looking at them.

Paralysis Shot, on the other hand, wears off gradually, but that's not a problem as long as I keep my Paralyzing Evil Eye on them.

Now that I've paralyzed the fire dragon, I've won. I can boil it, mash it, stick it in a stew…whatever.

No matter how high its stats may be, they're no match for my ability to inflict status conditions.

Now that I've captured it so beautifully, it'd be a waste to just let it sink into the magma.

There's nothing I can do about the sea horses and the eel that already sank, but I can't let any more valuable food go to waste.

Using some spider thread and a great deal of elbow grease, I manage to yank my prey onto land.

What a pain. The thread kept catching fire, so I had to keep making more and repeating the process.

Now then, I guess I should finish off these losers.

First, the eels.

Since they're already paralyzed, I go ahead and toss some Deadly Spider Poison right down the first one's gullet.

Despite its paralysis, the eel gives a final shudder before its strength runs out.

<Experience has reached the required level. Individual Zoa Ele has increased from LV 10 to LV 11.>

<All basic attributes have increased.>
<Skill proficiency level-up bonus acquired.>
<Proficiency has reached the required level.
   Skill [Spatial Maneuvering LV 8] has become [Spatial Maneuvering LV 9].>
<Skill points acquired.>

Watching this, the other eels' faces contort in fear.

Don't you worry. The suffering will only last a moment.

I pop more poison into the second eel's mouth.

<Experience has reached the required level. Individual Zoa Ele has increased from LV 11 to LV 12.>
<All basic attributes have increased.>
<Skill proficiency level-up bonus acquired.>
<Proficiency has reached the required level.
   Skill [Evasion LV 8] has become [Evasion LV 9].>
<Skill points acquired.>

<Condition satisfied. Acquired title [Fearbringer].>
<Acquired skills [Intimidation LV 1] [Heretic Attack LV 1] as a result of title [Fearbringer].>

I got a title. Man, it's another creepy-sounding one.

Geez, going by titles alone, everyone's gonna think I'm some kinda crazy person.

Oh wait, I'm a spider, not a person.

Well, I'll check it out later.

Same with this Wyrm Slayer title or whatever.

For now, I have to finish my business with these guys.

So here, third eel, I have a special present for you.

I worked really hard to make this, so you'd better appreciate it. C'mon, say "Ahh."

How was it? Oh, so delicious that you died? That's sweet.

〖Information brain, you're scary!〗

【Nice one! Keep it up!】

Oh, you guys are back?

【Yep. I don't think we need to be at max synchronization level anymore.】

"Max synchronization level" is a name I randomly coined for a Parallel Minds technique.

Like the name implies, it lets me sync all of my separate minds so we can act as one without the slightest lag.

Basically, it's like having a single mind that can do three different things at once.

I guess the only real downside is I can't have conversations among my selves when we're synced up.

〖We won more easily than I expected.〗

Yeah, I didn't think it was gonna go this well, either.

Maybe I've gotten even stronger than I thought.

Thanks to the new attack methods that magic enables, the range of strategies I can employ is much wider now.

Above all, now I know just how powerful status conditions like poison and paralysis can be.

Damn, dude.

I guess there's no way to avoid paralysis no matter how strong you are.

Like this fire wyrm here.

【Good thing that fire wyrm was so stupid.】

〖Yeah, if I were him, I'd have run away when things went south.〗

Totally. Why wouldn't you retreat when your losses start getting that heavy?

I suppose it was a muscle head who didn't know when to withdraw, just like the sea horses.

Maybe it's because it never got into such a pinch before?

〖Ohhh, maybe.〗

【Yeah, it probably didn't think it would lose.】

Exactly. I feel kinda bad now, so let's finish it off.

And so I give the fire wyrm what may have been its first (and certainly last) taste of defeat.

<Experience has reached the required level. Individual Zoa Ele has increased from LV 12 to LV 13.>

<All basic attributes have increased.>
<Skill proficiency level-up bonus acquired.>
<Proficiency has reached the required level.
  Skill [Destruction Enhancement LV 2] has become [Destruction Enhancement LV 3].>
<Proficiency has reached the required level.
  Skill [Destruction Resistance LV 3] has become [Destruction Resistance LV 4].>
<Skill points acquired.>

<Experience has reached the required level. Individual Zoa Ele has increased from LV 13 to LV 14.>
<All basic attributes have increased.>
<Skill proficiency level-up bonus acquired.>
<Proficiency has reached the required level.
  Skill [Rot Resistance LV 3] has become [Rot Resistance LV 4].>
<Skill points acquired.>

<Experience has reached the required level. Individual Zoa Ele has increased from LV 14 to LV 15.>
<All basic attributes have increased.>
<Skill proficiency level-up bonus acquired.>
<Proficiency has reached the required level.
  Skill [Impact Resistance LV 2] has become [Impact Resistance LV 3].>
<Skill points acquired.>

<Proficiency has reached the required level. Acquired skill [Demon Lord LV 1].>

Okay, body brain!
【Yeah, yeah. I've got some boring work ahead of me.】
Yep. I'm counting on you to de-scale these things.
It's nice to be able to foist work like this off on someone else now.
Meanwhile, I'll take a look at the effects of the skills and titles I acquired.
Starting with this Demon Lord skill.

Man, what's that supposed to mean?

<Demon Lord: Increases each stat by the number of the skill level ×100. Also raises all resistances.>

Ooh. That's a pretty sweet skill. Thanks, Demon Lord.

Next, let's check out these titles.

<Wyrm Slayer: Acquired skills [Life LV 1] [Wyrm Power LV 1]. Acquisition condition: Defeat a certain number of wyrm-type monsters. Effect: Slight increase in damage to wyrm- and dragon-type opponents. Description: A title awarded to those who bring down a large amount of wyrms.>

<Fearbringer: Acquired skills [Intimidation LV 1] [Heretic Magic LV 1]. Acquisition condition: Induce a certain amount of proficiency in Fear Resistance in others. Effect: Inflicts the heresy attribute effect "Fear" on anyone who sees the holder. Description: A title awarded to those who personify fear.>

Whoa! Wyrm Slayer's nice and all, but the effect of Fearbringer is crazy!

So just looking at me is fear inducing now?

That's not good!

I mean, it's great for enemies and all, but making everyone else scared of me isn't helpful in the least!

There's no way to turn titles on and off, is there?

Hoo, boy. Does this mean cowardly monsters like catfish are gonna run away as soon as they lay eyes on me?

Aw, man. Well, guess there's nothing I can do, since I've already got it.

Okay, shake it off. Time to look at the other skills.

I'm pretty sure I've seen them on the list before, but I don't remember the effects at all.

Ugh. I have the worst memory ever.

Should I grab the Memory skill or something? Oh, whatever.

<Wyrm Power: Temporarily gain the power of a wyrm>

Hmm? Hmm. I don't get it.

It seems to be the kind of skill that you have to activate, so I'll give it a try.

Oh? It looks like my stats went up a little.

And I lost a little MP and SP.

Guess this skill consumes a bit of MP and SP to raise my stats.

Unlike Magic Warfare and Mental Warfare, it also raises my magic stats.

Since it's level 1, it doesn't do much, but it might become pretty powerful if I level it up by keeping it on all the time.

The combination of Magic Warfare and Mental Warfare already has a pretty potent effect, but if you add Wyrm Power on top of that...

Niiice. Yes waaay.

<Intimidate: Inflicts the heresy attribute effect "Fear" on surrounding area>

You too, huh?

Unlike the title, I can at least turn this off and on, but wouldn't the combination of the two make pretty much any monster that sees me turn tail and run instantly?

Oh well. I can't turn the title off anyway, so I may as well keep this on all the time.

It doesn't seem to cost anything, in any case.

<Heretic Attack: Adds the heresy attribute "Rend Soul" to attacks>

Oh, great.

<Heresy Attribute "Rend Soul": An attribute that directly disrupts the soul>

This isn't just a "mental attack" anymore!

This is waaay creepy.

I'll have to try it out soon. Yep.

So Wyrm Slayer just ended up being a minor stat boost.

And Fearbringer... I'm not sure whether it's a good thing or a bad thing, on the whole.

It could be really good, but it could also be really bad.

Well, that's it for titles.

I have a bunch of skill points now.

And since I leveled up so much, I have quite a few.

Now I can get that skill I wanted!

Hee-hee. I didn't think I'd be getting it so soon.

<Spatial Magic (500): Magic that manipulates space>

There it is. Spatial Magic is a staple of cheating.

I'm sure I won't be able to use the kind of spells I want right away, since it'll start at level 1, but thanks to Ruler of Wisdom, my magic skills level up really quickly.

If I work hard at it, it should get to a useful level in no time.

Heh-heh-heh. I've got high expectations for you, Spatial Magic. I expect Teleport to be on my desk by Monday!

I mean, it's gotta exist, right?

What's Spatial Magic if not stuff like Teleport, Item Box, and hosting a villa in another dimension?!

There might be an Item Box–type skill that lets you store objects in another dimension, but I'm not in the habit of carrying stuff around in the first place, so it wouldn't be much use to me.

A villa would be nice, but given that's probably really high-level if it exists at all, I don't think I'll get it anytime soon.

But then there's Teleport. A wonderful spell that moves you to a different area in an instant.

If I can get Teleportation, I won't need to traipse all over the Middle Stratum anymore!

Thanks to Professor Wisdom, I have a map of the Upper Stratum!

If I can get it to work with the map, then I bet I could use Teleport to get there in a blink!

All right, Divine Voice (temp.)!

Spatial Magic, please!

<Number of skill points currently in possession: 500. Number of skill points required to acquire skill [Spatial Magic LV 1]: 500. Acquire skill?>

Hell yeah!

<[Spatial Magic LV 1] acquired. Remaining skill points: 0.>

Okay. Let's try out the level-1 spell right away.

Magic brain!

〖Aye, aye, sir!〗

Magic brain activates the level-1 Spatial Magic spell posthaste.

The level-1 spell is called Coordinate Designation.

Some kind of cube made up of green lines appears.

Magic brain can make it bigger and smaller, change its shape, and move it to the left and right.

Apparently, it's nonphysical because it sinks into the ground as well as magma.

It reminds me of selecting a range of objects on a PC. In fact, I think that's exactly what it is.

〖Looks like all this spell does is designate a space.〗

What good is it, then?

〖Maybe it's a preliminary setup thing for the higher-level spells?〗

Right, that makes sense.

So I guess this is another skill that won't be any use until it's a higher level, like Shadow Magic.

〖Yep.〗

Hmm.

Well, I wasn't expecting it to be useful in combat or anything right off the bat, so what really matters is that I got it for now.

We'll just have to level it up quickly.

You know what to do, right, magic brain?

〖Focus on this more than other magic, right?〗

Yeah. By the way, how many different kinds of magic can you activate at once right now?

〖Depends on the kind of magic. But Coordinate Designation doesn't seem too hard, so I think I could do two other spells at the same time as long as they're simple ones.〗

Gotcha. Try and stock up on proficiency while we're on the move as much as you can, then, 'kay?

〖Yessir.〗

Body brain is still busy with de-scaling.

Makes sense, since there are three eels, and the fire wyrm's about twice the size of one.

Looks like it'll be a while before we can do a fire wyrm taste test.

Man, though, I can't believe I beat a whole gang of monsters led by a super-strong wyrm.

In terms of stats, the fire wyrm was way stronger than me.

My chances didn't look very good at first.

But I managed to win by paralyzing them and dousing them in poison.

Just goes to show all over again that stats aren't the only thing that counts.

For example, a spider that specializes in abnormal status conditions can be an extremely difficult monster to deal with, if I do say so myself.

If my stats keep going up and I keep getting better at magic, maybe I'll become a high-powered all-rounder mega-monster?

Heh-heh-heh.

And I got the Demon Lord skill, too. Maybe I should really start calling myself a demon lord sometime?

I have the Fearbringer title already, so I bet it would suit me.

It is I, the Spider Demon Lord!

Just kidding.

At the time, I had no idea.

When I joked about becoming a demon lord...

...I didn't realize the significance of those words.

file.10 ELROE GUNESOHKA

LV.01

status

HP		1985 / 1985
MP		1522 / 1522
SP		1781 / 1781
		1964 / 1964

Average Offensive Ability : 1616
Average Defensive Ability : 1501
Average Magic Ability : 1199
Average Resistance Ability : 1196
Average Speed Ability : 1310

skill

[Fire Wyrm LV 8] [Imperial Scales LV 1] [SP Recovery Speed LV 1]
[SP Lessened Consumption LV 1] [Flame Attack LV 2] [Flame Enhancement LV 1]
[Cooperation LV 1] [Leadership LV 3] [Hit LV 10] [Evasion LV 10]
[Probability Correction LV 4] [Presence Perception LV 1] [Danger Perception LV 3]
[High-Speed Swimming LV 4] [Impact Resistance LV 2] [Heat Nullification]
[Life LV 8] [Instantaneous LV 4] [Persistent LV 5] [Strength LV 8] [Solidity LV 8]
[Technique User LV 1] [Protection LV 1] [Running LV 2] [Overeating LV 5]

Also known as a fire wyrm. A high-ranking wyrm monster that calls to mind an
Eastern dragon. Evolved form of the eel. On top of its extremely high stats, the
magma it lives in and the Imperial Scales skill provide it with excellent defense
against physical and magic attacks. In addition, its ability to gather and command
subordinates to surround its opponent makes it an exceptionally difficult monster.
Taking this into account, its danger level is A.

Interlude   THE DEMON LORD'S AIDE SIGHS AT A MEETING

I walk down a long corridor following a petite figure nearly two heads shorter than I am.

As a result, this individual's gait is quite a bit slower than mine.

Which means I have to be careful to proceed less briskly than usual.

It's not ideal, but I can't simply overtake the one I'm following.

Because the girl striding ahead of me at the moment is the current Demon Lord.

When we finally finish traversing the lengthy corridor, we arrive before a single door.

There, the Demon Lord stops.

To be perfectly honest, I do not want to open this door. However, I have no choice but to do so.

Taking care to swallow the sigh that threatens to rise unbidden from deep inside me, I open it.

Then I step aside to allow the Demon Lord to enter, bowing my head reverentially.

The Demon Lord doesn't so much as spare me a glance as she enters, as if she expected no less.

Once the Demon Lord has crossed the threshold, I fall in line behind her.

—After gently closing the door so it doesn't make a sound, of course.

The room we've entered is a sort of council room.

There's a circular table at its center, with a seat of honor reserved for the Demon Lord.

Ten other men and women are already arrayed at the table.

Half of them stand as the Demon Lord makes her appearance.

The other half remain seated.

The problem is that one of those who remained seated is my younger brother.

Once again, I have to suppress a sigh from escaping my throat.

I pull out the Demon Lord's chair so she can sit.

Again without even looking at me, the Demon Lord flops casually into the chair with an utter lack of elegance.

I notice a few grimaces in response.

I'm sure the Demon Lord noticed, too. She takes great pleasure in evoking that kind of reaction, after all.

Personally, I think it's in rather poor taste myself, but if I were to let it show on my face as well, there's no telling what she might say to me later.

The most effective way to deal with this Demon Lord is to keep a poker face at all times.

"Now, let's get this meeting started. Balto?"

"Indeed."

I give a brief reply to the Demon Lord's command.

To be frank, once she's given the signal for the meeting to start, the Demon Lord's role here is over.

All the actual work of conducting the meeting falls to me.

Or rather, it's forced on me.

"Well then, as our first order of business, let's hear your reports. We'll start with the First Army, shall we?"

As usual, we start the meeting with activity reports from the troops deployed in various locations.

At my prompting, First Army Commander Agner, who's served as the general for several generations of Demon Lords, rises.

Though Commander Agner would likely appear youthful by human standards, he is considered a senior even for a long-lived demon.

His power and competence are such that one wonders why he has never been a Demon Lord himself.

"The First Army has completed its preparations to advance toward the stronghold of the Renxandt Empire, Fort Kusorion. Supply trains have also been successfully deployed. We are ready to march on command. That is all."

As usual, Commander Agner gives a straightforward report without any extraneous information.

His fortitude and vigor make him the picture of a model military man.

"The Second Army is prepared as well. However, if granted a small amount of additional time, our shadowy dealings may bear fruit."

The next person to stand and report is an alluringly beautiful woman.

Second Army Commander Sanatoria. As a succubus, she's exceptionally charming and crafty, even for a demon.

The "shadowy dealings" she refers to are probably something along those lines.

"How much longer will it take?"

"As little as two or three days, perhaps."

"You are free to proceed, as long as it does not interfere with the advance."

"Thank you very much."

With a bewitching smile that could make your heart skip a beat, Sanatoria returns to her seat.

However, the Third Army Commander makes no move to rise.

"Commander Kogou."

"Weh... So, um, there really is going to be a war?"

The giant Kogou attempts to shrink down in his seat.

"There's no way we can, um, avoid that?"

"It is inevitable. If there were any way to avoid it, we would do so."

"Wha... No matter what?"

Before I can answer Kogou's insistent queries, a different voice echoes through the room.

"No matter what. But if you really want to avoid a war, Commander Kogou, there is one thing you could do."

It's the Demon Lord. She has a nasty smirk on her face, as if she's thought of a cruel prank.

"U-um, what is that?"

"It's easy. You and every last member of the Third Army can become the cornerstone for the world."

Kogou freezes at the Demon Lord's words.

"What's the matter? I thought you wanted to avoid a war? Well, that'd do it."

"I-I'm sorry. Um, I won't bring it up again. So, um, please forgive me."

Before the Demon Lord opens her mouth to bully Kogou further, I quickly cut in.

"Kogou, please let this be a lesson to avoid speaking out unnecessarily in the future. Do you have anything to report?"

"Um, everything is going well."

"Good. Next, please."

The Demon Lord looks a bit disgruntled, but this is for the best.

The Fourth, Fifth, and Sixth commanders give their reports without a problem.

Then it's the Seventh Army Commander's turn.

However, the commander, my younger brother Bloe, makes no move to stand.

"Bloe."

"I just don't get it, Brother."

Bloe crosses his arms and slouches back in his seat disagreeably.

"Why is this random chick the Demon Lord when you're the one who's been coordinating and managing us demons all this time? It doesn't make sense!"

"Bloe."

"And I don't get you, either! Why do you serve her, Brother?! She don't look strong enough to keep you under her thumb like this!"

"Fool! Don't speak of the Demon Lord that way!"

The Fifth Army Commander, Darad, erupts at Bloe's temerity.

Bloe and Darad clash often; their personalities seem to be at odds with one another.

Usually, one of their neighbors will step in, but this time no one is stopping them.

Some side with Bloe, some with Darad, and some prefer to watch and wait.

The commanders all have varying opinions.

However, it seems that this time everyone has decided to stay out of it.

"Have you forgotten, Bloe?! The providence of the world compels us demons to follow the Demon Lord no matter who it might be!"

"Who cares about that crap? She's no leader of mine! I've never even seen her lift a finger—have you?!"

"Do you think the likes of us are permitted to doubt the Demon Lord's intentions?! The inner thoughts of a Demon Lord are too complex for us to even imagine!"

"Maybe for you, but some of us have minds of our own, pal! What kinda chump follows every order without a second thought just 'cause it comes from the Demon Lord?! I don't wanna hear anything from a dumbass like you!"

"You, of all people, dare to call me such a thing?!"

Sandwiched between the arguing pair, Sixth Army Commander Huey looks very aggravated.

The other officers simply look on.

Among them, the only one whose thoughts I absolutely cannot guess is the Fourth Army Commander.

Commander Merazophis's pallid face doesn't show the slightest twitch of emotion.

Of all the villainous leaders in the demon army, this man is particularly difficult to understand.

I always pay careful attention to him, but thus far, I haven't noticed anything suspicious.

"Fine! Let's do this, then!"

Finally, Bloe puts a hand on his weapon.

Darad reaches for his own in turn, but his hand stops short.

"Wh...? My body..."

"Why can't I move?!"

Both of their bodies are frozen in place, not responding to their commands.

"Sorry, guys, but d'you mind not fighting over such stupid shit?"

These acrimonious words emanate from the Demon Lord, the very cause of the quarrel.

All the commanders, not just the two who are frozen in place, are overcome with astonishment.

None of them know how the Demon Lord is sealing the pair's movements.

Understandably so. The Demon Lord has always avoided demonstrating her powers in front of them.

Her method of restraint is silk too thin to be seen with the naked eye.

The threads are attached to the backs of their heads.

Marionette threads. Anyone captured by these strings becomes the Demon Lord's puppet.

And this isn't limited to living things.

To my knowledge, the Demon Lord can use these threads to simultaneously control ten puppets, developed specifically for battle, to wipe out hordes of enemies.

However, even I know no more than this.

The Demon Lord has yet to show her hand, even to me.

Bloe is sorely mistaken in thinking the Demon Lord incompetent.

The fact that she holds this station is no mere fluke.

She is the Demon Lord because she is worthy of the station.

"If you piss me off too much, I might have to use Abyss Magic, ya know."

A savage smile. After seeing that expression, there are none in the room who dare oppose her.

The Demon Lord gives the marionette strings a tug. That alone is enough to force the pair into their seats.

Then the threads separate from their bodies, and the commanders finally regain their freedom.

"I…I apologize."

"…"

Dalad apologizes, the color drained from his face, while Bloe seems incapable of speaking at all.

"Now, a report from the Eighth Army, please."

Though it may be cruel, I have to leave my deflated younger brother as he is.

"No problems here."

Eighth Army Commander Wrath responds curtly.

This man shows no interest at all in whether the Demon Lord is worthy.

He has all kinds of other problems to make up for that, but as they're not particularly relevant, I'll refrain from going into them now.

The issue at hand is the remaining two.

"The Ninth Army is prepared to advance."

If I were to describe this man in a word, it would be "dark." He is always clad in black armor and a black helmet, as if they were attached to his body.

What little skin can be seen underneath the helmet is dark. His hair is dark as well.

All that stands out are his eerily red eyes.

I don't even know his name. We simply call him Black.

"The Tenth Army has no issues to report."

The girl seated at the dark man's side is his polar opposite.

Her robe is pure white. Even her bleached skin is oddly white.

Her long, braided hair is white. And because her eyes are closed, no color is visible.

I do not know this woman's name, either. We simply call her White.

These two individuals were added to the staff of the demon army by the Demon Lord.

I know nothing about their identities.

However, I can make a guess.

I believe these two are Rulers.

Rulers are said to manipulate this world behind the scenes.

And these are two of their number.

Even I have no idea how the Demon Lord managed to turn this pair into her subordinates.

But I cannot help but be wary of their overwhelming unearthliness.

"I see, I see. Sounds like things're going well."

The Demon Lord nods, looking pleased.

"So...shall we start a war?"

With these words, the curtains open quietly on a great war, perhaps the worst in history, between demons and mankind.

All too aware of this reality, I cannot help but finally expel a quiet sigh.

J3   AND SO THE WAR BEGAN

The demon army is on the move.

I received this information just this morning.

The report came from a spy who'd infiltrated demon territory.

"So the time's finally come."

"Seems that way. Though personally, I hoped it never would."

"Come on, Julius. I know you don't like fighting 'n' all, but humans and demons are bitter enemies. You must've known this would happen sooner or later."

"S'true. The demons have been active since the previous hero died, so if anything, it's been a long time comin'."

Just as my comrades say, there's been a great deal of demon activity since the death of the hero before me.

Maybe we were just lucky it hadn't developed past little skirmishes into a full-blown war until now.

"So how long until the demon army arrives?"

"Hyrince went to find out. He should be back any... Ah, there he is."

At Yaana's remark, I turn to see Hyrince, the second son of Duke Quarto and my close childhood friend, walking toward us.

"Hyrince. What's the news?"

"Well...judging by the speed of their advance, it seems they're likely to arrive at this fortress tomorrow."

"I see. So it's really happening."

War.

Ever since I became the hero, I've spent day after day in the heat of battle.

This will be my first time experiencing combat of this magnitude, though.

And I'm not alone in that.

Large-scale warfare was unknown in the era of the previous hero, as well.

The only ones with experience facing such strife knew the hero from several generations back, and most of them have long since passed on.

Aside from those belonging to long-lived races, the handful remaining from that generation are far too old to fight.

In other words, none of the humans who'll participate in this conflict have ever experienced such a large-scale war.

Demons, on the other hand, live much longer than humans.

It's possible that some of them lived in the days of that hero—or may be even older.

How will that difference in firsthand knowledge play out?

On top of that, demons also have the advantage in terms of basic combat ability.

Both their physical and magical talents far exceed those of humans.

And their intelligence is equal to ours.

Humans can fight monsters with superior stats because of the power of their skills and their intellect.

However, we have no such advantage against demons.

Because, like humans, demons are able to make use of skills and intellect.

To be honest, I'm scared.

But as a hero, I can't let that fear show.

The hero is humanity's best hope. If I'm afraid, everyone else will be, too.

To hide my fear, I tug lightly at my scarf, a memento from my mother.

I lost her around the very same time the demons became active and I became the hero.

My father was grief-stricken at the loss of my mother, but as the king, he had no choice but to commit himself to his work while shouldering that grief.

Because of that, he became estranged from Shun and Sue.

I truly believe their familial bonds will surely heal with time, but right now, both my siblings are attending the academy.

My father will just have to bear it until they graduate.

Once those two graduate from the academy, I have no doubt they'll be a force to be reckoned with.

I wonder if I'll survive this war and get to see them again?

No, of course I will.

I can't just die here.

"If we survive this war, betcha the rewards'll be huge."

As if trying to prevent the mood from getting too dark, Hawkin speaks up in the most cheerful voice he can muster.

"I would hope so. Our compensation for that battle with the Nightmare of the Labyrinth wasn't nearly enough for the trouble we went through," Jeskan chimes in.

"Yeah, probably 'cause Julius went and crushed the damn thing into dust. If the corpse had been even slightly salvageable, we could've probably sold it as materials."

Hyrince glowers at me exaggeratedly.

Come on, what choice did I have?

"Really! I'm sure Julius did his best. Besides, I wouldn't have wanted to carry a dead spider back home anyway."

I can't help but smile at Yaana's offhand remark.

"You're probably right that the remains of a monster like that could've earned a good price, though. Bet the silk and such could make some clothes with pretty high defense properties, don't you think?"

Jeskan shakes his head in response to my banter.

"Not likely. Taratect thread is apparently generated by a skill. Even if you dissected a corpse, you wouldn't find any."

"Really? I didn't know that."

I instinctively reach for the scarf I always wear.

"Oh yeah, taratect thread. Y'know, I heard there was one time some adventurers brought back some taratect thread that weren't sticky, 'bout ten years back."

"I've heard that as well, when I was still just a young adventurer. They say a party burned down a taratect nest and found some intact thread inside. Apparently, it had ridiculously high magical conductivity and durability, so it fetched quite a bounty. And this part is only a rumor, but I've also heard they collected a dragon egg there. Dragon eggs are so rare, word is selling just one would be enough to allow you to live in luxury the rest of your days. As a fellow adventurer, I was rather envious at the time."

"Yeah, and then there was a craze of capturing taratects to get more o' that thread, weren't there? But nobody managed to turn up one that could produce it."

I froze during this conversation, still clutching my scarf.

Hyrince raises his eyebrows at me.

"Julius, you really didn't know how valuable that thing is? You're always wearing it…"

"I had no idea."

I answer awkwardly.

"? What's this, then?"

Overhearing our exchange, Yaana tilts her head inquisitively.

"The scarf this idiot's always wearing is made from the same thread they're talking about."

Hyrince's words turn all eyes toward the scarf around my neck.

Guess I'd better not tell them that Shun hatched the dragon egg Jeskan mentioned and is currently raising the product as a pet.

"Ho-ho! Is it, now?"

"I've never actually seen the material before. I did hear that some of it was even sold to a royal family, but I never guessed that family was yours, Julius."

"So it's that valuable? I always wondered about it, since you never take it off."

"Oh, no, I only wear it all the time because it's a memento of my mother…"

"Really? Ah, I'm sorry…"

"It's all right. It was a long time ago."

Shortly after she gave birth to Shun, my mother's health declined, and she passed away.

She knitted this scarf for me not long before Shun was born.

I knew it was made from taratect thread, but I had no idea it was such a rare material.

"Don't worry about it, Yaana. Julius just has an Oedipus complex."

"Come on, Hyrince, isn't that a bit much?"

I grin in response to Hyrince's light teasing.

Seeing this, Yaana feels relieved of her anxiety about upsetting me and giggles.

This is how it should be. A hero shouldn't be enveloped in a gloomy atmosphere.

I'm grateful to Hyrince for having my back. It's so important to have a close friend who really understands you.

Although I do think he could've picked a better phrase than "Oedipus complex."

True, I may have more intense feelings about mothers than most people, having lost mine when I was young.

That's evident from the fact that I see traces of my mother every time I look at Shun, who never even knew her.

I still remember the first time I met Shun.

It was the day before my mother died.

I was surprised by his steadfast gaze, the intensity in his eyes so unsuited to a baby.

His expression looked just like my mother's.

Mother was a strong-willed person, too.

She gave birth to Shun knowing full well that it could destroy her weak body.

"If anything happens to me, please raise your little brother right."

As she spoke, the radiance in my mother's eyes was just like the one I saw in Shun's.

Intelligent, gentle, yet somehow dangerous.

Those eyes…

When I think about it, the moment when I became strongly aware that I was an older brother was also when I accepted my position as hero.

When I first took on the role, I was terrified.

The realization that I would have to fight shook me to my core.

But when I lost Mother and met Shun, I felt the powerful desire to protect him.

I am his older brother, after all.

Even if I can't replace our mother, I can at least protect him as a brother.

That was the beginning of my story.

The origin of Julius the hero.

My thoughts are interrupted by telepathic communication from Hyrince.

[Julius, there's something strange about the way these demons are moving.]

[What's strange about it?]

【It's like they're dispersing all their troops to invade human territory all at once, but we don't know why they're breaking up their forces like that.】

【You think there's something behind it?】

【Yeah. It'd surely be better to concentrate on one front, so why divide their troops like that? It's best to assume they have a reason.】

【Any idea what that might be?】

【Not sure. It's beyond me right now. But we'd better not let our guards down.】

【Got it. Thanks.】

I have a terrible feeling about this.

As if we've somehow walked into some enormous trap.

Like being caught in a spiderweb.

It reminds me of the fight against the Nightmare's Vestige. I feel the same vague anxiety now as I did then.

But as a hero, I can't run away.

Once again, I tightly grasp the scarf made of spider thread.

S7 THE VOICE THAT ANNOUNCES RUINATION

"All right, class, today we'll be talking about wyrms and dragons."

Professor Oriza starts class with his usual disinterested tone.

Wyrms and dragons...

Hearing that, I can't help but remember that incident.

Hugo's attempt to assassinate me, and the wyrm's attack on the school.

Several years have passed since then.

Although few were hurt in either assault, it was still a shock to the academy.

However, Hugo was never definitively punished.

Before anyone could render justice, he disappeared from the school entirely.

The running theory is that Spatial Magic was involved in his escape, but nobody knows for sure.

At the same time, Ms. Oka disappeared, too.

In retrospect, she wasn't present for the fight against the earth wyrm, either.

Ms. Oka was strong enough to easily bring Hugo down.

If she'd participated in the subsequent battle, I'm sure we would've defeated the monster more easily.

So why wasn't she there?

With her gone, we have no way of knowing.

That isn't all that changed after the incident.

For some reason, Fei started devoting herself to leveling up, even though she hadn't been interested in it at all before.

She quickly achieved the evolution she'd once dreaded and now lives outside.

Something about witnessing the death of the wyrm that may have been one of her parents must have changed her outlook.

My own perspective changed a little after that encounter, too.

Before the attacks, I constantly aspired to be like my brother Julius.

But because of what happened, I learned a small fraction of the difficulty of his path.

Even now, I can't shake the fear lurking in my mind.

It may be due in part to the fact that I'm a reincarnation, but I'm afraid of killing—and of being killed.

But in order to live in this world, in order to walk by my brother's side, I have to conquer that fear.

Still, even if I have to overcome it, I don't think I should forget it.

Since then, I've had opportunities to participate in exercises and battle monsters.

These creatures are nowhere near as strong as the earth wyrm; they're so weak that they fall to a single swipe of my sword.

Still, the weight of killing them is the same.

I mustn't forget this weight. I mustn't get used to it.

I have to master my fears and go into battle fully prepared to take a life.

If I forget the weight of that act and get accustomed to taking lives, then I won't be me anymore.

Just a monster that happens to share my name.

It's possible I'm just being naive.

But even if I am a peace-loving fool, I don't want to feel any differently.

I want to respect and understand the weight of a life.

From there, I have to measure the balance between what I want to protect and the lives I must take to do so, and thus decide whether to fight.

It's easy to put into words but much harder to do in practice.

But my brother must fight with such thoughts held close to his heart.

He's far too kind to be oblivious to the value of life.

I hope to rise to the same heights as my brother someday.

But I'm not remotely prepared for that day yet.

It's not something I can just achieve overnight. I have to cultivate it little by little.

Until I find that resolve, I'll simply continue improving my strength.

That philosophy has helped me progress since that incident.

I've grown, and my physical stats have been enhanced accordingly.

My current stats are fairly well-rounded.

Thanks to my body's development, my physical stats have caught up with my magic stats.

I'm happy to have rounded out like this.

But it no longer elicits the same kind of pleasure as playing a game.

The stronger I am, the more frightened I become of wielding that strength.

But even so, I have to get stronger.

With the demons becoming more active, there's no telling when a war might break out.

If I'm not strong enough to act when that time comes, I wouldn't be able to bear it.

I may not be able to fight by my older brother's side yet, but I don't want to hold him back.

If possible, I want to at least get strong enough to protect Sue, Katia, and the others close to me.

Sue's been acting a bit distant lately.

She used to always call me "Brother" and follow me around, but that doesn't happen very often anymore.

Since she's becoming a young woman and all, it's not unusual that she'd want to distance herself from me, but it's still a little sad.

Still, she hasn't pulled away completely, and I can tell she still looks up to me, so I can't complain too much just yet.

My relationship with Katia has become a little strange, as well.

Ever since the incident, I've gotten the sense that she's trying to put some distance between us, bit by bit.

She denied it when I asked her about it.

But she avoided eye contact and backed away while she did, so I'm not convinced at all.

When I grabbed her arm to press the question, I was surprised by how thin it was.

It was too thin. So thin that I thought it might break.

On top of that, she gave an unexpectedly cute squeak of pain, so I let go instinctively.

Watching her face turn red as she rubbed her arm where I'd grabbed it, I couldn't hide my distress.

"S-sorry."

I didn't know why I was so flustered as I apologized.

But in that moment, even though I know Katia as well as I know myself, she looked like a total stranger to me.

Things have only gotten more awkward with Katia since then.

Yuri is just about the only one who hasn't changed. She's still as zealous about converting people to the Word of God as ever.

If anything, she may be getting more and more intense.

Whenever I see her harassing a student, I pull her away to let her prey escape, only to have her target me instead.

It's become a routine for us.

If Sue and Katia are around, they'll jump in to mediate, and we all get caught up in our familiar, friendly squabbling.

So even if there have been a few small changes, my life remains pretty peaceful.

<Condition satisfied. Acquired title [Hero].>
<Acquired skills [Hero LV 1] [Holy Light Magic LV 1] as a result of title [Hero].>

Until a voice shatters that peace.

"Huh?"

Since we're still in the middle of class, my confused mutter echoes through the classroom more loudly than I expected.

"What is it, Schlain? Is there some part of the lecture you don't understand?"

Professor Oriza eyes me politely.

But his voice doesn't register through the chaos erupting in my mind.

"Schlain? Schlain?! What's wrong?!"

I'm sure the blood must have been draining from my face.

But how could I not be shocked?

The Hero title is only held by one human in the world at any time.

And I know very well who that hero is supposed to be.

...ou acquire a title, you can never relinquish it for as long as you live.

...title of Hero is no exception.

...long as you live.

So that can only mean one thing.

There's no other explanation.

I can't believe it. I don't want to believe it.

But that title has undeniably been added to my status.

No. It can't be.

This can't be happening.

No, no, no no no no no no no no no!

That could never happen to my brother!

But that title obdurately reveals the reality.

On this day, a hero has died...

...and a new hero is born.

Interlude   SPIDER DEMON LORD

The Demon Lord holds a white piece of fabric in her hand, examining it with great interest.

A white scarf that, until a short time ago, was worn by a hero.

"White, take a look at this. Apparently, it's made of spider thread."

The Tenth Army Commander of the demon army, known only as White, turns her face toward the scarf in the Demon Lord's hand.

However, her eyes remain closed.

"I heard it traded at a high price among humans, but can you believe the hero was wearing it?" The Demon Lord murmurs sardonically. "Unreal."

She fiddles with the white fabric absently, then suddenly becomes still.

Her expression contains the innocent glee of someone who's just had a great idea.

At least, that's how she sees it. To anyone else, it looks like a wicked smile.

"Wasn't the hero's younger brother a reincarnation? Let's give this back to him, then."

As she speaks, she imbues magic into the scarf in her hand.

"Yep, yep. A little present for the hero's little brother, full of the Demon Lord's divine protection. Pretty slick, don't you think?"

White remains silent, offering no consensus.

"Ahh, I'd love to see the look on Yamada's face when he gets this…"

Picturing it, a malicious grin spreads over the Spider Demon Lord's face.

Final Act   GOD LOVES SPIDERS

Looks like she's taken a liking to Wisdom.

It's so nice seeing a present well received.

One can't help but be pleased by such a dramatic reaction.

We'll definitely have to save the image of her setting herself on fire and flying into a panic.

Surely, our special little spider will put Wisdom to good use.

Even with your mind divided, you can stay surprisingly calm.

Since you have two Ruler skills, Pride and Perseverance, I'm sure you can manage one more.

And someday, I hope you'll learn of my existence.

I have high hopes for you.

I'm sure you can entertain me for a long time.

For I am an administrator and an evil god.

Now then, what will you show me next?

How will you interact with this world?

How will you change it?

I'm very much looking forward to finding out.

AFTERWORD

Hello, everyone. It's me, the probably, maybe, hopefully beloved Okina Baba.

It can't be! You're telling me there are enough brave souls out there who bought the first volume to justify a second?!

I'm surprised there are so many weirdos out there who like spiders. What a wide world we live in.

Now then, a lot has happened since Volume 1 was released.

The series has gotten a manga, a commercial, lots of comments, and it started serialization on Kakuyomu.

It even got glowing recommendations from Mr. Ryohgo Narita and Mr. Satoshi Hase.

I never expected to receive such kind comments from such famous authors! It was petrifying.

Luckily, once humans surpass a certain degree of emotion, they actually become calm, assume it's a dream, and go to bed. Then, the next day, they think, *Looks like I'm still dreaming!* and go to bed again, and so on and so forth.

All joking aside, though, I'm sincerely grateful.

Just hearing that Mr. Narita and Mr. Hase enjoyed my work is enough motivation to keep me going forever.

Thank you very much.

To Tsukasa Kiryu, who illustrates these novels, thank you for always drawing such beautiful illustrations.

To Asahiro Kakashi, who creates the manga, thank you for being the only person alive who can give a spider such a wide range of expressions.

Finally, thank you to my editor Mr. K, everyone involved in the production of this book, and all the readers who picked it up.